For This Little Time

By
Pamela DeRaddo

KCM PUBLISHING
A DIVISION OF KCM DIGITAL MEDIA, LLC

CREDITS

For This Little Time by Pamela DeRaddo

ISBN-13: 978-1-939961-73-0
ISBN-10: 1-939961-73-4

First Edition

Publisher: Michael Fabiano
KCM Publishing
www.kcmpublishing.com

This story is dedicated in memory of my father Don Crosier who was humble, gentle, and loving to all people, at all times.

For This Little Time

"Could a greater miracle take place than for us to look through each other's eyes for an instant?"
—Henry David Thoreau

Contents

PART 3

Prologue

Spring 2011

It was sometime after eight in the morning on a Monday, a day in late March when the ice was beginning to thaw and you could feel the morning sun soak into your winter coat, providing a little warmth. The cars were wrapped around the doughnut shop like a half-eaten French cruller. It was the morning coffee rush for those heading in to work, and a quick cup of caffeine for tired moms with crying preschoolers, who would settle down after their first powdery mouthful of a jelly filled.

He seemed not to notice their eyes, darting quickly from his image back to the car ahead of them. It wasn't something people should stare at. Maybe one of those moms imagined their little "Johnny" in such a predicament, heaven forbid. There was no way these people would ever identify with a man like him. He tentatively kept at his search, looking up from the dumpster to the back door of the little shop. To the customers watching, they saw a hungry vagrant digging around in that army green pantry for whatever doughnuts he could find.

And it was true that this man was hungry and that he was homeless and that he came to this spot every Monday morning. But today he was late. He had never gotten there after 5:00 a.m. when the weekend manager, before leaving his shift, would leave a bag of day old baked goods in the front corner of the dumpster for him. This was arranged so that the man wouldn't be seen by customers or reported by workers and therefore told by the other managers to leave and not come back.

Somewhere in that line of cars, a woman sat at the wheel of her black minivan, watching the goings on. She had come for a "Number 2," a coffee and a bagel with cream cheese. This wasn't a usual stop, but she needed something after her blood draw earlier that morning. It was as she approached the area nearest the dumpster that things got curious. Despite the chill hanging in the morning air, she rolled down her window and appeared to be saying something to the back of the man's head. He cautiously lifted his arm out from the dumpster and turned a bent head towards the woman's voice. From their angle, several of the cars behind the woman's van could see one side of the garbage pickers' face.

He was a tallish man, and thin, wearing a dark canvas coat and tired blue overalls. His boots were speckled with all sorts of stains and weathered from use. His hair was short under his knit cap, shaved close to the skull and beginning to gray, and he had a thick, peppery beard that made him look older than he was. His hands were grimy with the trash he had handled from the dumpster. His left arm, though no one could see, was disfigured and its hand was missing two fingers. Arthritis affected the other digits, leaving them bent and swollen.

He said something back to the woman. It took him a minute and when he was done, he stepped away from the dumpster and off to the back corner of the building. You could just imagine the thoughts of those in the other cars. How bold she was to speak to that guy. Had she said something rude to him? That would have been uncalled for. Leave a guy like that alone, his situation's pitiful enough. Maybe she was one of those community lunch volunteers who told vagrants where they could get a hot meal. It wouldn't be the first time someone had offered that information to him.

But she pulled her van out of line and parked in the lot. With her purse over her shoulder, the woman, wearing a tight knit cap of her own walked to the dumpster and the man. A few people could be seen letting their windows down just a bit, attempting to catch a little of the conversation. A few moments later, the woman walked off toward the front of the shop. Strange, they thought, but the man remained in the corner, waiting. It seemed to interest a few of the patrons enough for them to pull into the parking lot after receiving their orders at the window. Some people are born nosy.

After a few minutes, the woman was seen exiting the doughnut shop carefully carrying two bags and three cups of coffee. She hurried along to the back of the building and the man peaked out from his corner. By now several people had their windows down completely, not worrying at how obvious their eavesdropping was.

"Here you go," she said with a smile. She held out the tray of coffees to him. He hesitated, not looking directly at her, finally taking it in his right hand. Then she set the larger of her two bags on the ground beside him.

"The coffees got cream and sugar in it. Hope you like cream cheese on your bagels. And there's a variety of doughnuts in there." She smiled as she reached out to him for one of the coffees. "Oh, and one of those is mine."

"It's all good to me," the man spoke to the ground. "Sure do appreciate it."

"Well, you have a good day now, and stay warm." The woman began to walk off to her car but not before unwrapping the scarf from around her neck and taking the mittens from her hands. Casually she held her knitted warmth out for him to take.

He made no hesitation in taking them, pushing them deep into a pocket of his canvas jacket. "Thank you for all of this." Still not directing his gaze to her he held up the bag of doughnuts. "And I love hot coffee." His words were quiet but said with feeling.

"I'm glad I got you the large ones then." The woman lingered just for an instant before quickly moving to her van and starting the engine. Without as much as a glance back toward the man at the doughnut shop, she pulled out onto the highway and was gone.

But that man hesitated for a heartbeat, holding the bag and the steaming cups of coffee there beside him. Then for the few who stayed on long enough to watch, they would have seen him limp around to the front of the building, walking over to one of several benches that were dotted along the side of the busy street. Sitting there sipping one of the warm cups, he watched the morning traffic. 'Real people with real lives,' he thought.

Then opening the bag, he reached for a bagel. It was then that he noticed a legal sized envelope tucked in along the inside of the bag, a bit of frosting having smudged it. Carefully he took it out from among the baked goods and he licked the bit of chocolate off of it. He wondered what it might be and he hoped it wasn't another one of those inspirational notes that people liked to hand out from time to time. He folded it neatly and tucked it into his overalls' center front pocket along with all his little treasures.

Some of the people present that morning found themselves thinking about what they saw several times throughout the day. A few even shared it with a co-worker or spouse. But many of them had put it out of their minds by the time they made it to their destinations.

Only one person thought about it long enough for it to make a real impression. That was the man at the dumpster. He had a name and it was James and he had a history and that was in part what led him to the place where he was that morning. People are often more complicated than they appear to be and James's life had been full of complications.

PART 1

Chapter 1

ames Gregory III was born just inside the emergency department doors of one of the larger city hospitals in Buffalo, New York. His mother was just twenty, barely an adult. His twenty-one-year-old father was not present because he had not been called away from his spot on the assembly line where he worked. It was only his third week at the job and the second job he'd held as a married man. Reliable he was not. In love with James's mother he also was not. And prepared to be a father he definitely was not.

Maria's pregnancy had been an accident, a most embarrassing situation for her and her Hispanic family. They were terribly upset when she finally came to them to tell them what she had let happen. But as upset and embarrassed as they were about what Maria had done, they'd said that they'd continue to have her at home until she did what they all felt was best and married the father of her child.

Maria had already made the decision after going to the priest in her church to seek guidance and forgiveness. After her tearful confession, Maria felt some small comfort about the shame she carried, quite literally inside her. It was that shame that motivated her to make things right. She was an adult and wanted to take responsibility, to make her parents see that she understood the shame she had placed on them as well. And so she knew she should marry her baby's father, even as her heart told her otherwise. James Gregory II reluctantly gave in and the two married on June 21, 1965 just three months shy of their son's birth on September 30th.

The couple took a small one bedroom apartment in south Buffalo where the Irish population had settled their families into close knit neighborhoods where work in steel and manufacturing was plentiful. James had made a meager attempt to learn a trade at a small machine shop. An uncle worked there and told James that there was a future for someone eager to learn and work hard, but James was neither of those things. He'd been the spoiled lazy kid of upper middle class parents. They'd managed to protect him from most any responsibility, indulging their boy and covering for his misdoings over the years.

College for James had been no more than a place to prolong his childhood. He took no pride in personal accomplishment and suffered as a student for it. His only apparent talent was the conquest of women. Unfortunate for Maria he had stumbled, literally, into a doughnut shop one night with a few of his college drinking buddies. The first thing he laid eyes on was the petite Latino girl at the front counter.

He found her striking. She had full red lips and brown skin the color of creamy coffee. Her black hair was heavy and flowed in waves down the middle of her back. He could only imagine the curve of her hip and the fullness of her breasts under the apron that covered her. James had always been an easy charm for the girls with his six-foot, muscular frame and eyes as blue as the clearest winter sky. His conquest began immediately and it was swift, leaving Maria no time to consider what she might be getting herself into.

Maria met James several times after her shift ended and each time they drove out to the lake under the light of the winter moon. One of those times Maria found herself half naked in the backseat with the handsome man; her life being changed that night forever.

When James came home four months later to ask his parents to get him out of a pregnancy that he had contributed to, he was shocked to learn neither of them would do anything about it. Even his pampering and doting mother offered little of her usual sympathies.

"Oh James," she said, "I tried for years with you. Didn't we give you the world? At twenty-one, we've taken you far enough. We've got to draw the line at killing babies. What an awful thing to suggest. You better do right this time James. But just make sure that you don't come around here with that Latino girl or her illegitimate baby either. We've got our reputation to uphold."

That was the last James saw of his parents for a good long time and the first time James found himself without an easy way out of something he didn't want to do. He felt shamed into marrying Maria, the sting of his mother's words hurting for the first time. And because of it all, he knew he needed to do something else he'd never done before...work.

The job at the machine shop had failed to interest James, but the owner, a close friend to his uncle, had given him ample opportunity to succeed. It didn't take long for the other employees to see the indulgences given James. He was chronically late and flirtatious with the girls in the office. On a good day he might accomplish half the work expected of the others. Complaints were rolling into the head office and James was smart enough to see what was coming. He quit after six weeks, before the boss had a chance to fire him. He didn't want the hassle of explaining his actions. That was something his mother had always done for him. And he sure wasn't going to let himself be humiliated. The Gregory's were not humble people.

So Maria, when she felt the first pains of child birth, did what she thought was best. They had no phone to call her mother or a doctor. The neighbor across the hall had offered hers just to make one call to James, but Maria thought better of it. She grabbed the packed, small, blue suitcase her mother had given her along with her purse and the only coat she owned and wobbled down the flight of stairs and out onto the street. She had thought about this ahead of time and had put aside money for cab fare. Maria's pain was intense and she didn't walk far before a cabbie noticed her obvious predicament.

The afternoon traffic was horrible and for a first child, Maria was progressing through labor rapidly. By the time the nervous driver managed to get clear of the traffic and arrive at the emergency room doors, Maria could feel the baby's head erupting from within her. Quickly two orderlies hefted Maria up onto a gurney they had brought out to the cab at the driver's request. As soon as Maria lay back she burst out in a shrill cry. A nurse turned to see Maria pulling up her dress to reveal a baby's head completely born. Without listening to the nurse's demand not to push, Maria did what her body told her it must. One screaming push brought forth a son and Maria's only child.

Immediately a mix of sobs and tears spilled from Maria. The new mother was at once joyous and petrified at what the birth of this baby would mean for their futures.

***

"He doesn't look like a James to me."

"I just thought that since he was a boy and your son, you would want him to be named James, after you," Maria explained.

"Yeah, well, I wasn't even here when you told them to put it on the birth certificate. You're lucky I could even get away to come and pick you up from the hospital. One of us has to work in order to put food in that kid's belly." James poked at the baby's round middle. "It would be one thing if he looked like me, but my God Maria, he's got dark eyes and all that black hair. I've got to trust you that he is even MY kid." As usual, James's sarcastic teasing came with his unsubtle desire to say what he was really thinking.

After that day Maria knew she would call her son Jimmy.

When it was decided that Maria and James would marry, Maria's father insisted that James come to the house to meet the family. She knew this was going to be hard for them all but she hoped at least that her parents would accept James on some level. Maria, her sister and brother-in-law, and her brother Edward and his family waited for James's arrival. Nearly an hour later he casually walked into the living room as Mr. Vazquez opened the door. Instead of an apology for his being so late, he had attempted to joke it off.

"Oh, the traffic is miserable today. I just about got out and walked. I imagine you understand. All that water traffic coming up from Puerto Rico must have been hell."

The mood was tense and Maria could see that it was all her father and brother could do to sit at the table with James. Mrs. Vazquez had spent the day preparing a table full of delicious food. James had not thought to compliment her on any of it, but had no problem filling his plate several times. The conversation was short and there was none of the music or laughter that was customary at gatherings in their home. The few words were mostly James's senseless talk about anything other than the obvious.

When Mr. Vazquez did manage to ask James what he intended to do about caring for his soon to be wife and child,

James spoke offhandedly about the "accident" that had put him in the position of becoming a husband and father.

"I know none of us wanted this," was his reply.

When he left shortly after eating, Maria's father vowed that James would never step foot in his house again.

"That young man doesn't care about anything or anyone but himself. He showed disrespect for me and your mother. And worst of all there is no denying that he doesn't want this marriage you are planning. It is hard for me as your father to think that my youngest child would be joined to such a person. I know that to marry is considered the right thing, that you're both adults. But I think this is very bad. It is a terrible, terrible thing you have gotten yourself into Maria. What good can come from it?"

Maria and James were married two weeks later at the city hall. No one from James's family came to witness the joining of the two. Only Maria's older sister, Naomi, and brother, Edward, made it. The whole thing was done in a few minutes and there was no party after, no celebrating. On their way out Naomi kissed her sister on the cheek while her brother shook James's hand, and Maria's siblings left the new couple at the door watching them walk away down the street. Maria's father refused to witness his daughter's marriage to James so he and his wife stayed home, Maria's mother left to cry on her bed. Maria felt betrayed by her father's actions and she stored the hurt away in her heart where it sat like a cold little seed, waiting.

Chapter 2

For the first few months, Maria was hopeful about their new little family. James seemed to be trying to be responsible. He was going to work on time each day and was coming home for dinner most evenings. The baby was sleeping well and at the first sound of him, Maria would jump to gather him in her arms. Most nights Maria was found sleeping with her hand draped over the baby's bassinet. Keeping him quiet and out of sight seemed to Maria to be the best thing for her husband.

James wasn't one for holding his son, but there were times when the two would meet in the kitchen in the morning while Maria made breakfast for James. There were moments when she'd find her husband peering over his newspaper at the tiny boy. He'd study his son as if he were trying to find a connection, something that would open his heart to this little person. James may have been trying in his own way, but it wasn't natural for him and Maria knew better than to hope for much right away.

Maria made up for the love Jimmy's father seemed unable to provide. She held and cuddled and kissed her baby whenever she could throughout the day. She talked to him constantly, both in English and Spanish. She sang beautiful lullabies to quiet him when he fussed. He was her joy.

And she did her best to keep their humble apartment as homey and welcoming as they had the means for. Pillows were fluffed and sheets were washed and ironed weekly. She had convinced the landlord to pay for paint as long as she did the work. The dingy gray living room was transformed into a more cheerful space with soft yellow walls and a few green throw rugs. The kitchen was an oasis of palm tree green with large orange and red hibiscus hand-painted along the border. She had successfully taken the tiny area and given it the breath of the home she grew up in, colorful and happy, that seemed to invite you in.

She always took extra effort with James's things. She starched his good clothes and ironed the rest, even his underwear, and put them neatly into his drawers. His papers and magazines were always refolded and stacked in a tidy pile next to his chair in chronological order. And every evening, before she expected him home, she set out a clean ashtray for his cigarettes and a small glass on the coffee table next to his coveted bottle of whiskey. She knew they couldn't afford the whiskey his family had been accustomed to drinking, but she did her best to keep him content.

There was a neighbor woman on the third floor that had begun to befriend Maria. The woman had taken interest in her when she had come home from the hospital with Jimmy. There had been a knock on the door a few mornings after. Maria had opened it to find a tallish woman with a pile of red hair pinned on top of her head holding a covered basket. She had a brown-haired toddler on her hip and a very red-haired girl of maybe three or four standing at her side.

"Hello," Maria had said with obvious surprise.

"Well hi neighbor. My names Donna Hennessey and I live in 3C. These are my children Liam and Patty." She nodded to each of the children. She noted immediately how very young this new mother was. "I just wanted to welcome you and your baby with a little something. Donna held out the basket for Maria to take."

"This is a very nice surprise." Maria took the basket from the overloaded mom and asked her in.

Donna made an obvious move of her head from side to side, taking in the living room and kitchen all at once. "You've done a beautiful job with this place. I didn't know these rat traps could come close to resembling a home. Mine sure doesn't look like this. You'll see what I mean when that baby of yours gets on his feet." She let her wiggling son slip down her side at that point, but she held his hand tightly.

"Oh, please sit down. Your children can play with the baby's things if they want," Maria pointed to the rattle and wind-up musical toy on the coffee table.

Donna began to chuckle. "My children will turn this apartment inside out if I let them have their way. It's best for this visit that I keep them close. I'm only staying a minute anyway. There's plenty for me to do before my husband gets home," Donna smiled at Maria. There was an awkward pause in the conversation that Donna knew she needed to fill. "My, it is very quiet in here. I bet your boy is sleeping."

"Oh, yes, I hear newborns do a lot of that. But come in and see him. His name is James, but I call him Jimmy because he seems so small for such a grown-up name. He is in the bedroom." Maria stood ready to lead Donna in. She was elated to have someone come to welcome her baby. No one in their families had seen him yet.

"Just for a minute though." Donna scooped up her thumb-sucking toddler and followed. "Patty, you must promise to be quiet if you come too."

"I will momma. I want to see the new baby," the girl looked up at her mother grinning.

Donna had oooed and aaahed over the sleeping baby in the center of the large bed. "Look at those long, dark, lashes.

Why is it that the boys always get the beautiful eyes?" she had smiled.

Maria had felt maternal pride for the first time since becoming pregnant. Her neighbor had stayed long enough for Maria to look through the gift basket. There had been two tiny flannel nightgowns and a beautiful hand-knit, button-up blue sweater for Jimmy. From the size of it, Maria realized that it was meant for some months later. There had also been a jar of jam with a box of those fancy crackers that the Gregory family might buy and a handwritten note. "Please call on me anytime you may need to. I'm just a flight of stairs away." The words at the time were a welcoming and kind gesture but would later become a lifeline for Maria.

A week later, a second visitor had come to see Maria's baby. Hoping to see her parents on the other side of the door, Maria had run to answer the knock. Her sister stood there with a small smile and a large unwrapped box by her side. Although Maria was glad to have her come, it was her mother that she had so wanted to see. She hadn't spoken with her since the day she left to join James in holy matrimony.

Naomi had been reluctant to come in. Maria knew she was uncomfortable with the living conditions. Although the Vazquez girls had grown up with little in the way of extras, Papi had worked hard to care for their simple home in the close knit Hispanic neighborhood on the west side of the city. Naomi and her husband had also bought a home on the west side and lived comfortably.

With some hesitancy, she entered the simply furnished living room and saw her sweet little nephew lying on a blanket on the floor. He turned his head to the sound and Maria was sure he had smiled for his aunt. She sat for a few minutes, holding Jimmy in her arms. While Maria opened her sister's gift, Naomi looked down into the baby's face.

"He really is beautiful Maria," she had said. "More beautiful than any baby except for my own. You will have to bring him to meet his cousins Carmen and Mateo."

Why hadn't Naomi brought her children with her? Maria realized she had never seen her sister without her niece and nephew. Before she left, Naomi hugged Maria and kissed Jimmy's plump rosy cheek. She promised she would be by again sometime. Her gift for the baby had come just in time. Maria had worried where she would find the money to get something for Jimmy to sleep in. The bassinet would fit nicely right next to Maria's side of the bed.

***

"You're his mother damn it! Stop him from crying like that. I shouldn't have to come home to this," James threw his newspaper to the floor.

"He's just a baby and sometimes, I don't know, they just cry. I've fed him and changed him. Maybe he's just tired and can't get to sleep. Donna told me some babies are colicky." Maria had Jimmy against her shoulder, rubbing his back and walking back and forth the length of the apartment. He was growing fast and she could feel the strain of his weight in her arms and shoulders. James had yet to offer to walk with him on the nights when Jimmy needed comforting.

"You know what Maria? I'm the one who's tired. I'm the one who gets up at six in the morning for work. I'm the one who does what he hates every day just to bring enough money home to support the two of you. I'm the one who had a good thing going at school before all this." James threw his arms out to each side, looking around the room. "And I'm the one who gave it all up to be responsible. But you know that, Maria? Do you?" James was right up against Maria now and had her and the baby pinned to the wall.

"James, I'm sorry. I don't know what to do," Maria pulled her face down close to the baby's. The baby seemed to recognize his mother's fear and his father's shouts were so close to his ear. He quieted almost immediately.

"Sorry shit Maria. What are you sorry for? You had choices before he was born. I'm the one who got dragged into this marriage. I'm the one who gave up my family. I had everything before this you know; everything." James punched the wall next to Maria and turned for the door, stopping to take a swallow of whiskey and grab his cigarettes.

"I'm not sorry about Jimmy." Maria breathed the words as James slammed the door behind him. "I'm not sorry about you my sweet boy." The tears she had been holding back came pouring from her heavy dark eyes.

This scene had been happening a lot lately. As Jimmy grew, he was more awake and busy. He wanted to lie on the floor and roll around. He wanted to grab at things and babble and be heard. He didn't sleep whenever it was convenient for his father. He was becoming a part of the family and he had needs and desires too. Maria realized James wasn't acting much different than his five-month-old son.

Weeks before, Maria had actually tried to talk to her mother about the deep sadness she felt at having lost her family somehow to the decision she had made. She managed to gather some change for the payphone across the street. She dialed the only number she knew…the home she had spent her first twenty years in and waited for the other end to pick up. Instead of her mother, she had heard the deep, tired voice of her father. Beginning to cry, Maria asked her papi if he would please come by sometime with mami, to see the baby. She knew she didn't dare complain about her circumstances to him, but she so desperately wanted to see her mother. She wanted to be held and comforted and reassured.

Papi's tone seemed strained and sad and she wondered if he too was struggling on the other side of the phone line.

"Maria, my dear mi-hija, you know mami and I cannot bear to see you right now." He broke off for what seemed a long time. "That man you have taken up with is to us a disgrace. But we know that as bad as he is, he is your husband now and you've taken your place as his wife, for all that means."

"But papi," Maria pleaded. "I did what was right. I married my baby's father. Can't you see I'm sorry for the mistakes I've made? Can't you see I've only tried to make things right? Won't you come and see the baby some day while James is at work. I am holding your grandson right now. He is beautiful papi." Maria's pleadings came in broken sobs.

"Maria. It is all too much for us right now. Seeing the child will only remind us of the pain you have brought on yourself. Forgive me Maria, but for now I cannot face it." Maria heard her mother's muffled sobs through the phone lines. She seemed a million miles away. "I'm sorry. I always pray for you mi-hija." And with that she heard the dial tone.

Maria decided that day that no one knew what was best, least of all maybe Maria herself. She had heard her father, the sadness and shame and pride in his words. How he couldn't accept her life as it was or that the baby was his grandson. She also had the hurt of his first betrayal still sitting like a seed in her heart, waiting. Her father had watered it when he hung up the phone that day, and it would begin to grow into something neither of them would have wanted.

It was Donna who Maria finally turned to for comfort and understanding. Donna had come by Maria's to check in on the young mother several times since her first visit.

She had been so open and friendly on her visits and her note had said "please call on me anytime." Maria knocked tentatively that first morning on the brown door with the cheap metal 3C nailed to it. Maria had made sure that Donna's husband had left for work and that it was late enough that she didn't think she would wake the children.

The door opened and immediately Maria wished she had not come. Donna was dark eyed and her hair had been quickly pulled back into a pony tail. She wore absolutely no makeup and her skin was shocking in its whiteness. Maria thought that perhaps she was ill.

"Oh Maria, how have you been? Come on in," Donna brightened and held the door open. Maria stepped into a large living room that could have been pretty if it had a fresh coat of paint and some neatening up. Liam was babbling as he rummaged through a laundry basket of tired looking toys that sat by the TV and Patty was running around in her underpants, a Raggedy Ann doll in her hand.

For its size, the place felt cluttered. There was a pile of fabric that lay next to a sewing machine just to the right of the door and an ironing board was set up with a few men's shirts thrown across it. Various magazines lay about and toys dominated the center of the space. Maria could see that this room served as the center of all the apartments' activities.

"I'm so sorry for just coming by like this. Maybe another time would be better. I just wanted to say hi anyway. Jimmy and I are on our way to the market. Could I get you anything?"

"Look at this little man of yours," Donna held out her arms to take the baby. "I see he is wearing the sweater I made him. But I will have to get busy with another one. Look at how big he is getting." She smiled broadly into Jimmy's face as she bounced him on her thin hip.

"Yes. I guess I didn't know how fast it all happens. He's been trying to talk since you saw him last and he just started to roll over."

"You just wait mommy. Just you wait." She spoke in a baby voice to Jimmy. "Before you know it, you will be coming to the door looking like me," Donna chuckled as she spun around holding her housecoat out with her free hand. She must have noticed Maria's embarrassment on her behalf because she handed Jimmy back and straightened her hair. "Don't think anything of it, Maria. Please stay for a visit. I'll put on some coffee. Some mornings are just like this. With kids and a husband and my sewing business, well I don't usually look like I do when I've visited you."

Donna was already walking into the kitchen where Maria could see her scooping coffee into the top of the percolator. Liam seemed curious about Maria and Jimmy, but hung back by the toy basket. It was Patty who ran over to see them.

"He's a cute baby. My brother is a brat. Do you want me to hold him?" Patty got up on the couch. "See. If I sit like this, I can't drop him. I used to hold Liam all the time for Mommy. But now he is too big and too bratty for me to hold onto. He pulls my hair and jumps on my stomach."

Maria moved a few toys off a section of the blue floral patterned couch and sat down. Not willing to give her precious baby over to Patty, she engaged her in conversation. "You are a big help to your mommy I bet."

Donna was back in the living room carrying a plate of chocolate cookies of some kind. She set them on top of an empty spot on the coffee table and walked over to Liam.

"Come see momma sweetie," she grinned. The toddler dropped his one-armed bear and ran into her open arms. She sat down in a navy, straight-backed chair by the couch, handing him little bits of a cookie.

"So, Maria, I'm glad you came to see me. I don't get too many visitors and I love to talk. I'm hoping you do too."

She smiled tentatively as if it was Maria doing her the favor by being there.

"I don't know. I just wanted to come by and thank you again for what you've done for me and Jimmy." Maria saw that her son was giggling at Patty who was playing peek-a-boo with him. "This is nice. You are all so happy and relaxed here. I guess lately things have been a little more stressing than I imagined."

"Life can do that to you. But you've got to have some perspective. You've got to have a place to take the 'garbage out' if you know what I mean," Donna said. She was shaking her head and lighting up a cigarette. "You're young and you've got a baby and a husband. Do you have family you can talk to? A mother or sister or something?"

Maria felt her chest tighten and she tried to choke back the emotion, but her tears overwhelmed her and she began to sputter out the story she had been holding back for all those months. The story of a girl who had been misled by a man; about the pregnancy and how by choosing to do the right thing, she had somehow lost the people she loved. She told about her fears, both of James and of motherhood. She confided that, although she loved her baby very much, she often thought of life before him and James. She shook as she told her new friend what it felt like to have no one love you.

Donna set Liam down and held Maria like her mother used to.

Chapter 3

"Look at you go, Jimmy. Isn't he doing great?" Maria had been using every opportunity to try and make conversation with James lately. The fact that Jimmy was up on two feet, holding onto the coffee table and bouncing on his chubby legs, seemed to be something worth calling attention to.

"Yeah, that's something," James mumbled without looking up. He was putting his sneakers on. It looked as though he had plans again today. Maria never knew or dared ask what he was doing from day to day. James hadn't appeared to be searching for work since leaving his most recent job about a month ago. He had told Maria the boss had unreasonable expectations. "I'm an educated guy and this SOB treats me like trash," he had whined to her.

"Will you be back tonight?" she wondered out loud.

"Doubt it. Stan and Benny have something going on at the shop. There may be something there for me to do." James was moving quickly to the bedroom, pulling off the tee shirt he had worn to bed and trading it for a clean, pressed one. He came back out with a stuffed duffle bag. He found his cigarettes on top of the TV and he stuffed them into the tee shirt pocket. Maria would bet she wouldn't see him until the next morning.

"Jimmy has a good-bye kiss for you daddy," she smiled as she held Jimmy out to his father. James begrudgingly dropped his bag and let Maria hand the growing boy off to him.

"Ok then. You be good for mommy," James managed a quick pat on the back and then Jimmy was back in his mother's loving arms. Without as much as another word to Maria, James turned and walked out the door. Maria went over to the refrigerator and reached up to the avocado green radio that sat there. She turned it on and let the fast tempo music spill into the apartment and drown out the empty place in her heart.

***

The next morning came and went without any sign of James. Usually he came back for food or to sleep. Maria had been worrying about money again. She had good reason to with the landlord looking for their past due rent and only a few dollars left in her jar on the refrigerator for groceries. She had thought about work. She had a little experience baking at the doughnut shop. But what would she do with Jimmy? Even if she could afford someone to sit for him she couldn't imagine leaving him.

Five days later when James hadn't come back, Maria realized she had to do more than worry about money. She had to go out and make some.

Maria could hear muffled giggles on the other side of the door. She kissed Jimmy on the forehead before knocking. He was pushing away from her hip, squirming to get down.

"Oh Donna, I'm so sorry to come here like this. But James hasn't been home in a week and I don't know what to do," Maria spoke to the open door, tears falling like rain drops.

"Mommy, mommy, Maria is here and she's crying." Patty yelled out. Immediately Maria realized who she was speaking to and began wiping her eyes with the back of her free hand.

"God Maria, come in. What the hell did he do to you now?" Donna moved quickly from the kitchen to the open door with a half-spent cigarette pressed between her lips. Her face was flushed as she coaxed Maria into the living room by the arm.

"He's gone, Donna. I mean, I haven't seen him in a week and I've just been pacing the floor every night waiting to hear him at the door. I've got nothing in the refrigerator and the landlord wants us out in ten days.

"Damn him. Damn that man. I should have known something was up. You haven't been by and I just got swamped with all this sewing," she gestured to the machine in the corner with a blue piece of cloth hanging from beneath its presser foot. "I should've come to check on you."

"Listen Donna, I've got to do something fast. Can you take Jimmy for a while today while I go out and look for work? I've got some ideas where I might go. I just need to go alone." Maria began to cry. "And do you have any milk to spare? Jimmy hasn't had any since yesterday. I brought his box of cream of wheat though."

Donna held her arms out to take Jimmy. "Come and see Aunt Donna, sweetheart. You will have lots of fun with Liam and Patty. Won't it be fun to have Jimmy come and play kids?" Donna smiled enthusiastically at Patty who was hanging on to Jimmy's foot. "Listen Maria, you go on ahead and don't worry about the baby. You know he'll be fine here with me."

"Thank you so much Donna. I don't know what I'd do without you," She gave Jimmy a long kiss on the forehead then set the baby bag on the floor and gave Donna, then

Liam and Patty each a quick hug. "I'll be back as soon as I can." Maria hesitated at the door just long enough to see Donna nod her goodbye.

***

Later that next week Maria began a job as an assistant baker for a bakery with several locations, one about three miles east of her apartment. She would work for the old head baker Mr. Deevers from 10:00 p.m. till 6:00 a.m. week days. Because the hours were considered a graveyard shift, she would be paid $1.70 per hour, which was $0.15 over minimum wage.

And it was because of Donna that Maria was able to do it at all. When she returned from her day of searching, having found several openings in area small businesses, the two women discussed the logistics of Maria working and of Jimmy's care.

"I hate the idea of having to leave Jimmy while I work. But it seems that if I have to, that the best arrangement is to take the bakery job. I can try to find someone who would take him while he sleeps and I'd be home with him when he's awake. I'd lose less time with him."

Donna saw the sense in that and understood as a mother how much it meant to Maria to be there for her child.

"I think you've found your job then, Maria," Donna had said. "And you've found your babysitter too." She reached out her hand to touch Maria's shoulder and smiled at the little boy in her arms.

***

Those first few years as Maria worked to feed and clothe the two of them had been exhausting for the young mother. Without the emotional support of a spouse and certainly nothing coming in financially or otherwise from

Jimmy's delinquent father, Maria had stretched her physical and emotional limits. She could almost bear to leave Jimmy during those sleeping hours with Donna and her family. At least she knew Jimmy's needs would be minimal and that he was being lovingly cared for.

The nights that Donna kept Jimmy during those first years, letting him sleep and rise with her own children, a bond began to grow between the boy and Donna's children. They started thinking of the baby and the boy as one of their own, like a brother and they protected him, as part of their family.

And naturally a bond grew between Jimmy and Donna so that she became a sort of aunt to him and when he found his words he referred to her as such. It was Donna who gave baby Jimmy his last bottle of the night and his first meal of the day. She arose to his middle of the night cries and his first nightmares. She was there when his teething brought on pain, she had changed diapers, supported Maria's efforts to potty-train him and he woke most mornings to her smiling face and morning hugs. As he got older she had tucked the toddler into bed with Liam, saying prayers with them and giving them soft kisses on their foreheads. Maria was eternally grateful for Donna's support and knew that because of her Jimmy had an extended family.

***

For nearly five years Maria worked this graveyard shift and indeed she often felt like death warmed over. The work was hard. She handled fifty pound bags of flour and made batch after batch of dough for cookies and doughnuts, breads, and pastries. And because of the schedule, there were precious few hours for rest. She had tried for a while to pick Jimmy up from Donna right after her shift but the lack of sleep wore on her and Donna insisted she let her keep Jimmy for a few hours so she could sleep.

Whenever she could Maria would come bearing gifts: a loaf of bread and day-old cookies or doughnuts and every week she brought a sealed envelope with a few of her very hard earned dollars. Her friend had argued about the money, telling Maria that her family didn't need it. She had a good sewing business and Jimmy just added more joy to their home. But Maria told her she absolutely had to give Donna something, as little as it was.

"I just can't bring him here if I give you nothing. You need to accept this small appreciation. After all, you have saved Jimmy and me."

"You save yourself every day Maria," Donna returned. "You're strong and devoted, but it upsets me that you have to do all this just to get by. You do know that you have the right to go after James for child support. And I think you should."

Maria looked at the sweet face of the little boy in her arms. "When he chose to leave us, to walk away from him," she kissed her squirming child on his forehead, "well then he chose to not be a parent. And I'm not going to go begging for money from someone who isn't a parent."

***

Two things saved Maria during those early years. One was her dear neighbor Donna. The Hennessey's were well respected in the neighborhood and their acceptance and close friendship with Maria and her son meant the Gregory's had assimilated into the community much better than they ever would have on their own.

The other saving grace came in the form of a new visitor. Maria's mother had shown up at the apartment door for the first time a few months after James had left them.

How she knew he was gone she never said and Maria never asked. It was a very emotional visit, the two hugging and holding hands and sitting on the couch with little Jimmy at their side, laughing and crying and telling each other about their lives since they had last been together.

Even with the new communication between mother and daughter by phone every week, there was nothing that would excite Maria more than her mother's occasional late afternoon knock on the door. They would exchange hugs before her mother handed her the basket she carried in her gloved hands. She'd step in to let Jimmy greet her, bending down to embrace him.

Mrs. Vazquez was a pretty, middle-aged woman. She was slightly full at the waist and hips and had a soft round face and big brown eyes. Her lips were small but plump and often accented with pink lipstick and she wore her neck length black hair curled and pinned back at the sides. She almost always had it covered in a scarf that tied under her chin which she'd remove only after removing her coat.

The basket she brought was always filled with food for Maria and Jimmy. Favorites were her lechon asado, pasteles and guineos en escabeche con mollejas. She told Jimmy that these were foods that his mother had grown up eating.

Every May 16th, Maria could count on her mother to visit, bringing along a brightly wrapped gift for her birthday. And somewhere within a week of Jimmy's September birthday his abuela would arrive with something for him as well.

Maria loved the little indulgences her mother purchased for their birthdays. Maria's gifts were usually something she would never consider getting herself like a pretty blouse or scented soaps and lotion and Jimmy almost always received pajamas and a toy that brought him hours of fun.

And Jimmy's grandmother always said the same thing when she saw her daughter. She missed her and she worried about her and now that her husband had left her wouldn't she come back to the neighborhood, maybe even live with the family. Each time Maria would hesitate, just for a moment before answering. "I can't mami, I just can't. Papi made it clear when I got pregnant and married James how he felt about it and what he thought it meant for me. I've determined to make a life for Jimmy and me."

"Mi-hija. You listen to me. I can talk to papi. He spoke from his anger and his hurt and I believe time has helped him to see things differently. Will you come? Talk to your father with me." Her mother would beg.

"No mami. I felt betrayed by papi, you know? I'm just not ready. And I'm not sure papi is either." Maria would make the statement sound final and her mother had to eventually accept that the two people she loved with all her heart were caught up in a battle of wills that she alone could not break.

Still, every December 23rd, Mrs. Vazquez remembered her daughter in a very practical way. After a long visit enjoying the cocoa and cookies she brought, Maria's mother would ready to leave. After buttoning her coat and tying her silk scarf around her head, she would hug Jimmy and then Maria as they followed her to the door. Before leaving she would unsnap her black purse and pull out a little white envelope. Handing it to Maria, she would kiss her before walking out the door.

That first Christmas Maria had been shocked to find the pretty Christmas card held five $20 bills. It was almost two full weeks of pay and it felt like a million dollars to Maria. A note in her mother's writing told her that she wished she could give Maria more, knowing how hard she worked to keep herself and Jimmy fed and cared for. She said that the gift was a small comfort to her as she waited until they would see each other again. Maria understood that her mother had as much need of giving the money to her daughter as she had need of receiving it.

She thought about her mother's visits and she believed that her father must have known about them. In his stubbornness, he may have been acting as though he didn't know what his wife were up to, but with the giving of money on Christmas, Maria realized that her father was likely silently helping their daughter in this way. From that small concession, Maria had begun to make a special pastry which she wrapped in red cellophane for mami to take back home for the Vazquez's Christmas celebration. The pastry she made had always been a favorite of her fathers and this she did as an unspoken thank you between them.

But what neither Maria nor her mother would have guessed was that papi had taken a good many long bus rides of his own over the years. He was dropped a block north of his daughter's apartment where he stood under the awning of a small grocer in the early evening watching for her. On several occasions, he was able to see the young mother and her son playing on the front walk. It wasn't until they went in that he finally walked back to the bus stop and at the back of the bus bowed his head and cried in his hands.

Chapter 4

"*O*h honey, you look tired. I have a pot of beef stew on the stove for tonight. There's more than enough for Patrick and the kids so you should take some back to the apartment with you for supper." Donna peered over her glasses at Maria who had just come in. She was feeding a pretty floral print through the sewing machine as she talked. Patrick was lying on the couch, snoring lightly. A piece of newspaper was still clasped in one of his hands. "The kids are in the bedroom watching TV." Maria had never asked why the family had a second television in Donnas' bedroom. It was not a typical indulgence but she assumed that with the sewing business in the living room, Donna needed the kids elsewhere.

Maria put on a weary smile for her friend. Her mind was still at work, but now she needed to change into her role as mother and friend. "Did Jimmy say anything about school when he came home today?" Maria questioned.

"No, just the usual stuff, but he did bring home a folder."

"Good. That's got to be from his teacher. He's been having a hard time with math again. I was thinking that maybe Patty could come over some evening and check his worksheets. He gets so upset when he's done something wrong and I just can't focus on it with him. But Patty, well, she's his big sister and you know how he feels about her."

"Okay with me. I'm sure she'd love to play teacher since, ironically, she recently changed her career plan to being one. Did you know that?" Donna shook her head and clucked. "I love her motivation. I wished her brother had a quarter of what she's got."

"He's only nine and he's got a big sister and a mother to take care of his every need. Can you blame him for taking advantage of that?" Maria smirked. She was walking past Donna and down the hallway to the kid's bedroom. The old black and white TV had its rabbit ears bent at several places in order to get a fuzzy signal but the jingle for Alka-Seltzer made it through loud and clear.

"Hi kids," Maria stepped into the cramped room. "Where's my little man?"

Jimmy looked up at hearing his mothers' voice and rolled off the side of Donna's bed. "Mommy," was all he needed to say. He was in her arms and all was well with both of them. They say that boys have a special connection with their mothers, but for Jimmy, his mother was everything.

There was no doubt that Jimmy meant the same to Maria. As her son had grown to school age and become able to express his thoughts and feelings, Maria had shared things about her days with him as she would have a husband or best friend. He was truly her "little man" and she realized just how much she cherished his companionship and presence at the end of the work day.

She did her best to act as a responsible mother and she held him to high moral standards, but often she would cater to his desires. He loved to help with the shopping and there were many nights that he ate his favorite sugared cereal in place of a proper dinner. Jimmy loved this about his mother and she was tired anyway, so meals were not a top priority.

And it wasn't uncommon to find Jimmy and Maria cuddled together fast asleep on the couch into the late hours of the night, still in their clothes, with the small black and white TV the only light in the room.

But Jimmy wasn't what one would call spoiled. He did for his mother whatever he could. At seven he was helping with laundry and washing dishes. Maria didn't need to ask. Jimmy just did them…out of necessity and love for his mother. He seemed to understand early on something of what his mothers work was doing to her and her sacrifices to keep him happy and cared for.

***

It had been two years before, when Jimmy had started kindergarten and was gone for the morning that Maria began to look for a new job. She was exhausted from her work-by-night and mom-by-day routine and as much as she appreciated the rest she got when he left, she didn't want to continue coming home to her son just getting ready to leave for school. Donna had been getting him up and dressed before Maria got home. She was left with a few minutes over breakfast before her son was out the door.

She had been disappointed that there were no openings to work days at any of the bakery's chains and as much as she had grown comfortable with her responsibilities and liked working alongside old Mr. Deevers, who had been a quiet but good natured boss, for the sake of a better home life she'd set off again to find a job.

It wasn't easy finding a job in the early 70's. Work had slowed in the steel and milling industries and people had begun to be laid off. There were fewer jobs for the growing number of unemployed.

Still, Maria had found a few places that were accepting applications. She knew that in wanting both day work and a good paycheck that she'd have to consider work she'd never done before.

She applied for an entry level position at a factory that made windshield wipers. The main plant was about five miles from her, not an unreasonable bus ride all things considered. It surprised her when the phone rang one morning two weeks after she had submitted her application to the factory.

The foreman called her in for an initial interview where he explained what the job entailed and what was expected. The job would pay $.10 less than her ending salary at the bakery but Maria had squirreled away a little money during the years having been given a few good raises as she mastered her baking skills.

He said that he had been impressed with her work history and that Mr. Deevers had given her a glowing recommendation. He walked her around part of the factory floor. It was a huge operation and he quickly pointed out some of the focus factories where different parts of the product were made.

It wasn't up to him alone though to decide if she were to get the job. He would recommend her to Mr. Reed the plant manager. If he were interested in what he saw on paper she would be called in for a second interview.

***

She stood at the open door of Bob Reed's office and rapped on it with her shaking hand. He had lit up a cigarette as he looked over to see Maria standing there. He motioned for her to come in and pointed Maria to a chair across from his desk.

"So, you are the Ms. Vazquez that I've heard about from Gary, my foreman." A tall, good-looking man in his early forties, Bob Reed picked up the application Maria had filled out for the job and pushed back in his chair, blowing smoke into the cramped air between them. "I see on your application that you work for a bakery, is that right?"

"Yes, I started there four years ago last June. My son was nine months old and now he's just turned five. I've been on a 10:00 p.m. to 6:00 a.m. shift but now, with my son starting school, I wanted a chance at day work if I can find it." Maria rolled her handkerchief between her fingers. She was sweating, but it was more from nerves than the heat.

"Gary tell you about the work? It's no bakery here that's for sure. The girls work on the smaller components and quality is everything. They quickly become good at the precision and the pace…or they are asked to leave. Are you up for that?" Bob seemed to sound skeptical about Maria at this point. He looked down from her eyes to her mouth, then to her full bosom and slender waist. She was still a beautiful girl even with the years of little sleep and the stresses of raising a young boy alone.

"I sure want the chance, Mr. Reed. I've been coming home from work with my son just getting up and then starting my day with him. I nap when he naps, and haven't had a bed time since I started. I'm hoping to just have a schedule…well, one that has me home with my son most of the time." Maria smiled shyly, willing herself to stay strong as she held the managers gaze.

"Well, that seems to make some sense I suppose, but you'd be taking a pay cut. Had you figured on that?"

"Yes, I know," Maria seemed to be thinking for a moment. "But my son and I… well, I think I have to consider all of it. Money will be a problem but a son not having a mother is a worse one." Maria's face showed determination as she said this.

"I'm not saying one way or another about things between mothers and their kids. I don't have kids, never thought I'd be one for fathering. But I guess you've given it all some thought and it's not why you take the job that I care about. But can you do it the way I want it done? I don't know if you've heard about me. I'm known as a hard ass and I'm ok with that because I am. So I'm gonna give you this job, but it's gonna be on my terms. I've got my way of running things and things get done because of it." Bob stood up and walked around his desk to Maria. Then he circled behind her where she could not see him. "So if I haven't scared the hell out of you, then I suppose you've got a job if you want it."

Maria turned to accept, smiling broadly. She saw that Bob had been looking at her with an amused expression on his face. It gave Maria an unsettled feeling. But this job was hers if she wanted it, and oh she sure did want it. All she could think of were the evenings with Jimmy playing games and watching TV.

"Yes Sir Mr. Reed. I would like to take the job. When can I start?"

"Ok then. This next Monday you'll need to be here by 7:00 a.m. You'll see the HR department. Oh, and there are papers you'll have to file with Doris on your way out," he took a drag from his cigarette and pointed through the dusty glass to a middle-aged woman at a small desk just outside his door. She seemed to sense his eyes on her and she turned away blushing.

Maria stood to leave, extending her hand to Mr. Reed. "Thank you again, Mr. Reed. I will do my best for you." Bob Reed held the door open as Maria stepped out, cigarette hanging from his bottom lip.

"I know you will Maria. That's why I am hiring you," as he closed the door behind her.

On Monday, Maria was given a small work station in an area of all women. They worked one behind the other using tools which they used to grind down metal burrs and imperfections left by the machines that had spit out the parts in front of them. The place was alive with the sounds of machinery and everyone kept their nose to the grindstone as it were even while quiet chatter was heard between them. And where Gary, the foreman, largely left them to their work unless there was an issue, Mr. Reed seemed to be very interested in what the ladies were doing. He'd come out of his office a few times a day and walk around puffing on his cigarette, telling the girls to keep their mouths shut and their thoughts on their work. And he'd stop at some of the girls work stations and watch them for a few uncomfortable minutes.

Maria had noticed that when Mr. Reed came out of his office and began his walk around the factory, Gary the foreman, if he was nearby would walk off in the direction of the more skilled manufacturing areas where the men worked.

The usual background chatter of the ladies talking stopped and the sounds of the machines and the ting of metal parts were all that was heard. Everyone was intent on keeping their eyes on their work. Mr. Reed would linger as he watched some of the girls and sometimes he'd reach around one of them to grab a part in a bin in front of them. From a distance, it appeared innocent enough, as if he was checking one of the parts or instructing a girl about something he wanted her to do. When he walked back into his office Maria noticed that, after some hushed whispers between the girls, the place seemed to take a collective deep breath and resume its volume of conversation again.

So when on the second week Mr. Reed came out for one of his walks and stopped to linger by Maria, she found out what he was really up to.

With everyone around her doing their best to keep their eyes off of Mr. Reed, he approached Maria from behind. Like the others, she had seen, he reached over her shoulder, leaning in to reach one of the finished wiper components she had in front of her. Close enough to smell the bitter coffee and musty smoke of his breath, he whispered into her ear, "Here Maria, this is how I would do that if I were you," and as he held a piece of metal out in front of the grinder he pulled his other hand back over Maria's shoulder and down her back to her bottom where he pressed his palm into her softness. Her head spun and she felt nauseous as he kept his hand there for what felt like minutes instead of seconds.

He finally withdrew his hand and whispered, "Thank you for letting me show you that Maria." He backed away and walked on down the line leaving Maria flushed and feeling sick. It took her a few minutes to shake off what had just happened and focus on her work again.

From that day, Maria went to work with a knot in her stomach. Bob Reed definitely crossed a line. But it was only with the single women that he made these inappropriate advances. If you were pretty but had a wedding band on you were ignored. Bob's behavior seemed to be an unspoken liability of the job. And as much as Maria hated it, she could not imagine any other option and, like most of the other girls who needed a paycheck, she was resigned to enduring the occasional advances of her boss.

Chapter 5

$\mathcal{F}$or several years things went really well for Maria and Jimmy. On weekdays after Maria picked Jimmy up at Donna's their evening routine would begin. It wasn't actually much of a routine, dinners were simple and unplanned. Like the stew, often Donna gave them a little of what she had made for her family. But on the other nights the two would snack when they were hungry on breakfast foods or peanut butter sandwiches over a glass of milk.

Maria was a soft and indulgent mother. TV was allowed as long as homework had been done first or if it was still light out, the mother and son would go outside to play a game of conkers or jump rope.

Maria had been sitting on the stoop one evening as she often did when she saw Patty and a few girls repeatedly getting caught up in the double dutch ropes that they were swirling. She wandered over to them and standing by the ropes she told them to watch her; that it was all about timing and if you swayed with the rhythm of the ropes, you'd find your way in. She demonstrated that she knew what she was talking about and the girls watched in awe as she jumped up, touched the ground and spun around inside the cocoon of those two whipping ropes. Her tight-fitting plaid bell bottoms whipped and fluttered around her ankles. After a while she had quite a following and sometimes when there was a knock on the door to the apartment, it was for her.

Patty persuaded her mother to come down to watch Maria and to her surprise the two women entered the ropes together and in perfect harmony ran through a complicated series of moves. They'd leave the ropes panting and out of breath but laughing at the childhood fun. Jimmy loved watching his mother play and he eagerly learned her game. After a time, much of the neighborhood was jumping together.

And while Jimmy didn't like to read himself, his mother had begun a tradition of reading to him. The two would usually go to the public library on a Sunday afternoon to pick out books. Maria had signed Jimmy up for a library card of his own and he had checked out a few of his favorite adventures while his mother did the same with her own card.

The two would curl up together on Jimmy's bed most weeknights after he had cleaned up and gotten into his pajamas. Maria would read a book from Jimmy's pile, usually a story filled with harrowing stories about pirates and men at sea. And Maria got to pick one from her pile too, finding that her son liked listening to her read about people in faraway places and heroes from times gone by. The tenderness between mother and son was soft and silent, like a bear cub nestled into its mother's warm fur for a winter's hibernation.

On weekends, when the weather permitted, Jimmy kept his mother busy with trips to the playground where they would kick a soccer ball around in the grass or throw a Frisbee. While Sunday was church and family time for the Hennessey's, on many Saturday's Liam and Patty came along and on summer afternoons they would often all go to the community pool where Donna would sit in a lounge chair dressed in light clothing and a wide-brimmed, white hat carrying on about the heat until Patrick and Maria came by and dropped pails of water on her until she surrendered and got in the pool.

When winter came, the outdoor play switched for the season. They would all bundle up in layers and go ice-skating at Humboldt Park. Jimmy would hold hands with Liam and Patty, all wearing mittens that Donna had knitted for them and they'd join others on the ice to make a whip, skating faster and faster until the kids began to break loose, falling away from each other. Donna and Maria would take to the ice, laughing as one would try to pull the other one up from a fall, usually bringing them both down together.

***

After Maria had been working at the factory for four years, one of the women who had been a focus factory supervisor when she started had quit. This opening wasn't as coveted as one might think considering the substantial pay increase. No one who worked at the factory stayed for any other reason than their desperate need for a paycheck, but if you took this job you had more contact with Mr. Reed and the girls knew what that could mean for them.

Maria wasn't surprised when Mr. Reed approached her about the position. She had done good work and her reviews reflected it. And as a single mother Mr. Reed knew how much Maria needed every dollar she earned. But she also knew that Mr. Reed had his eye on her for other reasons. She was one of his special girls, one who got an occasional inappropriate touch at their work station. She had managed to shut the episodes out and just continue on, remembering how good life was for Jimmy and her.

So Maria decided to take the job and the following week she began as a supervisor. She understood the responsibility, was very competent, and kept her reporting responsibilities to Mr. Reed as professional as she could for as long as she could. For his part, he initially treated her as a colleague and left her to run her area. He kept the door to his office open when she came in to report on things through the day. She was earning the money she needed to make home life more comfortable and she had begun to breathe again.

But slowly over the months, Mr. Reed began to want a little more from Maria. He decided her end of day report should be given at the end of the shift when everyone was clocking out. He'd been willing to pay the little overtime it would mean for Maria. And during work hours the door to the office needed to be shut. The sound was distracting and he didn't want Doris, the secretary to hear any issues that Maria might report about the girls on the floor. Discretion was needed. And while this all made sense and would have been reasonable, Maria knew what Mr. Reed really wanted. The little inappropriate touches started again. And Maria knew he held the power over her job, so she ignored them.

***

It was a Friday in April and a cold drizzle had started. Maria had run to the bus stop to find that the bus she would have usually taken home had left some minutes before. She had known as she stood in Mr. Reed's office that she would miss it. He had been carrying on about an issue with the foreman who he said some of the other supervisors complained was not pulling his weight. He wanted to know if she had had any problems with him.

She assured him that she had not. Secretly she suspected Mr. Reed wanted to get rid of old Gary and was looking to stir up issues that weren't there. By the time she got to her daily report, it was well past 5:30 p.m. and she hadn't walked out of the plant till almost 6:00 p.m.

She stood under the plastic canopy where one other person sat waiting for the next bus. Maria considered walking but knew she wouldn't get home before the next bus arrived. But she was frustrated, knowing the next bus route was not as direct and she would be sitting on the bus for close to an hour.

She heard the familiar voice shouting to her from his car pulled over just ahead of the bus stop and she looked up to see Mr. Reed motioning to her.

"Geez Maria. You missed the bus didn't you, because I held you so long," he sympathized. "When does the next one come?" he asked. Before she could answer he said, "Hell, forget about it. Let me give you a ride. It's crappy out and it's Friday."

Maria was tired and the last thing she wanted to be doing was to be standing in the rain leaning into her boss's car. "I'm okay. It's no big deal," she offered. But he told her that he felt bad to have been the reason she was waiting out in the cold. So she got in, and Bob Reed pulled away from the curb and drove down the street.

Maria gave him directions to her apartment and he said he knew the street.But instead of heading there directly, he drove north, away from Maria's house. Maria tried to correct him, to get him back on route but he said that she needed a little ride and for her to just relax and enjoy the drive.

"You work so hard and I know as a single mother you don't get any adult time. Consider this a little break, if only for a few minutes." With her mind racing and her heart pounding, they finally pulled into a parking lot looking out onto Lake Erie. It was close to 7:00 p.m. and nearly dark on the April night. Mr. Reed shut off the car and stared at the outline of the beach, the waves could just be made out crashing along the shore in the rain.

"Mr. Reed. Please. I just want to get back to my son. His babysitter will have expected me by now." Maria struggled to control the fear in her voice.

"I know Maria. I know. But you must remember. You have more than just a job now. You are a supervisor. And with that comes more expectations. He turned to her and reached for her hand. "We work very well together, you and me." And he moved his hand between the buttons of her coat. She pulled away from him and grabbed for the door handle but he held her by her coat until she turned back.

He held the edge of her coat until she turned her face to him. "Maria, the choice is yours," he said matter- of-factly.

With tears streaming down her face, Maria silently submitted to Mr. Reed's touch. Somewhere during the minutes that followed, Maria's body went numb and her mind left the car altogether, finding a place dark and silent where it could hide.

***

Maria was dropped off sometime around 8:00 p.m. She made her way to Donna's apartment where she thanked her and apologized to Patrick for being late. Jimmy and his mother went home where she poured him a glass of milk and asked him about his day. She sat at the little kitchen table with him as he talked on about his very hard spelling test and how much fun he had beating Patty at two games of war. Donna had made macaroni and cheese and it was very good. Maria smiled and nodded her head, hearing nothing. She got Jimmy into bed and went into the bathroom where she spent the night scrubbing and soaking in the tub.

The weekend went by as many fall weekends did. Jimmy played baseball for a few hours on Saturday but then the weather turned to cold rain and he spent the rest of it in the apartment. At one point Liam and another friend Danny came over and they played Monopoly and then soldiers, hiding and planning surprise attacks on each other. Sunday was quiet. Maria spent it lying on the couch. Jimmy chose the TV shows and his mother watched without seeing any of it.

On Monday morning the alarm woke Jimmy, but not Maria. She had not been sleeping but was sitting in the kitchen with a cup of coffee and her pajamas still on. Jimmy got ready as he usually did and somewhere in the process he noticed his mother had not moved.

"Momma. Are you going to work today?" He stood in front of her. After a pause, he gave her a little shake on the shoulder. She looked up at him as he repeated his question.

"Oh. Yes. Of course I am," Maria stood up and walked into the bedroom.

A few minutes later she came out with her work clothes on and her hair up in a severe bun. Jimmy had poured a bowl of cereal for his mother and was eating one himself. Maria sat with Jimmy for a minute and looked at her bowl but didn't even pick up her spoon.

Jimmy saw that his mother wasn't herself this morning. "Are you feeling okay, momma? It's getting time to go and you aren't eating."

"Not hungry, that's all." She drew in a deep breath and got up. "Guess I better get going. I will see you after work. Be extra good for Donna for me." And Maria pulled her coat off the chair where she had left it Friday night and walked out the door. It was the first day Jimmy could ever remember his mother walking out the door without him. And she hadn't giving him a kiss goodbye.

Back at work that week, Maria wasn't acting right. She was doing her spot checks carelessly, not asking the girls to show their progress sheets or checking calibrations. And she was yelling at them about little things like cleaning up the metal fragments that typically accumulated around them during the shift. When Mr. Reed came out to make his rounds, Maria would walk down the far side of the floor and into the bathroom where she would stay until she'd hear a knock on the door and Mr. Reed's voice telling her to get the hell out of there and back to work.

***

One afternoon while Jimmy was walking home from school with Liam and few friends, one of his mother's co-workers was on the phone with Donna.

"Is this Mrs. Hennessey?" a young woman's voice spoke urgently.

"Yes, I am Mrs. Hennessey. What can I do for you?"

"My name is Evelyn and I work at the factory with Maria. She gave us your number as a contact in case of emergency," the woman hurried along.

"Emergency? What's happened? Is Maria injured?" Donna rambled into the phone.

"No. There's no emergency. She's okay. But some of us are a little concerned about the way she has been acting at work the last few weeks. Honestly, I wasn't going to call. Everybody has personal things, you know. But Maria is always spot on here. Like every day she is 100%. So I'm just checking on my own. I remembered she's spoken about you taking care of her son. Is that right?"

"Yes. I care for Jimmy until she gets home from work. What exactly is going on?"

"Well, that's just it. I am not sure if anything is. She's just off, you know. She isn't doing her job really. Like her head's off somewhere else. A few of us girls thought we'd find out if you knew about anything or maybe you've seen that she's acting different in some way."

48

"Well, I don't know exactly. Her son mentioned that he thinks Maria has maybe been feeling sick, and I did ask her about it since I've noticed she's looked more tired than usual. She's been pretty quiet but said she's having a little trouble sleeping. Maria has a lot of responsibility as a single mother so I didn't think much of her not sleeping well. There are no issues that I know of with her family or anything. She's only really in communication with her mother. But if you are seeing her like that at work, then something's up. I know what her job means to her and she can't afford to lose it, that's for sure."

"Well." Evelyn paused for a moment. "I think I might have an idea of what might be giving Maria some stress." At this, the woman stopped talking like she seemed to be waiting for Donna to say something.

"What's going on? The kids are about to walk in the door any minute," Donna's voice was raised.

"I'd lose my job if certain people heard me saying what I'm going to tell you," Evelyn was very agitated and her voice lowered to a whisper. "The manager here. He's got a reputation. I'll just say he's kind of touchy with some of the girls. Maria makes daily reports to him and there have been times when he's called her to his office. I'd say that was just part of the job, but he's kind of handy with some of the girls down here. That's all I am saying.

"What are you trying to tell me? That this creep is messing with Maria? Is that what you're saying?"

"I'm not SAYING anything. Just some of us have had this feeling, what with the way Mr. Reed has been with some of us, but we don't work with him like she does. Some of the girls are saying that there's nothing Maria won't do to keep her job. We've got this one lady here, well she's like all Jesus all day, you know. She's been giving Maria a hard time about this stuff for a while. I don't know. Not saying I know anything." Evelyn seemed to be done talking at this point and she told Donna that she needed to hang up and get back to work. She must have said it three times if she said it once, "We did not have this conversation."

Five minutes later the kids walked in to find Donna pacing back and forth between the kitchen and the living room. She was smoking one of Patrick's cigarettes. She hadn't picked one up in years, but it was like she had never stopped. The boys ran right past her to the refrigerator. They began arguing about who would get the last piece of last night's chicken.

"Mom!" Absently, Donna had walked into her daughter who stood in her pacing path. "What's up? You just walked right into me…and you're smoking, and you don't smoke anymore."

Donna startled from her preoccupation. "Oh, hi honey. How was school?"

"Ok…but what are you worried about?"

"Nothing, honey. Really. It's just grown up stuff. Can you go get Jimmy for me?" Donna waved her cigarette hand behind her toward her bedroom in the back of the apartment. The boys had the TV up loud enough to be heard in the kitchen. Patty, who had become a strong willed fourteen year old, let out her frustration with a deep exhale and walked down the hall; a moment later, she had a reluctant Jimmy by the arm.

"Jimmy, I need to talk to you about something."

"See, I told you my mom wanted you." Patty sneered at Jimmy, who stuck his tongue out in response.

"Patty, go on and watch TV with Liam."

"Come on mom, really. They're watching some dumb cartoon we've seen probably a hundred times."

"Patty…. please." Her mother's tone and pursed lips were nothing to question. Patty turned again to the bedroom but looked back as she turned to go in. Donna was puffing hard on the cigarette.

"Let's sit for a minute Jimmy." Donna patted the couch seat next to where she had just sat herself. Jimmy shrugged and sat down.

"Jimmy, I was thinking that maybe we'd have you spend the night with us tonight. That would be fun wouldn't it?"

Jimmy looked surprised. "Sure, I guess…. but it's a school night and mom would never let me. I thought you both always told us that we had to wait for the weekend to have sleepovers." Jimmy was confused by Donna's unusual offer. She took a long drag on the cigarette.

"You're right. But even you said your mom has been tired lately. Maybe we could give her a quiet night. I thought maybe I'd go over and just have some grown up time for a little while."

"I don't know Aunt Donna. I don't think so. Mom has been tired a lot, but if I'm there I can help out with some things. I don't think she feels too good. I let her rest on the couch while I get us supper. I don't think she'd want to have you over until she starts to feel better." Jimmy started to get upset. He had been aware that his mother wasn't acting right. She didn't seem to care about things around the house and it made him nervous.

Donna thought through what Jimmy had said for a few seconds.

"Okay then. But I tell you what. Let's just see if your mom will let you stay for dinner and I'll tell her to go take a little nap or something. We'll have you go home before bed," Donna suggested.

***

That evening when Maria had come to get Jimmy, Donna met her at the door. They whispered a few minutes while the kids were playing in Liam and Patty's room. Donna asked Maria how she was doing and got the answers she had expected. She told Maria to go take a little nap and she'd keep Jimmy for dinner. Without any protest, she agreed and walked down the hall.

A few minutes later, Donna slipped out of the apartment and knocked softly at Maria's door. There was no answer so she unlocked the door with her own key and stepped in. She found the place dark and cluttered. She didn't see Maria in the living area. In the kitchen she saw that there were dishes in the sink and some of Maria's clothing lying over the backs of chairs. A few empty food cans were stacked on the counter and there was a sour food smell in the air. Donna called out for her friend as she opened up the refrigerator door to peer inside.

Suddenly there was a hand pushing the door shut. She turned to find Maria behind her, glaring at her with angry eyes. "What are you doing Donna? Didn't you tell me to rest? I don't need you coming in here checking up on me."

Awkwardly speechless, Donna tried to compose herself. "I just wanted to see if you needed anything. Jimmy's been a little worried you might be sick." Donna turned away from her and walked into the living room. Maria followed her, sitting hard on the couch.

Donna tried to pick her words carefully. "I think of you as my best friend Maria. And we've always talked. About everything. You would tell me if anything was going on, wouldn't you?"

Maria got up quickly and walked into the kitchen where she started pulling her clothes off of the chairs and folding them hurriedly. "Donna. There's nothing. Can't you just let me be a little tired without getting all worried?"

Maria stopped with the clothes but wouldn't look at Donna. "Honestly, I just want to be left alone. Okay?"

Donna felt there wasn't much she could say, but she wasn't going to let things stay like this. She would be quietly keeping an eye on her friend. "Okay Maria. But if you need me…for anything. Or just to talk"

"I know Donna. I will." Maria reached for the radio and turned up the volume on her favorite station, the fast tempo music bounced off the walls of the little room. She went to the door and opened it for Donna to leave. As Donna hesitated, wanting to give her friend a hug, Maria looked at her and said, "Would you send Jimmy home please?"

Chapter 6

Spring 2011

$\mathcal{J}$ ames was plenty hungry for one of the bagels in the bag, his stomach had been gnawing since sometime earlier the day before when he picked an untouched hamburger still in its yellow paper wrapper from a waste basket outside the fast food restaurant he had visited. It happened more often than people might think. Food was ordered for a child and then when the little darling didn't feel hungry or desired the toy more than the sandwich, it was tossed into the garbage rather than taken home and saved for later. It was something that upset James, yet it was the very waste of others that had helped sustain him for nearly a year.

But instead of sitting and eating James took one long drink from his cup and pulled a small thermos from his backpack. He emptied the second coffee into it and screwed the lid back on tucking the drink in between some of his clothing. Then he lifted himself from the bench and stretched his legs. He took a moment to rub feeling into the one that limped.

He realized that in the few minutes before he opened the bag he had been daydreaming. The winter had been very long and very hard on him. He looked and felt pretty rough and it hadn't helped that he had been forced to panhandle the last few days. He had made a little money, enough to get what he set out for and he hoped that it would help.

But having found the envelope and now wondering about it, he wanted to get back. He decided he would read it tonight, looking forward to any small diversion from the monotony of his life. And with that thought he felt an odd pleasantness, something like a small spark of anticipation, maybe even hopefulness…something he hadn't felt in a very long time.

Quickly now he moved out onto the sidewalk, limping along with a bag still full of baked goods. Eventually the sidewalk ended and he walked along the shoulder of the highway. He passed by an array of stores, restaurants, and gas stations that made up much of the city's downtown area. Finally he made his way into the quiet neighborhoods and turned off down a side street that dead ended with a small park, old and unkempt but neatly edged by the backs of old buildings and an overgrown treed lot. James had found this haven inside the small city and considered it one of his oases in the middle of homelessness.

This morning though, he walked through the park and the wooded lot that surrounded one side of it and out the other end. This opened up to a few old streets and abandoned warehouses that had been used years ago, when manufacturing had been a larger part of the economy. He studied his surroundings carefully, looking from side to side and behind him. Finally, nearing a group of old faded yellow buildings he quickened his pace until he rounded the backside of building B still clutching the bag in his hand.

Chapter 7

The next Friday morning Mr. Reed had called Maria into his office. She tensed up at the sound of his voice and by the time she had reached his door she was shaking. He told her to come in but keep the door open. In barely audible whispers he told Maria that she needed to get herself together. Her work was a mess and everyone was talking. This had to stop. "But", he said, "I've got these for you." And he pulled an old prescription bottle from his top desk drawer. "These should help with the edginess. Take them Maria. And take a week off too why don't you." Mr. Reed came around to where she was standing. "Keep your mouth shut, take the week off, and only come back if you can do your damn job."

Both Maria and Jimmy spent the weekend in the apartment. On Monday morning Jimmy asked to stay home with her and Maria didn't press him to go to school. She didn't have the energy. She couldn't move without Jimmy following on her heels. His anxiety over his mother had grown and he wasn't sleeping much himself, but Maria didn't notice what her son was feeling. She had started taking the little pills in the unlabeled bottle along with some over the counter medication for sleep that she had gone out to buy when she got a few groceries. Between the two she found it hard to keep her eyes open.

Donna had stopped by a few times, bringing food and attempts at conversation. She knew from probing Jimmy that Maria was taking the week off and allowing Jimmy to do the same. Donna worried where this all might be heading and what she should do for them. Her friend wasn't opening up to her and if this was about the boss, Maria was going to try to stuff it away for the sake of her job. Jimmy was being pretty quiet and Donna tried to comfort him, telling him not to worry. But he was a smart boy and very close to his mother and Donna thought this whole thing was bad for him.

Liam came several times to ask him about going to the park, but Jimmy wasn't interested. Maria was awake on the couch during one of the times Liam and a few of the neighbor boys came to the door.

"Jimmy, why don't you go out for a little while? Just let mommy get some sleep, okay."

Jimmy walked over to his mother who was lying on the couch. He whispered so the boys couldn't hear. "No momma, I don't want to today. I think I'm tired too." He smiled down at her and she simply nodded.

He walked back to the boys in the doorway. "My mom says she forgot she wants me to catch up on my homework. I'll go tomorrow if I can." Maria didn't hear his excuse, she was barely conscious at that point.

"Yah, well…. whatever. We could use you for third base. The kids from down the street want to play us," Doug hit his glove with his fist.

"Boy I wished I could but, my mom has been giving me a hard time about getting caught up for school. I'll try to get enough done so I can meet up with you guys tomorrow." Jimmy was at the door, trying to move his friends out of the threshold. Normally he'd be begging to get out on a nice spring day like this one was. But Jimmy wasn't feeling social and he was plenty worried about his mother.

"Stinks for you," Liam yelled as they backed into the hall while Jimmy closed the door. He could hear the ruckus of the boys pushing each other along the walls of the hall, laughing as they tromped down the stairs for the front door.

Inside the apartment, Maria moaned and turned to her other side on the couch. Jimmy sat down beside her on the floor and picked at the throw rug beneath him. For some time he sat there like that, watching his mother sleep, wondering when both of them would feel better.

The next few days Jimmy was lost in worry for his mother. He tried to let her rest which was what she seemed to be doing a lot of, but he wanted to see her getting better. He wanted her to wake up in the morning and make him pancakes, to mess up his hair and to tell him he needed to take a bath. He wanted to hear her say "Jimmy, it's time to get your homework done."

***

Two days before Maria was expected back to work, she had stopped taking the sleeping pills and was awake a little more. She had actually scrambled eggs for the two of them on Sunday morning and they ate together on the couch, watching cartoons. That evening she set her alarm, wrote a school excuse for Jimmy and packed him a sandwich. When he asked her about reading before bed, she curled up with him and told him to read to her. Jimmy was never so happy to pick up a book.

The next morning Jimmy woke early and felt the new familiar knot in his stomach and hard beating of his heart. He wasn't sure how his mother would be feeling and he wasn't looking forward to school. He anxiously waited for the alarm to ring.

Finally Maria groaned and slowly rolled over to the table between their beds, silencing the shrill beep of the alarm. She sat at the side of her bed for a few minutes, holding her head. But then she got up and walked over to the closet. She pulled out one of her work shirts and some pants and walked toward the bathroom. "Time to get up buddy," she said over her shoulder.

Jimmy was glad to see his mother up and getting ready. It was the encouragement he needed to start the day.

He was in the kitchen and had put out the bowls and cereal when Maria stepped out of the bathroom. He was relieved to see her dressed for the first time in a week. She looked tired, but better, he thought. Jimmy managed to eat a small bowl of cereal and asked if his mother was going to have some. She smiled absently and tousled his hair.

"You better get your teeth brushed and get going Jimmy. You've got your excuse in your backpack right?"

"Yes, I've got it. I'll be done in a minute," and Jimmy quickly went in to brush his teeth. Coming out of the bathroom he saw that Maria was in the same place he had left her.

"Are you ready mommy?" He questioned. Nervous for the answer he wanted to hear.

"I will be in a few minutes. I want to finish up a few things here. You go on along and find the kids and I'll see you tonight." She got up from her chair and walked back towards the bathroom. Again, they were not leaving together and she hadn't kissed him goodbye.

"Okay mom, but…" He wanted to hug her and shake her and make her be the mom she had always been, but instead he hollered back, "Love you mom." And Jimmy, with his heart pounding and his eyes tearing, walked out the apartment door.

Maria dropped to the bathroom floor when she heard the door shut. She had been waiting days to be alone. With Jimmy gone and no one looking over her she could finally express her silent pain. "I've got to get up now and go. I just have to," she chanted over and over again. She reached for the pills in the orange vial and swallowed two. She hated herself, the compromises she had made. And deep down somewhere she could barely reach she had begun to resent the reason behind her compromise... the very son she loved so dearly.

Jimmy waited in the alley by the apartment building, watching for his mother to walk by to the bus stop. After a bit Liam and the boys came out and started calling for him. He stayed back where they wouldn't see him and after a few minutes he heard their voices grow distant as they walked away from him towards school. He knew that if he waited much longer, he'd be late. He didn't want his mother getting a call from the school so reluctantly he slipped out of the shadows and down the street.

At the office, he held out the piece of paper Maria had written as his excuse. Apparently he hadn't been feeling well. With a slight fever his mother thought he might have one of those viruses going around. Old Mrs. Belcher, the school nurse seemed to accept the excuse but told him that he was ten minutes late. When she saw the desperation in his face and the tears, she told him to hurry on along, that it was okay this time.

Jimmy rarely missed school but the few times he had he'd stroll into class the next day letting the kids eyeball him as they did all the kids who'd been absent. It was actually nice to have the kids yell out, "Hey Jimmy, missed you in gym class," or "Man, where you been? I needed some help in math." This would be followed by laughter as everyone knew what a terrible math student he was. Today though, Jimmy didn't want to deal with it. He just wanted to slide in quietly.

When the teacher let them break for recess, Jimmy was the first one out the door. He had never felt like this before, but today he struggled to sit in his seat. He was sweating and feeling like a caged animal. The walls had felt like they were closing in around him. Maybe his heart would stop thumping when he got some fresh air.

Some of the kids ran for the basketball court while others were on the kickball field. A group of girls were starting the jump ropes in their whip, whipping on the pavement for a round of double dutch. Jimmy wandered over to the group at the court. Doug, his neighbor and classmate pulled him by the arm.

"I've got Jimmy," he announced to the other team captain as they picked sides.

"I'm still not feeling real good Doug. I'm watching today."

"Oh, come on Jimmy. You're not sick. No one is sick more than a day or two."

"Well, I am. Just leave me alone would ya?" and Jimmy pulled away. He walked off toward the chain link fence that separated the school yard from the street. He just couldn't shake the fear inside him. He wanted to see his mom and know that she was fine, that HE was fine. Five more hours and Maria would be at Donna's door, telling Jimmy to get his books and hurry along. Five more hours and they would have the TV on at home, talking about homework, probably math. Come on Jimmy…just five more hours. He was talking to himself. Everything was going to be ok. But Jimmy was pacing, like Donna had been a few weeks ago. For a quick second he thought he might need a cigarette too.

Just when the day was to the point of unbearable, mercifully the school bell rang. He should have gone to his locker to get books for homework, but he remembered after he had gotten outside and he couldn't bring himself to turn back into the crowded halls of the school. Everyone knew that Jimmy was fast, but this day his run home would have set cross country records.

Instead of going to the Hennessey's apartment where he spent the afternoon till his mother got home, he stopped short of the third-floor stairwell and ended up in front of his own apartment. He had a key. After all, he was ten years old and there were short periods of time when he stayed home alone. But he had always stayed at Liam and Patty's after school. It was better than sitting home alone and that was the way his mother had wanted it anyhow. But today he just had to get into his apartment. He had an uneasy feeling all day and he needed to see that everything was ok.

He opened the door and walked through the living room and into the kitchen where he saw that the cereal and the bowls were just where he had left them that morning. He didn't hear any sounds and was hopeful. He turned into the hall that led to the bathroom and the one bedroom.

Jimmy stopped a minute to calm himself down. He had been so worried that he'd find his mother home, never having gone to work. His breathing slowed a little and he was thinking about heading up to Donna's when he caught a flash of red out of the corner of his eye. There, on the mirror in the bathroom he saw the letters S L U T scribbled in some sort of paint or makeup. If it was a word, it was one Jimmy hadn't heard before.

He closed the door to the bathroom and got himself a drink of water. He was scared again. Had someone gotten into their apartment? If they had, they hadn't done anything that he could see, other than write those letters. He quickly decided that he wanted to go back to Donna's. He wanted to pretend he hadn't seen anything, or even gone into the apartment. So that is what he did.

***

That evening Maria had picked Jimmy up at Donna's. The two women spoke for a few minutes and he heard his mother say that everything had gone fine and not to worry. Jimmy had watched his mother as she opened their apartment door and immediately headed for the bathroom. He could hear her moving around, the cabinets opening and closing. In a few minutes she came out and he pretended not to see the red stained washcloth in her hand. She dropped it in with the dirty laundry.

They had fried bologna sandwiches with mayo and no lettuce. Maria asked Jimmy if he had gotten some help from his teacher with catching up on school work. She smiled when he said he had some worksheets to do, but that it wasn't so much work. Together they cleared off the table and Jimmy did up the few dishes while Maria turned on the TV. He told her that he was going to sit out on the front stoop and do his work. He would be in before dark. Before he walked out, he turned and bent over to his mother, kissing her on the cheek. She smiled at him.

He came back a few hours later after watching some of the kids play hopscotch on the sidewalk. It was an unusually warm, breezy evening with birds chirping and cars gliding past on the street. Enough people had walked by interrupting the girl's game that they finally got tired of it and took their chalk home with them. When he finally came in Maria was asleep on the couch and that bottle of pills he had seen over the last week was open on the coffee table.

***

So it went on for some weeks, the two of them going through the motions. Maria made it to work with the help of the contents of the orange vial. Somehow it seemed she never ran out of them. Bob Reed had left her alone after that, recognizing that the new Maria was edgy and unpredictable. She performed her duties like a zombie but was still easily provoked. She looked like hell and everyone noticed.

For Jimmy's part, he slept fitfully. At school, he had struggled not to run from the room when they closed the door at the start of class. When it got real bad and he was sweating and breathing fast, he grabbed the bathroom pass. He had gotten his mother's okay to let him stay at home after school. It didn't take much to persuade her of anything lately. Donna had more objections about it than Maria had and the two women had a small confrontation regarding Jimmy.

Jimmy had hated upsetting Donna but he used this freedom to keep her from knowing too much. A few times he had actually walked to the corner where the school stood, looked at the kids in the yard, and turned back home. He'd sat in the dark apartment, keeping the TV real low. He'd watched the hours tick by, waiting for his mother to come home. He had managed an acceptable forgery of his mother's signature and written up a few excuses for the school.

But no one was holding up real well. Maria's personality change seemed unreasonable and Donna was very concerned. Liam had also confessed to his mom that Jimmy had missed school a few times but he had told Liam not to tell his mother. People began to interfere. Maria was being asked a lot of questions at work and ironically it was her boss Bob Reed who came to her defense, making the girls shut up and get back to work.

***

And then May came and the apartment was its usual mess. It was Sunday and Jimmy had decided to make breakfast for his mother. He had gone out very early to the corner store for bread, eggs, milk and some bacon. Shopping had become one of Jimmy's unspoken chores, another role he had taken on so that the two of them would eat. There were pots in the sink, a fry pan on the stove, and dishes in the living room when the knock came on the door. Apparently neither of them remembered that Maria's mother would be coming by this afternoon. After all it was only once a year that her daughter had a birthday.

Mrs. Vazquez looked almost square into the eyes of her ever growing grandson when he answered the door. The surprise in both of their eyes was evident as Jimmy let her in. Maria was on the couch, curled up with a blanket and napping lightly. The curtains were pulled across the windows and the television cast a soft light on the dark walls of the room. The scene confirmed her suspicions after having several strained phone conversations where Maria seemed more distant; less like herself. It seemed obvious to Mrs. Vazquez that her daughter wasn't feeling well. It would have been a shock to anyone who knew Maria to see the place looking like it did. Jimmy was instantly embarrassed.

Jimmy shook his mother's shoulder, waking her with a start. Mrs. Vazquez was standing next to her grandson, looking down at the drawn face of her daughter.

"Are you sick sweetheart?" her mother spoke with quiet concern.

It took Maria a minute to put together in her head that it was her mother standing over her and that it must be her birthday visit. "Oh mami, I am so happy to see you." And Maria's inflection was genuine. It was when she stood up to hug her that Maria realized what her mother must be seeing.

She quickly pushed her blanket aside and motioned for her mother to join her on the couch.

"Honey, you don't look well. And you're so thin. I suspected something was going on. Have you been sick?" Obvious concern was in Mrs. Vazquez's voice. "I knew to bring some asopao along for your dinner."

"Oh, no mami. I'm fine. But things have been very busy. I've been working some extra hours and with all of Jimmy's school activities… well, I'm sorry for how the place looks."

Jimmy listened to his mother lie her way through his grandmother's questions. Was she getting enough sleep, taking a vitamin, still finding time to visit with her friend Donna? "A good friend is worth her weight in gold," abuela reminded.

"Yes, I know," Maria sighed.

"I didn't even wish you a happy birthday yet sweetheart." Mrs. Vazquez hugged her daughter again and turned to where Jimmy sat silently in the chair. "Come over here Jimmy. Give your abuela a hug and see what I have brought your mami."

Obediently Jimmy approached his grandmother's outstretched arms. Although she was small she was strong and the safety he felt in her arms was a comfort he didn't realize just how much he had been missing. She hugged him tightly and when they parted he turned away. He hadn't let himself show much emotion since his mother first became sick and he didn't want his grandmother noticing him struggling for composure.

Abuela went into the kitchen and, pulling up the sleeves of her dress, she filled the sink with soapy water. Although Maria protested, abuela worked on the dishes and wiped the table and counter clean.

"You rest Maria. I just wished I could help you more."

They spent some time talking about Maria's family. Her father had been laid off as they suspected he would, but even so he was quietly upset about it. He was pretty sure he'd be able to pick up work pouring concrete especially this time of year. And they had sold the house, thank God. The upkeep was just costing them too much and with papi laid off, the decision for an apartment was a good one.

Maria's sister's boy was playing baseball with the varsity team even though he was only an eighth grader. Naomi and her husband Joey were very proud of him. Naomi sent her love as always and promised to come see Maria this summer. Jimmy thought about the last time he had seen his aunt. She came around the New Year and stayed for about an hour. She wore a white hat and gloves that looked like cat hair. Her coat was black and long, and the buttons were shiny gold. He felt sorry for his mother. Her coat was from the Salvation Army store and it was missing one of its buttons. She had found one that almost matched and sewn it to the missing space. Jimmy had never met Naomi's two children.

Mrs. Vazquez had bought her daughter a white floral blouse, which was beautiful but looked too big, and a little basket of soaps and lotions. Maria thanked her mother for them. Too soon it was time for abuela to catch the bus home. After hugs and a promise from her mother to come by sooner than usual, Maria closed the door. She went into the bathroom. Jimmy listened at the door for the familiar sound of the medicine cabinet creaking open and the tiny "pop" of the vial that held his mother's precious pills.

When she came out, Maria saw the look on Jimmy's face and she approached him. "What Jimmy? What are you looking at me like that for?" When he tried to look away she took his face between her hands. "I am your mother for

God's sakes. Don't you look at me like that," and Maria turned and walked into their bedroom.

As Maria lay on her bed, brooding over the visit with her mother and the lie she was living, her mother had been one floor above them at Donna's. She had knocked firmly on the door several times before resigning to the fact that no one was home. But the gnawing feeling that things weren't right with her daughter wouldn't leave her so she pulled a piece of paper from her purse and with her tiny printing she wrote a note to Donna. They had met only one time and for only a few minutes but from what she had heard from Maria, Donna was her most reliable friend. Mrs. Vazquez tried to convey her concern in a few sentences and then she signed it leaving her telephone number and address at the bottom. She folded the yellow sheet in half and slipped it under the door, but not before printing "PLEASE READ" on the outside. She prayed all the way home that it would be found, but she planned to find her way back to her daughter's apartment very soon.

Donna did find the note. Actually, Liam was the first one in the door that evening. The family had been to a spring event at the park. Patrick held to a tradition of spending Sunday afternoons doing something together, and a day at the park was a family favorite. Liam saw the paper, read the outside and handed it immediately to his mother. She had been surprised that he had not read its contents first considering the urgency of the words.

Donna was very relieved to read that Mrs. Vazquez had been to visit and that she had found reason to be concerned. 'Thank God' she thought as she read that Maria's mother wanted to be contacted about any problems Donna may be aware of and that she planned to be back to see Maria soon.

Donna held the note for a minute before deciding to call the woman the next morning.

***

Donna couldn't get the kids out the door fast enough that morning. She grabbed Mrs. Vazquez's note and dialed the number she had left. Maria's mother seemed to be expecting this call and she asked a lot of questions about her daughter. Donna expressed her concern and told her as much as she could without making the woman panic. Maria was not doing well and it wasn't about being sick, not physically anyway. This had been going on for a while…at least a month. Donna thought she might be having some sort of breakdown.

And Jimmy was no longer staying with her after school. There were a number of days that he had missed school altogether. Maria wouldn't normally let that happen. He wasn't playing with her son Liam and his other friends much either which was very unusual because Jimmy had always been a very active boy. Donna had tried to talk to Maria about these things, but nothing had changed. Maria was staying in almost all the time as far as Donna knew and there was little contact between them now that Jimmy was staying on his own after school.

When she hung up the phone, Mrs. Vazquez's hands shook and she began to cry. And because of her reaction Mr. Vazquez asked her what was the matter. Tearfully, she told her husband of how she had found Maria and what her neighbor Donna had just said. To his wife's surprise, Mr. Vazquez's face turned red and he began sputtering obscenities. Why hadn't she told him before this that Maria was in trouble? Mr. Vazquez had been well aware that his wife had been going to see their daughter and although he didn't ask questions, she should have known that he'd want to know if something were wrong. As much as Maria's father had hated the life she had chosen to live, he wasn't going to let his daughter fall apart because of that horrible man. And that boy Jimmy. His grandson. Well, he supposed he'd have to do something about him too.

Chapter 8

Jimmy's last day of school felt like most of them had for the last five weeks. He had vomited in one of the alleys down the street from the school before going in. He was wired, nervous with his surroundings and preoccupied with things at home...namely his mother. Most of the kids had given up trying to talk to him and he was okay with that.The teacher had noticed the change in him and she had reported her concerns to the nurse who called his mother about it. But Maria was already absorbed in her own depression and self-loathing and she found it hard to muster extra emotional energy for Jimmy even as she knew that wasn't fair to her son. So she did talk to him one night after dinner, trying to assure him as much as she could.

Jimmy went on pretending as his mother was doing and both of them were secretly aware of it. It was easier, Maria found, than to try to face down more problems. She simply was not well. But the pretending was killing Jimmy and going to school took every ounce of fortitude the young boy had. He was able to get through by marking the time hour by hour, till lunch, then recess, then the last bell.

At home, he felt more in control as he was able to see his mother, care for her, behave for her, and know that she was okay for another day. This was how Jimmy had been living until he came home one day to find his grandmother waiting for him at the door. Inside his mother was crying on the couch while a short, thick-chested, older man with a head of greying hair walked back and forth in their living room, talking animatedly in Spanish.

Maria saw Jimmy and she called him over. He was shaking and feeling nauseous, thinking with dread about what might be happening. He reached for her outstretched hand, and Maria held him tightly yet tenderly, and it was like a dream to Jimmy who hadn't felt his mother's affections in a long time. He looked at her and saw that she was trying to smile for him in that way a person does when they have something they need to tell you that they think you're not going to like.

When she let him go, she introduced him to the man that stood inside the kitchen doorway. "Jimmy, this is your abuelo Vazquez. My father. He has come with abuela to talk to me about some things." And suddenly she wasn't smiling anymore, but looking serious, making no eye contact with Jimmy or the man.

What was he supposed to do? Here was his mother's father, someone she had never talked about and he had never met. Was it good that he was there, or was it bad? Was Jimmy supposed to approach him, hug him? Say something? He just didn't know how to feel or act about the man. It was his abuela who stepped in to save Jimmy from the awkwardness.

"Carlos, come here and see your grandson," and she took her husband by the arm, guiding him to the couch where Jimmy sat by his mother.

His grandfather stood above them, looking hard at Jimmy as he scratched the back of his neck. Abuela whispered in his ear and he slowly extended his right hand.

"Hello Jimmy, it is good to meet you."

Jimmy had picked up some social graces, mostly from watching Mr. Hennessey so he stood up and put his hand out allowing his grandfather to shake it.

Jimmy could hear his mother behind him on the couch, crying again. Was his mother happy to have her father there? To see him shake hands with his grandson for the first time? Abuela gave him a short hug and a kiss on the cheek and motioned for him to sit back down with his mother.

Jimmy's head was racing with ideas as to why his grandfather, for the first time in ten years, had come to the apartment and his immediate thought was that his mother must have gotten sick and called her parents. He became afraid again, thinking this. Maybe someone in the family had died. That might be reason enough for his mother to come home from work and her parents to be there. Had the school found out that Jimmy had made those fake excuses and called his mother?

"You must be wondering why your grandfather and I are here suddenly like this," abuela began. "We were just talking with your mother about how we think she is very tired from her job and how we would like to help her out."

"Mami, I really don't think now is the time to be talking about all that," Maria interrupted.

"Do you think we are just going to walk out of here, knowing what we know and let you just continue on living this mess you call a life?" Jimmy's grandfather was angry, his voice loud and high for a man. Jimmy felt an instant dislike for him. "Maria, look around you. Anyone can see you need help."

Maria flew to her feet. "YOU say I need help? YOU say you can't let me go on living like this? You. The father who wrote me out of the family ten years ago. I can't believe you stand here now insisting on helping me. And you think I'M the crazy one," she threw her hands up over her head and walked out to the kitchen where she sat with her head in her hands. "Go on papi. Tell your grandson what you are going to do to help us. Tell him you've come to take him from his home, his friends, his school." Maria shouted from the kitchen.

Jimmy felt the sick panic rise up and his chest got tight as he tried to sit there, piecing this information together. His abuela was at Maria's side the next moment, standing over her, hugging her.

"My sweet. You know I love you. I couldn't walk out of here and leave you like this. Jimmy is young, he will adjust. Maria, it is time we try to become a family again. Your father has been burdened by all this. He was hurt and worried for the life you were going to have when you married James."

"And I was right! That man ruined your life and then he left you."

Jimmy was only ten, but smart enough to know that they were talking about him and his father. He always thought his dad was a bad guy for not sticking with them, but he hadn't thought about what it was like for his mom… to have been left with him as a son. As he understood it, his mother had a good life before she got married and then when Jimmy was born, everything went bad.

"Quiet with all of this! You don't know what you're talking about," Maria saw that Jimmy was crying and she tried to diffuse the situation. But at this point a bomb had gone off inside of Jimmy's head and the shrapnel would be with him for years.

Maria went to Jimmy, but he pulled away and ran for the door. "There you go papi. So this is your help? What can you expect Jimmy to think after all of that?

"That's what boys do, they walk out. He's got to think. He'll be back. But come on now Maria, we want you to get some things together and come home with us. I should have insisted on it years ago. You can find work. There's good work for women back home in your old neighborhood. You belong there. It's not good for you here where James brought you.

"People will be glad to see you back home. And I will love to have you back. Come Maria, pack your things. I will go out and look for Jimmy." Maria's mother waited until Maria nodded consent, and then went out into the hallway to find her grandson.

PART 2

Chapter 9

Maria did go to pack. She had put up a reasonable argument about the whole thing, but secretly this was exactly what she wanted. She knew she wasn't in any shape to continue caring for the two of them. She needed someone to take care of her for a change. The thought of it brought tears of relief. Tears she wouldn't share with her parents, especially her father whom she resented for his years of absence. And Jimmy would be better with this change too. He'd be among a close-knit Latino community and could start fresh at a new school.

Maria figured that it was Donna who had gone to her parents with her concerns. Part of Maria wanted to go to her apartment and tell her she had betrayed a friendship and that Maria would never consider her trustworthy again. But part of Maria, the part she'd struggle to admit to, wanted to give her friend a hug and thank her for doing for her what she would have never done for herself.

Jimmy's first feeling about the move was relief. The thought of having adults now looking after his mother, getting her better, left him hopeful. He had been carrying a load of responsibility that a ten-year-old wasn't meant to shoulder.

But the sadness of it, leaving everything he had ever known just about broke his heart. On the day they left, Liam and Patty stood on the cracked sidewalk watching abuelo, uncle Edward, and aunt Naomi's husband Joey load the last few furnishings into a truck. Jimmy knew he had to be helpful but he just wanted to go off and be with the friends he had neglected the last few months.

Maria and her mother finally came out of the apartment and Donna was waiting in the hallway for them. Mrs. Vazquez shook Donna's hand and whispered a thank you to her before walking down the stairs. Maria struggled with her emotions. She felt awkward around Donna for the first time, trying to decide what to do.

It was Donna who had reached out, grabbed Maria, and embraced her in a long, tender hug. Maria couldn't hold back the tears in that moment. This woman had been her lifeline and only real friend for so many years. When they parted, Donna pulled a tiny wrapped package from her cardigan and held it out to Maria. Jimmy had come back inside in time to see the two women embrace and their silent goodbye tears. Donna pulled Jimmy close into one of her tender embraces and whispered that she loved him to the moon and back.

Settling into his grandparent's apartment that evening, Jimmy and his mother put their clothes into their dressers and hung a few things in the bedroom closet they would share. They set the old, avocado green radio on Maria's dresser where they could hear the familiar music that they had played in their apartment.

Abuela kept apologizing for the apartment's smallness. She regretted that they had had to leave the home of Maria's childhood for this place. Still, Jimmy did notice that the apartment was bright and colorful like his mother had decorated theirs. His grandparents had many pictures with thick gold frames on the walls, a good number of them were religious. He saw icons of the Virgin Mary throughout the place and a small shrine was set up on a table in the corner of the living room.

Emotionally and physically exhausted, Maria and Jimmy each made up their twin beds and Jimmy lay back on his. Maria walked over to her coat where she had tucked away the package from Donna. Sitting on her bed, she removed the pretty paper. She found a note and a shiny silver necklace. Jimmy could see it was a cross and as his mother held it up, he realized it was a Celtic knot. It looked identical to the one he had seen hanging from Donna's neck for as long as he had memory

His mother ran it through her fingers and laid it across her thigh while she read the note. Jimmy could see Donna had drawn her signature string of hearts down the right border of the paper. His mother held the necklace up again and studied it before putting it around her neck. The note she slipped into the little wooden box where she always kept her special things.

***

In the weeks ahead Jimmy worked hard to adjust to his new life. Abuela and Maria had taken him to register at his new school and he finished out his last few weeks of fifth grade feeling overwhelmed. Fear, like the old ugly thing that it was, had found Jimmy again and he fought against it.

And at home things were not much easier. Even though he shared a room with his mother there was nothing of the privacies he was used to having. Living with his grandparents and having aunts, uncles, and cousins coming by all the time; there was very little time for just Jimmy and his mother. For all the anxiety her illness had caused him, at least he had had his mother all to himself.

Maria had found work in a grocery store and sometimes wasn't home until after dinner. Jimmy especially missed her on those nights. He'd have to sit at the table for dinner, his grandmother all full of questions while his grandfather barely looked up from his dinner plate. And they spoke Spanish all the time. While Jimmy had heard his mother and abuela use the language when they were together, he had to concentrate now to pick up threads of conversation.

Then there was the issue with his grandfather. Abuelo rarely said a word to his grandson and he avoided being in a room alone with him. When he did speak, it was usually to yell at him about something. Jimmy had quickly picked up on the sad fact that his grandfather didn't like him and Jimmy was genuinely afraid of the man.

And every Sunday, every single Sunday, the family went to Mass. There was a large stone church less than a block from their apartment and it was so full of parishioners that many stood along the cold mortar sides through the forty-five-minute ritual of song, homely, and receiving of the Eucharist. Up and down, kneeling and sitting, the people performed these movements in harmony and without prompting. It was a Mass for Hispanics, everyone and everything was spoken in their native tongue.

Jimmy would learn that going to Mass was for the Vasquez family and many others as essential as air. It was where you brought the worries and cares of a hard life. You came to celebrate the Eucharist and eternal life through the giver Jesus. You came to pray and to weep for lost family, and for some, you came out of obligation and the fear that in not going you would be called to judgement in the life after.

Maria followed along during those first months. She made the sign of the cross and genuflected as she entered the church right along with everyone else. Abuela smiled, pleased as they sat together on the hard wooden bench. Jimmy was put between the two women so that he could learn the timing of the movements, the prayers that were said and the strange little songs sung in response to the Priests chanting's. Here even abuelo never complained, but silently followed the rest.

But years ago Maria had lost her heart for the church, for God and His mercies. She had slowly stopped communicating with Him until eventually, over the years, she felt abandoned by Him.

And with her family, like with God, she would begin to withdraw. It was a slow fade and not obvious to them for a long time. Jimmy was the only one that recognized when his mother was slipping back to her troubled ways. He could see it in her distant eyes and in the words she did not speak, but he trusted his grandparents to know if his mother needed anything and he did everything he could to believe, like they did, that everything was fine.

***

Donna had faithfully sent notes to Maria that first year; you could count on seeing her big, loopy, curling cursive on a pretty envelope every few weeks. Jimmy found himself watching his mother after she would read one of the notes. A mix of sadness and longing would show on her face and in her slow movements around the apartment. She seemed lost in the past for a few hours, quiet and pondering.

His mother never talked about what Donna had written and Jimmy didn't push her for information even though he wanted desperately to know what was happening back at the apartment and in the Hennessey home. But eventually Jimmy couldn't stand it and decided to read the letters after seeing his mother had been sliding them into her top dresser drawer.

Jimmy could hear Aunt Donna's sweet voice in the opening words. Words that told Maria how much they were both missed but assuring that things would all work out and that she was so happy that Maria had found her family again. "How was Jimmy? Liam asks about him all the time and I hope that soon we can get the boys together." When Jimmy read the words, his heart leapt. He didn't realize how much he wanted this too. Why hadn't his mother asked him if he'd like to see the Hennessey's he wondered.

The second letter was four pages long. Donna told Maria all about the old neighbors, the kids, her sewing jobs, Patrick's schedule and the search they had started for a little house of their own. "Will you call me soon Maria? It would be so good to see you. Liam misses Jimmy….and I do too."

Jimmy savored every word. They were candy to him and he wanted to reach through the pages, through the words, and give Donna a hug. It had only been a few months but he realized he desperately missed the family.

After reading them all, he guiltily tucked them away in the drawer and tried to take his mind off of what he had read. But he couldn't, and he decided he wouldn't. He wanted to see his friends and he would bring it up to his mother somehow. It would be a good thing for her as much as for him he decided.

The next Friday afternoon, they met Donna, Liam, and Patty in the park near the Vazquez's apartment. Maria made the call after Jimmy began nagging her about his friends. "We will do this…but," she said, "we will ask them to come here to our park."

Jimmy had hoped to go to the old neighborhood, but didn't argue with his mother. He was just so glad they were going. He couldn't know how hard this was for his mother, that she was trying every day to forget the last months of her life. That it would be difficult for her to see Donna and to have things come rushing back.

Jimmy ran when he saw the figures of his friends by the swings. Getting hold of him first, Donna hugged him close, lingering to whisper in his ear and give him a tender kiss on the cheek before releasing him to the kids. Maria allowed a hug from Donna and greeted Liam and Patty with kisses as well.

The afternoon was one of a wonderful few that first summer. Always the same place and time, the meetings were a sliver of joy in the hard months after the move. And Maria seemed to respond as well, warming slowly to conversation with Donna. Her guard was down, if just a little and for those few hours.

***

Near Jimmy's eleventh birthday that fall, the first of seven annual birthday cards came from Donna and the family. In it was $10 for "whatever he might like, just as long as it was fun." But better still was the letter, a page written from Liam and one from Donna, just to him. Jimmy sat down to write his thank you that very night and made sure he wrote a letter too. He repeatedly said how much he looked forward to their next visit. "Where do you want to meet now that it's getting cold?" he asked.

But as weather changed, so did Maria's motivation to keep up with the Hennessey's. They met a few more times before Christmas, taking the kids to a museum, to pick pumpkins, and finally to a winter festival. And Jimmy could see his mother struggle each time, waiting till the last minute to leave and then hardly adding to the conversation. Jimmy found himself filling in for his mother and making excuses to his friends.

So as the New Year came and Maria continued to grow more distant even as she balanced work and family, Jimmy backed off. He was coming to realize that he had to let go of the things and people that made it harder for his mother and he had to move on, whether he was ready for it or not. The winter festival was the last they saw of the Hennessey's for a very long time.

Still, he worried about his mother who he thought should be doing better after being back with her parents. Not able to ignore the silent tension and tired of worrying, Jimmy found himself questioning abuela about her. He needed to know if she was seeing the changes in his mother that he was or if maybe he was somehow worrying about things that weren't there.

He snuck around the subject with simple questions and casual comments: Do you think mom likes her job at the grocery? I thought I heard mom crying in the bathroom last night. Is she sad about something? I wonder why mom doesn't write Aunt Donna much anymore. I miss doing things with them. And remember when we first moved here how she would walk with me to the park? We haven't done that in a long time.

Abuela always assured Jimmy but he knew she also considered what he said. Several times he had heard her speaking in hushed tones to abuelo, but he would just shush her off telling her to find something else to worry her time. Abuela was beginning to see what Jimmy was seeing and in an effort to help, she tried to make things as easy as possible for her daughter. But when Maria began to go out on the nights she didn't work, coming home into the morning hours and then finding excuses for not going to Mass, abuela became upset. Even abuelo seemed to consider that maybe his daughter was in some kind of trouble again.

They prayed for Maria, lit candles for her, and invited the priest to their home. Abuela asked Naomi to come by and talk to her sister. But as Jimmy saw it, Naomi was the worst one to reach out to his mother. She'd come with her husband and two perfect little bratty kids who said and did all the right things. How could his mother relate to her? If anything, Naomi was pushing Maria further away.

For a while Jimmy believed as his grandmother did, that going to mass, lighting the candles and praying would somehow fix his mother. He recited and memorized every prayer and knelt on the kneeler, fervently asking God, Mary, and Jesus for his mothers' problems to be lifted, carried away. He was strangely comforted by the ritual of it all and didn't complain when abuela told him it was time to go to church. Jimmy thought he was doing something, that by his prayers, his mother would be healed. It gave him purpose and hope.

But after a time, when Maria was not only not better, but becoming less and less of the mother he had known, Jimmy began to doubt the whole thing. This God of his grandmother's wasn't listening. And while abuela prayed all the more and abuelo lit more candles, Jimmy tried to distance himself from his mothers' problems and abuela's God.

Chapter 10

"Where are you going?" Abuela yelled down the street after Jimmy.

He didn't bother to look back, to try to say something to set his grandmother's mind at ease. He knew it was mean, and he'd upset her. He knew that he'd pay when he got home, but for a little while Jimmy was in control.

It was a Sunday afternoon and the neighborhood was busy with people out on their porches, men talking and smoking in their white tee shirts. Kids were running everywhere along the rutted sidewalks playing chase or hopscotch or bouncing on pogo sticks. A few of the lucky ones drove radio-controlled cars up and down the street or sat on apartment steps with little electronic games in their hands. Still others balanced on the crumbling curb of the street like it was a tightrope, arms extended, wobbling from side to side.

Music came out of many of the open windows and young mothers in tight bell bottom jeans with babies on their hips were talking to other mothers holding babies. Jimmy didn't notice much of it. He'd lived in this neighborhood of lively, talkative Hispanic families for over two years but hadn't embraced much of the culture or the friendliness of the people.

There were a few guys a couple of years older than him that he'd recently been spending time with. They were kids his grandmother would have said were trouble, problem causers. But she hadn't met them and he had no intention of bringing them by the apartment.

Miguel and Antonio were out in front of the market when Jimmy rounded the corner and he saw them immediately, Antonio with a lit cigarette between his fingers and Miguel kicking a can on the sidewalk. These guys could be found most any day hanging out somewhere along this stretch of the street. Jimmy had first met them when he walked by them after school one day. It wasn't his normal walking route, but he had been trying to waste time, not wanting to go home.

"Hey, what's up?" Miguel looked up from his can kicking when he heard Jimmy approach.

"Nothin'. How 'bout you guys?"

"The same. But we were just talking about going over to the school. Antonio left some smokes under one of the slides. Want to come with?"

Jimmy hesitated for a minute, unzipped his Yankees sweatshirt and tucked his tee shirt into his jogging pants, trying to look older. "Yeah, I guess. But why did you leave them there? Aren't you afraid someone from school will find them?"

"Nah. I mean, even if they did, they don't know whose they are and they don't really care. Smoking is nothing to them." As if on cue, Antonio pulled one last drag from his cigarette and snuffed it out with his sneaker.

"I don't leave my cigarettes anywhere near home. Some parents might get pissed about them, but for me… my dad, well, he don't give a damn if I smoke. Only thing is, he'd probably smoke 'em himself. I can't be stealing cigarettes both for me and him, so I hide them places, like at school."

Antonio didn't talk much, but when he did it was usually about his dad.

"So come on, let's go. I'm tired of just standing around." Miguel kicked the can out into the street and started walking in the direction of the school. The boys quickly followed as they usually did when Miguel wanted to do something.

About a block from the school, Miguel bent down suddenly to tie his sneaker. The boys were following close and Jimmy ran into Antonio before he realized it.

"What the hell, Jimmy."

"Sorry, Antonio. Didn't know we were stopping."

Miguel talked low so people passing by wouldn't hear him. "Jimmy. Antonio and I've been walking around most all day. We're thirsty. Why don't you go in there and get us some sodas." He looked up and jerked his head toward the small corner store across the street.

"I would, but I don't have money. Abuela had to stop giving me my dollar allowance when my abuelo told her I didn't deserve it. Said I was lazy and not doing my chores right. He's such a jerk. I hate him."

"Don't care about that Jimmy. Only know that we're thirsty and want soda. We let you hang out with us and here you are only thirteen. Why don't you just go in and get them? You know, the way we do."

"I don't think he's ready, Miguel. He's got scared all over his face."

"Jimmy. Do you like hanging out with us?"

"I guess."

"Really, Jimmy. 'I guess?' You've been coming by every couple of days for weeks and following us like a little puppy and now you're saying 'I guess' to hanging out with us." Miguel stood up and looked down into Jimmy's face.

"No. I mean, yeah. I like hanging out with you guys. You're my friends"

"Well then, Jimmy, why not just go in to that store and get your friends a drink."

"Well…ok. But what do I do? I've never taken anything before."

"Bad idea, Miguel. If he screws this up, we're all in trouble."

"Not so, Antonio. He's got to go in there for himself. Anyone ever hold your hand first time you took those cigarettes?"

"Yeah. Guess not. Jimmy, it's something you just got to do for yourself. You just got to be confident. Like it's no big deal to go in the store. Walk right over to the sodas and take a few. Kind of wait around a minute. When the cashier's busy, that's when you slide 'em under your shirt and walk on out of there.

That's right. Just slide in and slide out. Nothin' to worry about. It's no big deal. People are taking little stuff like that all the time. I heard store owners got insurance for it. If something comes up missing, they tell the insurance guys and they just write them a check for it." Miguel grinned convincingly.

"I guess I can do it." Jimmy stammered. "You guys gonna wait out here for me?" Jimmy tried to sound confident but his voice betrayed him.

"Yup. Just around the corner there. We'll watch for you. Be sitting right against the first building." Miguel stepped away from Jimmy and pulled Antonio along with him. "See you in a few."

Jimmy was left there, staring across at the small store with the dirty red awning. Every minute or so someone would either enter or leave. He thought about it for a moment, of what might happen if he were to get caught, but then he walked across the street. He zipped up his sweatshirt and waited until a young woman with a small boy pushed open the door. He followed closely behind, hoping to appear to be with the woman.

When she headed down the canned food aisle, he did too. She stopped part way down but Jimmy walked to the end and turned right. The sodas were along the wall ahead. It was the far end of the first aisle and the cashier was at the front end of the aisle, by the entrance. While the old man checked out a customer, Jimmy quietly opened the cooler and grabbed the first two bottles he laid his hands on. Then he turned and walked along the back wall of the store, waiting a minute before pushing them one at a time down into the elastic waist of his pants. His sweatshirt hung over loosely and for the first time he was grateful that it was a size too big.

Luckily when he walked back around the corner he saw that the young woman was in line with a few items in her hand. He walked up front, waiting back a few feet while she purchased her things. The pop was ice cold against his hot stomach and he could feel the wet run down his skin. Then as the woman went to the door with her boy by the hand, Jimmy followed along too, right behind them as he had when they entered. Outside the door he followed them along the first few buildings before turning back towards the corner where the boys were supposed to be waiting.

He wanted to run, but he didn't dare. The bottles were inches from slipping through the waist of his pants and onto the sidewalk. He hugged himself, using his arms to hold the bottles up as he made his way past the few store fronts to the corner. Turning onto the side street he saw the two boys leaning along the wall of one of the apartment buildings. Realizing he had successfully stolen the sodas, he let out a loud sigh and quickly pulled the bottles from his pants pushing them into the hands of the boys before they could say anything.

"Damn, Antonio. The kid did it. I wouldn't of bet on you though," Miguel gave Jimmy a poke with his elbow. Both boys emptied the bottles before saying another word.

"Ok, Jimmy. But for the record, I don't like orange pop so much. Next time get colas, ok?" Miguel laughed as he rolled his bottle along the length of the alley. It curved to the left and stopped about ten feet ahead in the gutter.

Jimmy was feeling weak and his hands were shaking. He stuffed them into his sweatshirt pockets and wordlessly nodded. He felt like pacing and he was sweaty. It was the same as he'd felt when he was in class sometimes, thinking about his mother. It was his damn thinking that made him feel bad. When he didn't think about things, when he just did, then he was fine. It was like Antonio had said. You just got to slide in and slide out like it is no big deal. It was about confidence.

"So let's go get my smokes."

Miguel nodded and the two turned back toward the street.

Antonio looked back to where they had left Jimmy. He seemed to be mumbling to himself. "Hey. Are you coming?"

Realizing someone was talking to him, Jimmy lifted his head and nodded as he jogged up to the boys and quietly took his spot behind them. He tried as hard as he could not to think about anything that had just happened or anything about what would happen when he got home.

***

He hadn't noticed the time and as he approached the apartment he could see abuelo sitting on the stoop. That was what he did most evenings after dinner. It was a place for him to get away. To think or not to think. There abuelo was, sitting and smoking, oblivious to the few children left playing on the street. Jimmy hated abuelo, but he was also afraid of him. He couldn't think of any way of getting by him and he'd hear about it for missing dinner.

Abuelo stood when he saw Jimmy coming. "Where in the hell were you?" he bellowed. "Don't you have a thought in your head for anybody but yourself? I ought to lay you out for what you've done to your abuela in there. She hasn't stopped talking about you since you left." Abuelo was hotter than Jimmy had ever seen him and the kids on the street knew enough to head into their apartments.

"I went to the park with some friends. We were playing ball and no one checked the time. I'm sorry I missed dinner. I'll go in and tell abuela I'm sorry."

"Oh, so that's how you do this? You apologize and then everything's ok? Well I've got other ideas for you." Abuelo grabbed Jimmy by the arm.

Jimmy suddenly felt a new kind of hot. Not sweaty, but hot in his face and he was shaking, but not his usual nervous shaking. This was anger and he found it was harder to control. He pulled hard to free himself from his grandfather and then he looked him in the eye. "You are out here yelling at me. Telling me I'm only thinking of myself because one time I forget and miss dinner. Well I'll tell you what I think. I think you take all your meanness out on me. All the things you can't fix get to be my fault. Why don't you get mad at my mother when *she's* gone? How come she can go off and leave and never say where she's going or when she'll be home. How come you let her do that? How come? How come?" He was trembling, and immediately he regretted betraying his mother in this way.

Big heavy tears fell from Jimmy's eyes and he slid down onto a step with his hands over his face. His grandfather didn't say anything and Jimmy sat there with his tears running down his cheek and collecting in the palms of his hands. Suddenly he felt a set of hands over his own and he fought the instinct to look up. But then he heard abuela's soft voice in his ear and he wiped his eyes and lifted his face to her. She was upset he could see and she hugged him tenderly. Abuelo was on the other side of his wife, sitting on the same step as Jimmy, with his head down, hand on his mouth. Jimmy thought he saw his grandfather's back shutter. Could it be possible the mean old man was crying?

Jimmy went to his bedroom where he spent the next several hours alone. His grandparents hadn't come in or tried to get him to come eat dinner. The house was quiet except for the muffled voices of the television far off in the living room. Sounded like M.A.S.H to him. Jimmy began to feel hungry and, as he sat there, realized maybe he was at some fault for what had happened on the porch. But he just didn't feel he had a place he belonged anymore. He so wished his mother would come through the door. He wanted her to sit on the end of his bed and tell him she was sorry. She was sorry because she had forgotten they had a relationship, because she had abandoned her position as mother and left him wondering what he had done to deserve it all.

The next thing Jimmy remembered was waking up to the light on the nightstand. He turned instinctively towards his mother's bed and was surprised to see her sitting there staring back at him. He wondered what time it was and why she was sitting there, awake. It wasn't often she was in the room other than to sleep. But as he woke more, he noticed that his mother's eyes were red and ringed like a raccoon's and his thoughts went back to what he had said earlier to his grandfather. Had abuelo spoken to Maria? Jimmy thought they would have had to say something to her about his behavior. He felt embarrassed and wished he could start the whole day over.

Finally it was Maria who spoke.

"Jimmy, honey. I'm so sorry about how things have been going. I guess I just didn't know how bad you were feeling about…" her voice trailed off and she sniffed back tears. "It's just that, I guess I'm not sure about some things myself. It's not about you. It never has been, but I'm not so sure I can be the mother I wanted to be to you." Maria bowed her head and wept quietly.

"No, Mom, don't cry. You *are* my mother. You *are!*" He went to her bed and sat carefully on the end of it, waiting. He was afraid for what she might say next.

Maria quieted after a minute and looked up at Jimmy. "Yes, I'm your mother and I will always love you. But when I was a little girl I had two parents and they knew what to do. Abuela was always a good mother. She just knew how to be one. And I know you think your abuelo is mean and unloving, but he wasn't like that when I was a kid. He played with us and he told me stories and always took care of our family. And he talked to abuela every night. I could hear them in bed. She always knew she was loved. They were happy and they were good parents because of it."

"But you're with them now. They love you just like they used to. Nothing's changed," his voice pleaded.

Maria sighed and moved to Jimmy, taking him into her arms. "I wish it were true. That nothing's changed. I wish it were true."

Jimmy didn't understand his mother but he knew she was struggling with something that was too deep maybe even for her to understand. But for now, he had the warm loving arms of his mother wrapped around him and, although he somehow knew that this was only for this moment, he wasn't going to ruin it.

***

For a while after that day, the family seemed to be especially good to each other. Abuelo let up some on Jimmy, not finding fault in every little thing he did. He even asked him about his friends and things at school. Jimmy found it odd to the point of being uncomfortable. It wasn't the way he knew his grandfather and it felt like an act to him. He suspected that abuela was behind it and he knew it was because of what happened that day on the front stoop.

When Jimmy went off with friends, abuela didn't ask him to be home for dinner although he knew how important it was to her and that he often upset her. And when the Sunday came when Jimmy pulled the blankets up over his head rather than get up to go to church with his grandmother, she restrained herself from jostling him awake as she had done in the past. She left for the church silently and alone.

Maria had been trying as best she could to be the mother her son deserved and the daughter her parents had raised. It seemed to Jimmy that she would hold up for a while, sometimes months at a time. During one of these especially good periods Jimmy came home to find the sweet smells of baking and the unusual sound of laughter spilling from the kitchen. As he entered the doorway he saw his mother standing with her arms outstretched, her face and torso covered in flour. Abuela looked as though she had had an encounter with the baking ingredient as well and she was swatting at her powder covered clothes with a hand towel, the two of them laughing.

As soon as Jimmy stepped in to the room he was blasted from the side with a cloud of white. Looking for the source he was startled to see abuelo standing a few feet away with a near empty bag of flour in his hands and a challenging grin on his face. Maria went to Jimmy as though she was going to help him, but then she hugged him tight, rubbing more flour on to his clothes. Then just as suddenly she turned toward abuelo and with a quick move she popped the flour bag out of his hands and upturned it over his head, his grey hair becoming white. Jimmy held his breath wondering until he heard his grandfather's chuckling grow into a deep hearty laugh as he acknowledged that he had gotten what he deserved.

There were a few times like that one, little happy moments that broke through like a tiny ray of sun reaching through a cloud filled sky. And Jimmy knew to hold on to them and to love them because his mother always fell back into the despairs of her mind. And when that happened she withdrew from everyone again.

Finally, the sadness won out and the inevitable happened. Maria lost her job. She didn't tell anyone, but it wasn't hard to figure out. Jimmy saw the high platform shoes and the impossibly tight jeans, the heavy makeup his mother was wearing. She began going out more nights and coming back well into the morning hours when the house was asleep. Jimmy's grandparents didn't know where she had been and they didn't dare to ask because at this point no one wanted to push Maria over the edge. Jimmy wondered why it was that he seemed to be the only one who knew that his mother was already teetering on the edge and without someone putting their arms out to pull her back, she was going to fall.

Chapter 11

Spring 2010

James had only been approached on a few occasions in his first weeks living as a homeless man. Few people bothered him and most did their best not to notice him and he liked it that way. Occasionally, though, groups of kids on their way to nowhere would stop to throw insults and even pieces of trash at him while he limped along the streets, looking for something to eat. They were mostly young and typically just trying to get a laugh at his expense.

But one evening in April in the oasis that was the park, just weeks into James's new life, a large kid in his late teens thought it'd be fun to push him around a little. James tried to tell the boy that he didn't want any trouble, but he had at least five friends with him and they circled around him, taunting and poking at him. There was another transient sauntering around the playground but he wasn't interested in saving anyone's hide but his own. He moved along into the dark recesses of the trees.

Just when James thought he wasn't going to get out of it without a beating, they were all startled to hear the high pitched screams of a woman. The kids turned to see the outline of a small figure coming up fast from behind them. Each of them, even James, were startled to see an insane looking girl running towards them with hair long and ratty nails filed like claws, her chest bare but for a bandana tied around her, breasts hanging heavy beneath it. She held one hand up in front of her and in it she had a hypodermic needle held like a knife.

"Get the hell away from him! Right now! I've been using this needle for my crack and you don't want me stickin' it in your arm, that's for sure." She smiled then, and they all saw her front teeth which had each been filed to points so that they all looked like canines. In that moment he thought she was the most horrific thing he had ever seen. The kids must have felt the same, for not one of them stopped running until they were far from sight.

"That works every time." She laughed and topped the syringe with an orange tip she had in her hand, carefully wrapping it in a rag and pocketing it in her ragged jeans. "Guess I scared the hell out of you too." She grinned and held out her hand. James was too afraid not to shake it, so he did. "Name's Molly," she said casually. "Hang on a second, I've gotta' go get my coat, it's cold as hell out here. You'd have to be crazy to walk around with nothing but a bandana for a shirt." She laughed a teasing little laugh and retrieved a much used black leather coat from behind a bush. James didn't know what to think, but was relieved to see that this woman appeared to have some sanity after all.

Molly looked over each side of her back to see that no one was within ear shot. Then she leaned in toward James who bowed his head to her. "I've had my eye on you since you started staying here. I've got a little place I'm working on over there in the back of those buildings. Great plans for it!" She turned her head slightly to the left where there was a grouping of long, narrow, yellow buildings that looked like abandoned warehouses.

"Found my way in there one night. I'm not gonna tell you how I get in, but I do. Found a great place for keeping out of the cold and away from the crazies. Haven't told anybody about it, don't want cops breathing down my back or junkies knocking on my door and I've got great plans for it. Like I said though…I've been watching you and you don't look like you know much about living out here. I figured you weren't the type, you know. Then I saw those kids starting in on you and you with no idea of what to do. That's why I came over… looking like this." Molly smiled that horrific grin and pulled her coat back to show her bandana shirt, breasts and all.

"Well. I guess I should thank you." James acknowledged bashfully.

"Yeah, well. You've got to come up with something to keep people off your back. If you're gonna make it without shit like THAT happening, you've got to either look completely put together, like you never go without a shower and you get three square meals or you've got to disturb people. I mean *look* like you shouldn't be messed with." Here Molly opened her mouth and pointed at her fang teeth. "Did this myself back when I was living in Chicago. And yeah, I scared the shit out of myself the first few times I looked in a mirror, but they've kept people off my back so I just stopped looking."

James couldn't help but take a step back. "They *are* pretty awful. But you sure had those kids running. Like I said, thanks for that."

"We're neighbors in some twisted way, I guess you could say. But even out here back away from the city you need to be careful. Doesn't hurt to have someone watching your back. You planning on staying out here like you've been?"

James was hesitant to get into a conversation with this young woman. "I don't want to be sleeping on the streets. And I don't plan on staying homeless, you know. But out here… I don't know. At least I feel like maybe I am just camping until I can figure things out."

"I get it about the sleeping on the streets thing. But dude…homeless is homeless, even if you ARE gonna make it back into suburbia, you aren't there yet. You've got to save your ass." Molly slapped her rear with her hand for emphasis.

"Guess you had me right. I'm new to this whole thing," James was embarrassed to admit this to Molly. That, he thought was crazy. Shouldn't it be the fact that he was homeless that embarrassed him and not the fact he wasn't good at it.

"Well, if you stay on here, you'd be better to make yourself invisible." She stopped and looked James over, head to toe. "You'll never pass for the threatening type. Cops won't bother you much as long as you stay quiet. There really isn't much of a homeless community here, not more than a few of us I've ever seen. But the kids, well they're another story. They come through here when they're bored and all full of anger. Kids are such jerks sometimes. They've got no clue, you know. At night you've got to either get yourself out onto a street where everyone can see you or get undercover where no one sees you. Get yourself hurt or worse, the way you're doing things." Molly shook her head vigorously for emphasis.

James was surprised at Molly's take on young people. She looked maybe a few years out of high school herself. "Well, it's been kind of one day at a time so far."

"Well, I know people who've tried that but if you know you're gonna be out here a while, do what I say. Maybe you are one of the few that just got screwed on a job and will leave when you get another one. Don't know your reasons, but as I see it most of us are bound up with something, say drugs or alcohol or maybe just messed up about something.

People run for all kinds of reasons." She stopped her talking and touched her chest with her outstretched hand. "If you got one or more of those things going on then you'll be calling yourself homeless soon enough."

James didn't know what to say. Molly understood more about his condition than maybe he did himself. He hadn't wanted to think about all that had brought him to where he was standing that night. But from that conversation and at that point in time he realized that for now he was a homeless man.

Molly had bounced back down the road after talking to him, babbling on about needing to get some more supplies. She was in the middle of something and needed to get back to it. Jimmy was relieved to see her go. He had decided that he was going to go through this time alone.

To his surprise the young woman came to him the next day. She had shown up at the park just before sunrise and woken him from his fitful sleep under his tarp-covered picnic table in a cluster of trees. She had cleaned herself up just a bit from the day before. Her hair, while still stringy, was in a ponytail and she had on a paint-speckled sweater in place of the crazy, breast-bouncing bandana. She handed him a crumbly biscuit and told him to get up, she was taking him on a tour of the city. Jimmy, not wanting to hurt her feelings, ended up spending much of the day doing the best he could to keep up with her as she set off in flurry of sightseeing information.

Molly took him to a diner where the owner had a soft spot for her and left a bag of day old breads by the back entrance from time to time. It was hers if she came by to retrieve it. "That biscuit I gave you came from here," she exclaimed. The manager would even pour her a cup of coffee at the counter during business hours and let her sit there and drink it, no charge. Then there was a little Italian restaurant that was known to leave carryout containers of pasta and meatballs just outside their back door in a bag on the ground after closing every Saturday night. Molly had come to know this when she had first come to town and started stalking one of the few vagrants for a couple of days. She saw him stop at the restaurant, bend down on the back stoop and grab a container out of the bag. She came back every night until she figured out that it was a once a week thing and there was plenty for the few who knew to come by.

Molly seemed to do everything at one speed. She walked very fast and talked even faster, gesturing and laughing as she told him how she figured out this life during her own first months. James found it impossible to keep up with her and after a few minutes he was trailing a ways behind. Eventually she would become conscious of this fact and turn back to him, skipping and bouncing down the street. She had an extreme amount of energy, especially considering that she told him she had been homeless for more than two years. But she was so full of positivity and exuberance that he was carried along by her attitude.

By noon, all the walking left James's leg in terrible pain and he had to tell Molly he was returning to the park to rest. She apologized for pushing him too much and promised to bring him back some food by nightfall. Off she went, in a jog down the street. James sat on a bench he found in front of a bank and silently watched the cars and people pass him by. Had it been that not so long ago he had been one of those people? It was too painful to consider.

***

James didn't see anything of Molly for the next week and when she did find him again in the park one afternoon she looked like she hadn't slept much. She wasn't bouncing

102

around, but instead slumped like she carried a weight across her shoulders. She had dark circles under her eyes and had cut back her filed fingernails. Her hair appeared clean but was sloppily pulled back and she was wearing an old, oversized cardigan, fitted jeans and sneakers. And her teeth. They were perfect rectangles and unnaturally white. She looked like a different person.

"Sorry about the last few days," she said. "I was working on some things and time gets away from me sometimes." She sounded like she was talking while sucking on a hard piece of candy.

"You don't have to explain Molly. You were very nice to me and I don't expect anyone to take care of me."

"Yeah, well. That's probably for the best. I'm not so good at it as I may have seemed to be," her voice was a whisper.

"You look a little tired and…well different. Your teeth. How did you do that?" James rubbed his index finger across his own front teeth.

"This is a fake. A dentist saw me shortly after my file job and pulled me aside, right there on the street. Said he had something I could wear if I met him the same place the next day. I showed up and so did he, with this thing." She pulled at the front of her mouth and extracted some sort of plate. It looked like a thin white half ring, the plastic shaped like perfect white little teeth.

"Neat!" James exclaimed. "Looks good on you."

"Well, I get enough attention for my liking without my teeth being my mouth piece. No pun intended." She said seriously. "Think I'm going to go lay low for a while. Just wanted to check on you I guess."

James didn't know where to go with the conversation and seeing that Molly was not acting like the same girl he had met last week he knew he needed to let her go. But surprisingly, he didn't want to. "I may go look for a little something to eat. Can I bring you something if I have luck?" James got up off the ground and stretched before hoisting his pack onto his back.

"No, don't bother. I'm going to go walk around, clear my head for a while. See you later sometime." And Molly went off toward the group of buildings she had mentioned all those days before.

James managed to find a bag of fries and an apple pie in a trash barrel outside one of the fast food restaurants he had been watching from a distance. And someone who apparently saw him reach in for it gave him a coupon for a free burger from the same restaurant. He hated this part of being homeless. If people offered him something, he would humbly accept. But never, he vowed, would he beg for anything. He didn't like being out on the streets for any longer than necessary and he headed back to the quiet and seclusion of the small park.

James couldn't help but think of Molly when she hadn't shown up those first few days. There was just something about her that left him wondering…and worrying. She had come to his rescue and exuberantly shared some of her street smarts with him and then she had returned days later looking tired and drawn, maybe even sick. As much as he thought it would be best to just put her behind him, he knew that he couldn't. He'd made impulsive decisions and meddled where he should have left well enough alone before, and he was about to do it again. So with the apple pie and some water in his backpack, he limped off down the path that led from the wooded lot to the abandoned warehouses.

Chapter 12

Not surprisingly, the day came when things would not hold up any longer in the Vazquez family. There was a line that they carefully walked with each other. Jimmy's grandparents continued to entertain their family and friends even as Maria came and went as she pleased. Jimmy couldn't understand how abuela could cook for birthdays and smile at gatherings. Jimmy found it harder and harder to be around his aunts, uncles, and cousins. He was tired of pretending. He knew they all saw the changes in his mother, how her eyes were dark and sunken and her body so thin. He heard the whispers in the kitchen and he knew they were about her… about him.

Maria was in such a state that it seemed enough for her to bathe and feed herself some days. She hadn't worked for nearly a year and she slept a lot of the time she was home. But still she went out many nights. What she did they didn't know, although Jimmy had his ideas about it. But asking questions or confronting her was out of the question with abuela always protecting, always keeping the peace.

But peace came at a price and it was an unrealistic expectation. When Maria would go off, sometimes for days at a time, abuelo would become angry. Like Jimmy, he had a hard time walking the thin line abuela had drawn for them. Not able to pretend any longer, he let his anger surface. He'd pace the house, swearing and smoking and threatening abuela that this was the last time he'd put up with it. And if Jimmy was around…well, he'd get a dose of his grandfather's anger too.

"Get the hell away from that refrigerator, boy. I'm the only one around here making any money so that food is mine."

"Go on now, Jimmy. You've had dinner. Go on and find something to do. I'll bring you something later."

Jimmy would look at his grandmother with stone cold eyes and walk away.

Then there were the times when abuelo would seek Jimmy out. No matter where he might be, sitting out on the steps, or laying across his bed his grandfather would come looking for him. And it didn't matter how innocent he was. Abuelo wanted someone to pay for his pain.

"What in the hell are you doing?" Jimmy would look up at his grandfather's frame in the doorway. "I said…what in the hell are you doing?"

There was no right answer Jimmy knew. He'd tried them all. It didn't matter his reply, only that abuelo needed to drain the fury from his blood.

One time when Jimmy provoked his grandfather by turning his back on him in the middle of one of his rants, abuelo had pulled him by the ear and dragged him out to the tiny patch of yard in the back of the apartment. He'd pulled his belt swiftly from his pants with one hand while continuing to squeeze Jimmy's ear. Then he'd pushed him away with the command to stand with his face to the tree. It was more frightening than usual, seeing abuelo this out of control.

The belt snapped against Jimmy's shirt and he howled and moved his hands to cover his back. He turned, but by then the belt had been snapped a second time and it connected with his cheek. The sharp, piercing pain had made Jimmy cry out again. The sound of it, sudden and shrill like a distressed animal, must have jolted his grandfather back from the dark place he had gone because he stopped abruptly. Without a word, he left the yard, pulling his belt back through the loops in his pants. He never laid a hand on Jimmy after that.

After the shock and the pain of that day, Jimmy knew the fallout of his mother's problems was ruining more than just her life. Surprisingly, Jimmy didn't hate his grandfather. Not for this thing, because he too felt the strength of his own emotions and knew he had to find his own way of purging it. But after that beating, Jimmy had looked up and seen his grandmother in the upstairs window. She had looked out and she had seen him with abuelo and she had turned away in silence. Abuela. The one who cooked his favorite dinners, who made sure he had a packed lunch and said prayers for him at night had been watching. That hurt more than any crack of the belt ever would.

Jimmy needed something more. Something that took up time and got him away from his grandfathers pained anger and his grandmother's refusal to do anything about their problems. He needed to get his mind off of his mothers' absence and the ache it left in the pit of his stomach. He needed to get rid of the frustration and hopelessness that were becoming his new identity.

Kids his age fell into one of several groups. The adrenaline junkies were reckless, always plotting their next dangerous adventure. The punks got their kicks out of stealing and vandalism. Jimmy had stolen those sodas a few years back and the thought of it, the ugly feeling after, still haunted him. He drifted away from those kids after that.

Most of the good kids collected in the streets or the city parks where they'd get a game of ball going. They were full of energy and talk about girls and sports, their part time jobs, and their futures. And they irritated Jimmy. While he would occasionally step out to join a game of baseball or throw the football, as he got older he increasingly found that he didn't identify with any of them.

When he wanted to be alone, and that was much of the time, he'd start walking, setting out with no plan or destination in sight except to get lost for as long as he could. He'd pass people, shops, ball games, busy workers, and mothers herding restless children. But none of it really registered with him. He became intent on the process of moving, of feeling his heart pump and the blood come to his face. If sweat trickled down his brow and his muscles tightened with his fast, long strides, it was all the better. It was a release of emotion and a high to be going somewhere, anywhere fast, and to feel what his body could do when he pushed it.

Jimmy soon started carrying small hand weights that he found at a yard sale and at home he kept a dumbbell under his clothes in his closet. He discovered that these workouts gave him a new energy and focus and that his sixteen-year-old body was responding by getting stronger and his muscles by getting large.

He began to turn his walking into jogging and then running. He'd come home, usually after dinner with a blissful body fatigue. When he finally lay down to rest he could sleep and some nights there would be no dreaming. At its best, he would be spent to the point of not hearing when or if his mother came home.

***

Was it possible that there was a God that saw one's distresses and eventually, when it looked like there was nothing left in them, decided to step in by way of providence? Jimmy thought just maybe it *was* possible. That this great Father that abuela had prayed to had finally stepped off his thrown to attend to a lost young man. Whatever the workings, a little break in the clouds of Jimmy's life came in the way of an old pickup truck that broke down on the street he happened to be jogging down one afternoon.

"Damn piece of junk," a short, skinny old guy dropped out of the driver side of the truck, kicking the door shut. "We need to get these to the market before they cook themselves." It was a very hot midsummer day and it was debatable whether the truck or the skinny guy was more overheated.

"God knows this thing's been on borrowed time since I've worked for you." A young, strong blonde kid was popping the hood of the pickup, a rag between the hot metal and his bare skin.

"Hey kid. Come over here. Think you could give us a push?" Jimmy had stopped and approached the truck.

"Sure, okay. Where do you want me?"

"I'll take the wheel," the old guy said. "Bob, you and the kid get back there and give her hell."

Jimmy followed the young man around the back of the truck and positioned his hands on the top and mid left side of the tailgate. Bob gave him a quick nod and the two threw their backs into it. A few grunts and a slip or two of foot on pavement and the truck was pushed over to the side of the street. Bob slapped Jimmy's back on his way around to the driver who was cursing as he pushed the door open.

"Damn bit of luck. And we're only maybe a block away...son of a" and the little man gave the truck the side of his boot. "We got to get to a phone and call the farm. Let 'em know about the truck."

"Chuck, give me a few dimes and I'll find a phone. Hey buddy, what was your name? Thanks for the push," the young man looked at Jimmy.

"Oh me… I'm Jimmy. Your truck's steaming pretty bad. You think some water on the engine would cool it down?"

"Shit no kid, that's not how it works." The skinny guy was laughing despite his temper. "She's a bitch she is, this truck. The radiator's shot. We've been giving it IV fluids for weeks. Can only do so much."

Bob looked at Jimmy again. "Water is more for putting out fires. This is like a cooker gone dry. Needs special fluids to keep it cool and moving. Jimmy, was it? Do you know where we can get to a phone?"

"Yeah. Just down past that corner there in front of Kay's Kandy store." Jimmy pointed in the direction they had just come from. "You want me to run down there and call someone?" He surprised himself at his willingness to get involved.

"Hmmm…no, but thanks," the tired old man answered. "I'm gonna have to talk to Betty if she hasn't already left. The market is her thing. We only help set up and tear down. She's gonna have to come with a truck, and soon if she wants to make any money today."

"Chuck, you want me to maybe start pushing a few crates with the dolly. I mean it's only a block or so and I can take three at a time on this thing." Bob already had the tailgate open and was pulling the dolly out.

"I'll help." Was Jimmy really saying this? He seldom committed himself to anything.

"Yeah maybe, Bob. But wait for me to get back." Chuck turned in the direction of the store but stopped. "Hey kid. You said you want to help. Bob, give him the canopy and the sign. He can run those down to the market, set them up for us."

"Gotcha boss." Bob motioned to Jimmy to come around the front of the truck. He pulled out a boxed tent and a tote bag. Chuck had already started up the street.

"Good of you to offer, man," Bob grinned. "Markets just a few blocks over on…"

"Oh I know where it is. I run by it all the time."

"Cool. When you get there, you'll see people setting up. Go to the left and just a few vendors down there should be an open area with a sign reading 'Hope Grows Farm.' If you can, set up the canopy in that box and try to put the sign up along the top. There's clips and stuff in there." Bob pointed to the bag.

"You can tell the girl and her mother in the next booth that we broke down but still hope to get there. They know us. Maybe ask them to tell customers that we'll be opening late. The girl. Her name's Suzie and her mom is Nancy. Just tell them Bob is asking."

"Okay. Shouldn't take me long." Jimmy headed down the street and around the corner, barely breaking a sweat.

As Jimmy came upon the open market area he saw that there were a lot of people in various stages of setting up. A few trucks had their tailgates down, young kids swinging off the ends while adults and older kids unloaded their wares. There was boisterous chatter between neighbors and some amazing smells coming from the back of the lot. Jimmy liked it.

Finding the area with the farm's name scribbled on a piece of paper and taped on a cement block he quickly went about figuring out how to construct the yellow canopy tent in the box. Only after assembling it did he turn to the vendor to the left. Sure enough there was a young girl boxed in by four tables setting out all sorts of cakes, pies, cookies, and other good things.

"Umm, Hi." Jimmy approached her quietly. "Bob wanted me to tell you that they are going to be late but they are still hoping to get here so he asked if maybe you could tell customers that they will be late." Jimmy spoke bashfully.

"Yeah, definitely… okay. We can do that. But what happened? Usually those guys are here by now." The girl who spoke, Jimmy realized, was probably close to his age, but she was tiny. Really tiny. Her face and hands were miniature, doll like. Her light brown hair was pulled up in a fat ponytail that bobbed up and down as she moved about.

"Oh right. Well, their truck broke down just a little ways back and I told them I'd run down and set up while they waited for someone from the farm to come get them. They still want to sell whatever they can get here."

"Aww, that truck. Huh. I'm sure not surprised to hear that." She laughed as she shook her head. A tiny gesture but her ponytail went swinging and she caught it, twisting it in her doll hand.

"I've got to get back there though. Bob might start out with some crates soon and I can maybe help them load up when the truck comes." Jimmy stopped and looked at the sign for the farm that he was holding in his hands.

Suzie was crawling under the back table. She popped up and came around to the front where Jimmy stood. "Listen, I can do the sign. No big deal. Let me see if my mom can drive you over there. We've got the station wagon. Could load it up and maybe a few trips would get your produce here in time." She turned and ran off, not waiting for a reply. Jimmy paced around, feeling unsure what to do. But not a minute later Suzie had a short, slender woman with a similar ponytail striding up the path alongside her.

Suzie was smiling. "My Mom said she'll drive you over and see what you can get in the car."

"Hi, I'm Nancy and yes, let's go see what we can do." Like her daughter in looks and manner, she turned toward the lot where cars were parked and motioned for Jimmy to come along. He left the sign with the girl and followed like a puppy, eager to please. Suzie was already putting up the sign, waving at them as they drove out the back entrance.

Nancy took a right onto one of the many one-way streets in the city. "So where we going? Oh, and what's your name by the way?" She was a fast talker and kind of hyper, he thought.

"They're just a few blocks over. Take the next right. Then up one block."

"Okay. And your name?" Nancy was smiling as she turned to look over her shoulder at traffic.

"Jimmy. Jimmy Gregory. Oh, and thanks for doing this. I don't know these guys but I saw them break down and thought maybe I could do something. I think the older guy, Chuck, is pretty upset."

Nancy nodded knowingly as she took the next right. They were easy to spot with the awkwardly parked truck and Chuck sitting on the edge of the curb, looking defeated. A group of kids were hanging around and all eyes were on the station wagon as it pulled up behind them. Jimmy jumped out and ran down the street where he had spotted Bob, who had just started out with the dolly. Nancy had joined Chuck on the curb.

"Looks like you could use a lift. That is if you still want to go to market today."

"Hey Nancy. Really nice of you to come. I made a call to the farm but Betty had already started out with the car. If we can get some of this over there now it will be easier for all of us." Chuck stood up and gave Nancy a pat on the back.

He walked over to where Jimmy and Bob were waiting. "Nice job, kid. You did good by us bringing Nancy over here. Still got some time? Could use your help loading up."

Jimmy grinned. He was hoping to be asked. It made him feel like he was part of something important. "No problem. Glad to help."

"Well then, shall we boys?" Chuck followed Nancy to the car and the younger two carried crates behind them.

They managed to stuff the car to the point that Jimmy and Bob had to slither into gaps between crates where they could find them. They couldn't take any tables, there just wasn't room. They would have to sell right out of the crates. Chuck stayed back with the remaining produce and waited for a farm truck to show up for the rest. Bob brought along the money box and brown bags. It seemed impossible that Nancy could possibly see from any window, but she drove confidently around the first corner, her four ways flashing.

The car was backed into an open space not far from their booth and Nancy pulled the door open to let the boys free. "There you go guys. Guess you've got it from here." Bob shook her hand as Suzie ran over to ask what she could do. Nancy gave her a quick pat on the shoulder before walking over to watch her own booth. The first customers were milling about outside the market entrance waiting for it to open. Bob handed Suzie the money box and bags and she ran over to their booth, and Jimmy saw she had borrowed and set up a table for them to use.

Without talking Bob and Jimmy started unloading the produce. Jimmy didn't have to be told what to do and when he saw Bob standing with a hand on one side of a large crate, he grabbed hold of the other side. In this way they moved quickly and had everything in their area in no time.

"That's great. Thanks a lot you two," Bob said. "That's about as good as we're gonna get for now. Betty will be here any minute and I know she'll appreciate it." Bob turned to talk to a customer but held up an index finger to signal for Jimmy to wait. He noticed that Suzie was taking some change from someone in exchange for a few tomatoes.

After a quick transaction where Bob took a dollar for a bag of beans, a few tomatoes, and some squash, he turned back to Jimmy. "Don't go until I've got your name and a phone number. Chuck made me be sure I asked. He said that if you wanted something to do the rest of the summer he was pretty sure he could pay you something for working some of the markets with Betty. It's usually my gig but extra help here means more of my greatness back at the farm."

"Wow, really. Sounds pretty cool. I don't have anything going on until school starts in September. When do you think I can start?"

Bob laughed. "I think you already did kid. If you want to do more of this, then make sure I get your information. They won't pay you much but both Betty and Donny, the owners, are super people. And Chuck, he's Donny's cousin. Well, he's good enough. Just needs to sputter from time to time. You get used to it."

Jimmy knew plenty about the reality of that last statement. He turned back to Bob who continued to help customers when they came by. Suzie had seen how busy her mom was and told them she had better get back over to her and help there. So Jimmy carried on, following Bob's lead until Betty showed up a few minutes later. She was a woman well into her fifties, her short, silver hair lay every which way on her plump head. Quick introductions were made and Bob explained what happened. Chuck showed up about a half hour later with the rest of the produce, the old truck was towed back to the farm.

***

Around five, a silver station wagon pulled over by the side of the street where Jimmy's apartment stood among the many others. One of the moms who lived there was sitting on the steps smoking a cigarette and watching her two girls skip rope. Abucla was in a second-floor window shaking out a throw rug when Jimmy stepped out of the passenger door. He looked up for just a second to see abuela watching. He quickly turned back to the car and thanked Betty and Bob for the ride home.

As they drove off he thought about his day and he wanted to be back at the market, busy with the produce and the vendors. Bob and Betty had talked to him between customers about the farm, the work, and what Betty thought Jimmy could do at the markets and at the farm. He had made a friend in Bob he thought… and liked the feeling of being part of the whole thing. And then there was the tiny girl and her mom in the next booth.A few times during the afternoon it had slowed enough for Suzie to stop over. She brought them a few cookies and Betty had given Nancy a large bag of vegetables. They all exchanged conversation and some laughs about how the day had started. Bob thought Chuck might have blown a gasket when the truck blew its radiator and he told Jimmy he should try out for the track team at school.

It was the first time in a very long time that Jimmy remembered being around so much laughter or laughing himself for that matter. Suzie was so nice. She did everything with gentleness and such ease. She seemed like a balloon floating around the market. She smiled and laughed a lot but not in a silly or loud and obnoxious way like most of the girls in school. He found her fun and easy to talk to and he hadn't experienced that in a girl before. Jimmy was looking forward to next Thursday he realized, for a number of reasons.

Chapter 13

Jimmy mentioned his new job to a few of the kids that played ball at the park around the corner that evening. He didn't often go looking for them but when he heard them out that evening he actually grabbed his sneakers and ran to catch up with them. When they all started on about their sports, unfair parents, or some girl they liked, he felt excited to have something real to share.

He hadn't said anything about the day to his grandparents, even when abuela asked him about his ride home during dinner. He just kept his mouth shut and ate. Work had made him very hungry.

But when Saturday morning came around and Jimmy went to wait for his ride, abuelo was out smoking on the front stoop. Abuelo gave him a typical dismissive look as he puffed away. Jimmy returned the look and walked out to the curb to wait. When he finally saw an old truck come slowly up the street, he waved it over. Jimmy knew his grandfather was watching. So as Bob pulled up and called out to him, Jimmy looked over his shoulder. "Won't be home for a while. Gotta go to work." The satisfaction in that moment was something he remembered for a long time.

Jimmy discovered that Thursday's market had been small in comparison to where they went on Saturday. There were many more people and double the produce to sell. It was hard work, but good work. And to his surprise, there was Suzie again. Apparently, she and her mother worked more than just the Thursday market and he would be seeing them most of the summer.

That night, abuelo actually asked Jimmy about this job of his and what was he doing. Jimmy kept it short and tried to play cool. But inside he was busting to talk on and on about the work, the guys, the farm, the girl. Abuelo appeared to listen with interest and before he walked off he gave his grandson the smallest of grins. He found Jimmy in his room later that night and handed him a pair of work gloves. "These will help," was all he said but his eyes said more and Jimmy was proud.

This job had given Jimmy confidence and purpose. His grandfather had not only softened but Jimmy sensed a new but unspoken approval from him. Abuela was packing him hefty lunches and baking his favorite desserts and even his mother, tired and troubled as she was, had a twinkle in her eye when she asked him about his work. And so it seemed that this job with Hope Grows Farm had grown a little hope in the Vazquez home just when it was desperately needed.

***

The rest of July and August went by in a flash. Jimmy was getting paid under the table. No paperwork and no commitment but Donny and Betty, and even old Chuck, loved his enthusiasm and energy. By the last week of August, Chuck had told him that the markets, while still continuing on through September would quiet down considerably and Betty could handle the customers on her own, but Donny wanted to offer him some hours at the farm on weekends if he wanted them. At that point they would put him on the payroll and get him an official work cap.

And as good as that was, Jimmy was a little saddened to think about moving from days at the market to weekends strictly on the farm. He had been to the farm many mornings helping to pick produce from the thirty or so acres they liked to call "Betty's market garden." He loved how alive everything was there. He sensed a pulse coursing through the furrows in the long acres of fields he had been taken to see. And there was a smell there distinct to the farm. An unusual sweetness came from the cow barns with all that straw and hay mixing with milk and manure. The morning soil when damp had its own musty earthy odor. Jimmy discovered that green was more than a color, it was a smell and the tomato vines had a distinct sharpness that stayed on your fingers all day. These were smells that Jimmy had never experienced in the city.

There were endless rows of green with their blooms of ripening vegetables, growing stalks of golden corn, and delicate wheat for as far as the eye could see. The farm trucks had worn dusty tracts into the grass as they made their way out to the fields. Tractors moved gracefully with a predictable rhythm along the open land and the whole thing came together into a beautiful landscape. All this was his to behold, to touch, and to work. And he was being paid for it. It was a dream to him. But still he couldn't help but wonder if he would ever get a chance to talk to Suzie again.

On his last day working at the market, a Thursday ironically, Jimmy thought he might ask Suzie for her phone number. He knew it would be a bold move on his part since he hadn't really sensed that she had been interested in him in any special way. She was friendly and fun with everyone. Actually, she seemed to talk to Bob the most when he was there to help set up and occasionally stayed to work a Saturday market. To his surprise Jimmy found he was jealous about it. But as this last day came to a close and Bob pulled in to the market with the truck, Jimmy quietly walked over to where Suzie was putting a few last pies into boxes. Nancy was helping a customer.

"Hey. Hi Suzie. It looks like you had a good day today," Jimmy scanned their almost empty tables.

"Yeah, we did. I think people bought more knowing that this was their last chance for the summer. You guys do good?"

"Definitely. But I wished we had more market days. Summer went by fast and now school, you know." Jimmy was feeling pressed for time and started to sweat.

"Yes. School. At least this is your last year Mr. Senior. You're one up on me. I like school but still I can't wait to graduate and maybe start up a bakery of my own someday." Suzie smiled dreamily as she said this. It was a smile Jimmy wished was meant for him.

"That would be amazing. You would be so good," Jimmy encouraged. "Everything you make is absolutely the best. Everyone thinks so." Jimmy had spent some of his paycheck buying pies, cookies, and cakes each week from Suzie. He always found a reason why he needed them. A lot of summer birthdays in his family he had said. "I guess I better get back over and load up," Jimmy turned to see that Bob had already started. Betty was looking at him with some sort of strange grin but when she saw Jimmy looking her way she quickly turned her head the other way.

"It was really good to get to know you, Jimmy. But hey, I could set aside some of the day-old doughnuts or cookies for you sometime. We can't sell them but we always find friends to give them to."

"I would love that. So yeah, that would be great." Jimmy put out his hand for Suzie to shake. It was all he could think to do.

She looked right into his eyes then and smiled. It was all for him and he blushed. She shook his hand, and as he turned to go, she tapped him on the shoulder. "Here Jimmy. You might need this. It's the bakery's phone number. If you call to check, I'm sure we will have some of your favorites. Oh, and I wrote when I am usually there just in case."

He realized his heart was racing, and he knew his face was red. So he smiled and thanked her quickly before turning back to where Betty and Suzie's mom Nancy were talking in muffled voices, doing all they could not to be noticed watching the two teenagers.

***

A week before school started Jimmy still hadn't found the nerve to call the bakery. The possibility of someone other than Suzie picking up the phone paralyzed him. He knew another option would be to actually go there but he felt himself overwhelmed at the thought of walking in and asking Nancy if he could see Suzie. And he knew if he waited another week school would start and his weekends were already tied up with work.

But still he hesitated and suddenly it was Monday and the last day before school resumed. By midafternoon he had talked himself into making a move, literally. He took a quick shower and grabbed the little pencil map his mother had drawn for him a few nights before.

Maria had been especially quiet, struggling to answer for a few minutes when Jimmy asked her for directions to the bakery. She quickly figured out what the back story was since she'd heard Jimmy talk about the girl who sold baked goods all summer at the market. She hadn't asked him any embarrassing questions which he was relieved about. But the one thing his mother did do made the moment feel important to Jimmy. He knew it from the way she came across the divider that separated the room they shared. He knew it from the way she grabbed his shoulder and looked up at him with her tired, bloodshot eyes.

"You be *good* to that girl Jimmy. I mean, you always be good. Listen to her. Remember what it was like when you were little. What love looked and felt like. That is the goodness you give to a woman." A tiny tear slid down his mother's cheek. She wiped it away and told him to bring her a pencil and paper.

Looking down at his mother's map, he was all the more determined. He jogged to the bus stop and waited impatiently for it to show up. He sat near the front, tapping the paper with his finger while the bus stopped and people got off and on at the speed of snails. Frustrated, he jumped off one stop early and began running, referring to the map for street names and landmarks. Finally, he turned the corner to the street that his mother had highlighted. He found the bakery just a few buildings down on the left. It was easy to spot with its pink door and black awning with the name "Bea's Big City Bakery" stamped in pink lettering He found himself standing in front of a pretty display window with a tiered wedding cake in its center surrounded by some tiny, brightly frosted cookies and a display of some ornately latticed pies. Inside he could see that it was dark and there were no signs of people. His watch told him it was 4:00 p.m.

It was then that he noticed the door with its little "closed" sign dangling from a string. There were store hours painted in tiny white lettering on the glass. Apparently he wasn't too late, but he had picked the only day they were closed. He suddenly recalled that Suzie had written down the shop hours for him and when she would most likely be there. In his excitement to get there he hadn't thought of it. How could he be so stupid? He was so disappointed he didn't know what to do. He didn't want to give up, but he knew it wasn't likely Suzie was going to be anywhere nearby. 'Damn,' he thought. And as he started back for home he lost his nerve all over again.

What he didn't know was that as he was standing there and looking in the window someone had been in the alley throwing empty bags of flour and sugar in the dumpster. And he had been spotted with his hands in his sweatshirt pockets, walking past on his way back home. He didn't know that when a bakery is closed for the day there is usually some serious baking going on in the kitchen.

Several times during the week Jimmy picked up and then hung up the phone on the wall in their kitchen, stopped by the thought of who might be on the other end of the phone and if it were Suzie, how he'd begin a conversation. Everyone in the house, even his mother knew that Jimmy had a crush and was having a hard time getting the relationship off the ground. It was abuelo who several times patted him on the shoulder when he saw him sitting on the stoop of the apartment, watching the kids go by.

***

Thankfully Saturday came and Jimmy's thoughts were diverted to work and the busyness of harvesting produce from Betty's fields. The place was busier than usual with the help of a few seasonal hires. Donny was everywhere it seemed. He would be spotted bouncing along the bumpy tire tracks in his old blue dodge, coming from the dairy barns out to check on the few guys in the corn fields, and then back again to the group picking vegetables. He was a thoughtful man and understood that cold drinks and a little something to eat was appreciated when he came to check on their progress. So it was no surprise to see him coming down the path midmorning in the field where Jimmy's group was busy loading a flatbed. Bob was the first to notice Donny and that he had someone with him.

"Well, look at this. Looks like Donny's hired more help. Maybe you ought to come meet the new kid Jimmy," Bob laughed as he walked past Jimmy who was head down in the field, picking some cucumbers to fill out his crate.

Jimmy turned and looked over to the truck and the guys that were already starting to collect there. And as if one of his dreams had materialized, he saw the figure of a little doll-like girl with a big shiny brown ponytail standing against the side of the truck, holding a large white box in her tiny hands. He felt his heart start to pound and his face blush red with excitement. 'Suzie! For real,' he thought. Tossing the vegetables in his hands into the crate, he made his way through the field to her.

There were a few guys mumbling thanks to Suzie as they took huge bites from doughnuts, the fillings seeping out the corners of their mouths and the powder on their fingers made them look like little kids.

"Hi Jimmy. I saved a few jelly-filled in the truck for you. Oh, and half-moon cookies too," Suzie's smile was brighter than the sun.

"Ooooh, Jimmy. Doughnuts just for you," Sam mocked in a high-pitched voice. "Wished I had a girlfriend like that." All the guys started laughing and poking at Jimmy whose face was burning up at this point. If it wasn't for Suzie being there, he would have crawled under the truck.

"Hey Jimmy, why don't you take the flatbed up to the barn? Take your break there and I'll send someone up shortly to help unload. Take Suzie back up to the house too, would you? Her mom will be there with Betty." Donny lured the guys away with another box of pastries and a jug of lemonade.

Suzie grabbed the bag she had stowed in Donny's truck. "Come on, break time. The boss said." She came alongside Jimmy and waited for him to walk towards the flatbed. He had learned how to drive since being on the farm, but today he was afraid he'd not be able to hold down the clutch his legs were so wobbly.

They climbed in and finally Jimmy found his voice. "I'm really surprised to see you here. Do you know Donny or something?"

"Yes, of course. Actually, my mom got to be very good friends with Betty over the years at the markets. The Eddinger's have been to our house many times since I was a kid."

"Oh wow. That's awesome. So that means you come here sometimes?" Jimmy sounded hopeful.

"I don't usually come with mom, but since someone hasn't bothered to call me and I haven't seen him in weeks, I asked her if we could make a delivery." Suzie turned to him, her arms crossed, trying not to grin.

Jimmy took a deep breath as he moved the truck forward, "Yeah. I know. You got me. I guess I was just nervous about it for some reason. I tried a few times. And I even went to your bakery. Thought I might catch you working, but…"

"Oh, I know. It was a Monday and we were closed right?"

Jimmy was surprised. "Yes. It was. But you weren't there were you?"

"No, but my mom saw you walking by. She does most of the baking when the store is closed. She's the one who said it was about time she come by and bring doughnuts for the crew. I'm glad she saw you." Now Suzie was doing the blushing.

They made their way up to the house where Jimmy saw the old station wagon parked in the lawn by the back door. He wasn't looking forward to her leaving. He had just gotten his voice back and wanted to ask Suzie about going out sometime. So it was a relief when Suzie told him to keep going and head to the barn. "My mom's not expecting me for a while. That whole 'get me back thing' was just Donny trying to give us some time to talk. Maybe we should do what the grownups want this time, you think?" Suzie reached across the cab and touched Jimmy's arm."

Jimmy couldn't talk again. But he could smile and that he did.... from ear to ear for the rest of the day.

Jimmy managed to ask Suzie to get a pizza the following Friday evening. She happily accepted and they made plans to go to a little shop she liked somewhere between the bakery and Suzie's house. He would pick her up around 6:30 p.m.

Bob asked about Suzie on the ride home and Jimmy was grateful for the gentle intrusion in the matter. Since Jimmy knew nothing about girls, dating, or any of what Bob called the 'do's and don'ts, Jimmy listened intently. He had a few questions for Bob and Bob had good answers, Jimmy thought. Bob was as close to a big brother as Jimmy was ever going to have and he liked the feeling.

When they pulled up in front of his home, he thanked Bob for everything, promising he would fill him in on how things went the next Saturday at work. He bounded up the steps to the second-floor apartment and walked in with a rush of excitement. But the smile he was wearing dropped immediately when he saw his grandmother sitting awkwardly by his mother who was curled up in a ball on the couch, rocking herself and looking blankly at the far wall.

He approached his mother cautiously. She'd spent time on the couch before but usually she was sleeping and abuela's face indicated that this was more serious. Jimmy bent down to meet his mother's face, trying to get her to focus on him.

"Mom, I'm here. Do you need anything?" He ran his big, tanned hand gently across her shoulders where he felt a little shudder. Abuelo had come into the room and approached them from behind. His hand now on Jimmy's shoulder.

"Let's go into the kitchen for a minute."

Jimmy gave his mother a kiss and followed his grandfather into the back of the house. "So did something happen?" he asked impatiently.

Abuelo sat down at the table and motioned for Jimmy to do the same. "Your mother has had some sort of breakdown the best we can guess. Some man dropped her off out front about an hour ago, according to Rosa who was outside at the time. Rosa said the man pulled her out of her seat and left her on the curb. She just sat there and wouldn't move, so Rosa called us down to get her up here. We've tried to talk to her but she won't speak."

"So what did you do? Did you call her doctor?" Jimmy was upset and angry.

"Yes, Jimmy. We just got off the phone with him. He wants us to take her to Buffalo Psychiatric center for evaluation. We've called for a cab." Abuelo looked down at his hands.

"Damn. Damn it to hell." Jimmy got up and started back for the living room. Abuelo followed behind him.

"Stop sitting there looking like that abuela. Mom's gonna be fine," Jimmy reached out and pulled the afghan off his mother. "Mom it's time to wake up. Wake the hell up mom." Jimmy's words shook with frustration and fear.

Abuela ran out the front door and abuelo grabbed Jimmy, pushing him into a chair where he told him to wait and they would all ride in the cab together. Maria continued to sit and rock and stare at nothing, seemingly unfazed by her son's pain. But if you looked closely you could see a tiny tear that had collected in the corner of her eyes.

A few minutes later Rosa was at the door telling them that the cab had come and abuela was waiting in it. It was abuelo who was able to coax Maria off of the couch and, with his arm tightly around his daughter, he guided her out the front door. Jimmy fell into step behind them and closed the door.

Chapter 14

Spring 2010

As James got close to the group of abandoned buildings he could see how they had once likely been part of the same business. There were six of them, each equally long and built to create a quad with two central buildings, all with similar weathered yellow paint and large windows. They were each stamped with a letter A through F and he would learn that they had been part of a clothing factory and warehouse.

He was hoping to find Molly without being noticed and without startling her so he tried to get his hands through a small break in one of the boarded doors, but even with his fingers making it through, there was nothing reachable on the other side. He eventually gave up and began to walk the perimeter of the buildings, finding a few windows without boards.

The little day light that made it into the factory was so dim that all he could see was the outlines of what appeared to be skeletons of old sewing machines on tables in a corner of the building. In another building, there were several very long rows of tables and benches where it wasn't hard to imagine women standing to fold and box the newly made clothes.

James continued to stare inside, hoping for some movement but seeing none. Finally he went around rapping on any exposed sections of glass. He knocked on the boarded doors as well and stepped back to sit in the quad, watching against likelihood for Molly. But after just a few minutes he turned to the sound of crunching in the graveled lot and there was Molly looking nervous as she moved quickly toward him.

"What are you doing out here?" her voice was low and she looked around her instead of at him.

"I was worried about you and wanted to bring you something to eat."

"Well, that wasn't a good idea. Come on out of here, I don't want anyone seeing us. It's still daylight for God's sake." Molly walked off toward the park and James knew to follow. Part way there she turned to him and said, "Look, I appreciate what you're trying to do, but I am not an easy person. Who you met a few days ago…well, I'm not often like that. Mostly I'm best when left alone."

James saw that she was upset, maybe even crying, and he felt bad. He told himself that he had stepped in where he wasn't welcome. But, he decided, this young woman looked as frail as a robin's egg and he was determined to figure her out. "Here." He reached into his backpack. "Take this at least." He offered her the food and drink. "And I don't mind telling you that I'm not an easy person myself. You aren't the only one with a complicated life and so telling me that doesn't scare me. But look. If you need your space, I get that. But everybody needs a friend. So call on me when you're up for it. You know where to find me." James looked at her until she returned his gaze. He smiled softly and then continued walking into the quiet of the park.

Molly watched him walk away, and then she did the same. But she couldn't return to the factory, at least not until dark. So she walked along the streets for a while, grateful for the pie and water. It had been a day or more since she had last eaten. After a few hours, she felt the little energy she had was all used up and she found herself heading back into the park. She sat, leaning up against a large tree hidden behind a group of tall shrubs, and fell into a fitful sleep there.

A few hours later Molly woke to see that evening had arrived and the cold was settling in. She rubbed her arms and then her legs and stood up, pulling her hands up into the arms of her thin coat for warmth. Then she peeked out onto the grounds of the park and saw that it was quiet, no kids sitting around or passing through.

Just as she considered looking for James, she saw the frame of a man sitting on some sort of chair by a tree on the edge of the opposite side of the park. She was sure it was James and she thought only for a moment before she began crossing the park towards him.

He saw her coming and slowly rose, shaking out his stiff legs but otherwise staying in place. He waited for her. After all, he had left it up to her as to when they might see each other again. Only as she got close to the wooded edge did he step out into the waning light of the cold evening.

Almost shyly Molly approached. "Hey there. Um. Listen. I was just thinking about what you did earlier. Guess I was kinda mad about you getting too close. To my place I mean. I've been in this town for a while now and making it on my own." Here Molly stopped to look at James. He was listening but she couldn't read his thoughts. "Anyway. You said something about needing a friend. I haven't had one of them in a long time…a friend I mean. I'm complicated. Like you said. But sometimes I've wondered what it'd be like to have someone to talk to. You know?"

She waited a minute before continuing but she saw that James was nodding his head. "So maybe, well, maybe you might want to come back with me tonight to the warehouse. There's tons of room and you could find a decent place to sleep."

James didn't speak until he was sure Molly was done talking. "Molly. I don't want you to feel that you've got to put me up or anything. I wasn't asking for that."

"No. I know that," she continued. "But I think it might be good to have someone else around. I get pretty down sometimes. Maybe a friend would help with that. But I don't want to freak you out or make you feel like I am all needy, because I'm not." She added with a little edge.

James smiled then. "I don't think you're needy Molly. You stood up for me and saved me from a beating, you're tough when you need to be. But…well, no one can be tough all the time and I saw you yesterday when the fight had gone out of your eyes. I just wanted to help."

"Yeah, well…Okay then. If you want to come back with me to the factory, you can. It's up to you. I'll be going over after dark. So maybe a few hours from now. No one has ever bothered me there. It's the safest place I've found in a long time. But I think it might be time to share some of the space. But you absolutely have to promise NEVER to tell anyone about it OR EVER go over there in daylight." She stopped and waited then said, "Do you promise?"

"Yes, Molly. I promise. It's your place and I'm the visitor. Friends don't snitch."

"Well, all right then. I'm about spent for the night, so when we go over I'll be going to sleep. I think I'll just sit back where I was and wait. I'll come and get you when I'm about to leave."

"Since we've got time, I want to look for a little food… maybe coffee or something. I'll see what I can find and be back soon." James didn't wait for her to answer, but handed her his little camp chair and grabbed his backpack. Slinging it over his back, he went out and down the road toward town.

Molly watched him and when he didn't turn around she pulled his chair back into the treed lot and sat with her arms tucked under the blanket he had left with the chair.

It hadn't been an hour when James returned, his limp exaggerated in the darkness. He found Molly wrapped up in the blanket, sleeping. Very quietly he called her name, and then gently touched her shoulder. She woke slowly and it took her a moment to realize where she was, but then she saw James and her sleepy mind remembered.

"Ready to go?" he asked. "I've got a little dinner in my bag. Not much, but it's food."

"Yes, it's late enough and damn, it's cold out here," she wiggled out of the blanket and folded it as James grabbed the chair and waited for her.

They walked along silently for several minutes as they left the park and moved out to the block where the factory loomed in the distance. As they got close Molly whispered for him to get himself up against the wall of building B. He did as she asked and slithered with her around the back side, away from the parking lot and street. It was a cold and clear night and James imagined he could see small puffs of Molly's breath hanging in the air around her head. He watched her closely, trying to be quiet and not upset her even as he felt a little ridiculous about the way they were moving, like robbers casing a joint. But he understood what a trust this was for a homeless person to be taking and he respected her for it.

Molly motioned for him to come up behind her. She was standing in front of one of the many boarded windows pointing up at it. Without a word he watched her slither again along the building until she retrieved some sort of pole from the ground and coming back with it she stopped again at the window. On tiptoe she reached with the pole and stuck it up under the bottom edge of a board. It was obviously not nailed down there and after a few crowbar type moves, a slender fold out stool fell out from behind it onto the grass in front of her. She stood it up by the window and then climbed up, using the pole to pull the corner back.

There was an opening large enough James could see to allow Molly to wiggle under it. She looked back at him on the ground before hoisting herself up and through the opening. Almost immediately she was peeking out the opening and motioning for James to get on the stool.

He was concerned about his ability to not only balance on the stool, but to fit under the loose sections of board. It all looked like an obstacle course to him. But he knew he had to try. Molly had gone so far in trusting him up to this point, so slowly and carefully James steadied the stool and climbed. He managed with the help of warped pieces of wood along the building that he used as handholds. He found he could push his head up and through the boards and surprisingly it was fairly flexible and he could bend it as he pushed up under it. Molly moved his hands to a large opening where glass should have been and he felt the sill of the window. He hoisted the rest of himself up and rested on the sill, the top half of his body inside the building. Molly had lit a candle just inside and he saw that there was a pile of blankets beneath him. He dropped onto them, exhausted but grateful he made it.

While James caught his breath, Molly was again leaning out the opening and fishing around with another pole, this one with a hook on it. She was successful in landing her catch and he saw she was pulling in the stool that they had left outside. She grabbed hold of a piece of it and dropping her hook behind her she wiggled the stool through the magic door of sorts and into the room.

He couldn't help smiling then, realizing what Molly had managed to do. It was almost burglar like and he was impressed. Molly sat on the mess of blankets with James for a minute before saying anything.

"Well. That's how it's done. I worked to get it right for a while. I'm glad you were able to get in here…. you know, with your arm and leg and all."

"You are an amazing little woman Molly," James tried to look at her so she could see that he was serious. The candle's light flickered from where it sat on a table in the middle of the small room.

"It's my home, James. And I'll do what I need to protect it. I'm not even sure why I told you about it or showed all this to you. I hope I haven't made a mistake." She stopped and looked him square in the eye.

"I'm a lot of things, Molly. But I am not someone who would ever intentionally hurt or take advantage of anyone. I still have some integrity. But you hardly know me, so I can't expect you to be okay with me here. I'm fine with going back to the park. And I will *not* share this with anyone."

"No. No. Forget it. What's done is done. It's a big place and there's room for both of us as long as you do it right. The whole entrance after dark part I mean. I can show you around tomorrow when there's some light in here. Right now though I think we're both tired and I think I have a place where you can crash." Molly got up and with the jar candle in her hand she motioned for him to follow her.

***

James settled himself onto his wool blanket which he laid out in a corner of a smaller room next to the room they had entered from. This room was completely dark and

136

Molly had given him a jar candle with just a little wax in the bottom. Thankfully the one little flame cast enough light to help him set up his indoor camp.

"Keep the door shut. I've got traps in here for the mice and rats, but they're everywhere," she had instructed before leaving.

He set the candle and a few matches on the floor near where his head would lay and then he blew into the jar and the smoke from the wick made him cough. The dark of the room was peaceful and warmer than he had been used to and he was so tired that, after kicking off his shoes and placing his head on his backpack, he fell into a deep, restful sleep.

He woke many hours later but with little sense of the time. There was a haze of light that had filtered into his room from cracks in the window boards and he could see enough to make out the corners and the door across the room. Rubbing the sleep from his eyes he sat up and stretched his aching limbs. Last night had been a bit of a workout. But the sense of safety that came with sleeping under a roof and four walls had been worth it.

He decided to step out into the hallway and maybe see if he could find his way to Molly. With his shoes on and the lit candle in his hand, he walked in the direction he had come last night. Molly's door, which was on the other side of the room they had entered from, was shut and he hesitated, but then knocked softly on it and waited. From the other side he heard a moan and then eventually a shuffling sound. Molly pulled on the door until it came free from the warped frame and opened in a rush.

She told him to come in as she moved back to a crib-sized mattress that she was using for her bed. There was a fair amount of light squeezing through various cracks and holes in and around the rooms two windows. James blew out his candle and found a chair in a corner to sit in.

"It's still early, James, and cold. I'm not moving from here for a while yet." Molly said flatly.

"No problem. I just woke up and couldn't tell what time it was. Didn't think to look at the watch in my pack."

"Well, it's after 9:00 a.m." She pointed to a table and a small windup clock that faintly ticked there. "Since we slept into the morning light, it's going to be an indoor day. You need the bathroom or anything?" she asked in a muffled voice from under her blanket.

James had not expected to be offered a bathroom, but come to think of it he would need to get to one sooner than later. "Well, yes, I will soon. You have a bathroom in this place?"

"Not exactly what you're thinking maybe," Molly rolled to face him. "It's more of a room that was once a restroom and now has a bucket for a toilet. I've made it work when I stay in here for periods of time. May as well show it to you." Molly got up, wrapping herself in her blanket. Looking like a taco with a head, she shuffled to the doorway and waited for James to follow.

It was so dark in the hallway that James wished they had lit a candle. He struggled to follow Molly. He finally asked her if he could hold on to the edge of the blanket she was wrapped in. With that he was able to navigate the turns and distances until she stopped him in front of a closed door. "This is it," she motioned with her head. "You'll be able to see decent in there but there is a candle in the sink so go ahead and light it if you need to."

James felt uncomfortable but needed to ask, "So Molly. What do I do with, um, with the bucket?" At least she couldn't see him blush.

"Oh. Right. Well I take it to a certain window that looks out on the little grassy quad. No one sees that way. It's not been boarded up like most of the others and I broke out enough glass to just tip it over and out. But I don't bother with it too often unless it's, well, you know, if it's solid waste. I'll wait for you out here and you tell me if I need to go down there after or not." Molly didn't sound especially uncomfortable with the conversation. "Everything you need is in there though." And she motioned to the closed door again.

Jimmy was grateful that at this time anyway, he would not be filling the bucket with anything that needed to be walked to the window. "No…you don't have to wait for me. And I can make it back. I kept track of turns I think." James began to open the bathroom door.

"Here. Take this then." She held a pen light out to him. "Use it sparingly. These are hard to get." Gratefully, James reached for it. As he opened the door Molly could be heard shuffling back down the hallway.

The inside of the bathroom surprised James. It was brighter than he expected and he could see that light was coming in from two small windows of uncovered glass high up on the wall. More light filtered in through small holes that had been bore through the wall in various places, straight through to the outside apparently. On this day, it was enough to see without straining. A bucket was placed just outside of each of the two stalls, one which had been used but left no smell. A third bucket half filled with what looked like water was on the floor next to the sink. There was even a towel and a sliver of soap next to it

But as amazing as all of this was, as James' eyes adjusted to the low light, he became aware of a garden that was growing up the sides of the walls. Not a garden in the traditional sense, but one that had grown from a paintbrush. The walls around the sink and across from the stalls were filled with blossom-filled vines that wrapped around the porcelain and ran in long trails along the larger wall. There was a weeping tree that hung heavy with pink flowers and something like a meadow of wild looking poppies, buttercups, and baby's breath with tiny butterflies hovering above the grassy edges. This beautiful mural had captured the best of a spring day and brought it into this drab bathroom of sorts. James was awestruck and couldn't help but use the penlight to focus light onto it, finding its bright colors all the more alive.

He added to the used bucket and lingered at the door before leaving the spring day behind. With the help of the penlight he managed the hallway and found his way back to Molly's room. She had left the door ajar and he entered quietly and sat again in the chair. She was sleeping and so he waited, nodding off himself until hunger eventually woke both of them.

Chapter 15

A lot had happened in those first days after Maria went to the hospital. Her brother had been called and he showed up with his wife Kate, carrying some pink and white flowers. Edward had always stayed quietly informed about his sister's mental instability even though he never once spoke of it in Jimmy's memory.

And his Aunt Naomi knew about Maria as well. She and her family had moved to Pennsylvania a year ago. His uncle was said to be a sales manager for some big company there. Jimmy didn't miss them a bit, the family with money and attitude. He could see it in his cousin's clothes and the things they did for fun. He could hear it in the words they used and the things they talked about. The oldest, Mateo, played trumpet, first chair, for his middle school. And Carmen's attention to dance had landed her the part of Clara in *The Nutcracker Ballet*. Abuela always seemed a little uncomfortable when Naomi's family came by and when they left, Maria would sputter obscenities under her breath. It was just as well that they weren't close enough to get involved.

A few neighbors had come by with casseroles for them to eat and concerned questions. Abuela, who was always so warm and friendly had gotten to where she ignored the knocks on the door. She was finally worn out from trying to keep up appearances.

A psychiatrist had taken pages of information that first day. He had decided that based on the history he was given by Maria's doctor and the things her parents were saying about Maria's long-term behavior that she would be best helped through an "in house" treatment plan. A blood test revealed his mother had drugs in her system and it was assumed that she had likely been using them for some time. Even as Jimmy heard it, knowing that his mother had struggled and needed help, he hated this new reality. He hated her, he realized, for not getting well on her own and for abandoning him. And he hated himself for not having been enough for his mother.

But it wasn't just Jimmy who was struggling with what was happening with his mother. Abuelo, the strong, stubborn and sometimes angry man that Jimmy knew him to be was suddenly quiet, a new sadness and resignation hung in the air around him. It was in the heavy silence of his walk and in the bend of his shoulders. It was in his dark, downcast eyes.

Jimmy hadn't stopped thinking about Suzie and how that day had started. He had been so happy, so excited to think about their date. He would daydream about just the two of them: being able to hear her talk and see her smile, a chance to maybe reach out and hold her hand and to tell her how pretty she was. But by the middle of the week he wasn't sure if he could do it. If he could bring himself to sit with her and be happy, to pretend, when his mother was competing for a place in his heart.

***

After dinner that first Wednesday night, the house was quiet except for the hiss of steam coming from abuela's iron.

She had been working feverishly on anything and everything she could around the house and she wasn't talking to any of them. Jimmy had offered to help with dishes after dinner but had been dismissed, leaving him with little to do but think. It was a surprise for him to find his grandfather at the door of his bedroom that evening.

He quietly poked his head in the room and asked Jimmy if he had a few minutes. Before Jimmy could answer, abuelo had shuffled in and sat on the edge of his daughter's bed. From there Jimmy really couldn't see him so he picked up the divider and leaned it up against the wall. Jimmy realized the whole thing was awkward for both of them, so he held his tongue and waited.

And then the tears began. At first just a wet streak on abuelo's cheek, then a stream, and a few choked gasps as the older man tried to compose himself. Jimmy waited. He hadn't seen anything like this from his grandfather. And he didn't know what he could possibly say.

But then abuelo dried his face with a thin handkerchief and found his voice. "When your mother was young I was a good father. I used to give her nickels for popsicles and take her to the park to swing. She wanted to play catch with her big brother so I showed her how to hold the baseball and keep the glove close to protect herself. She was very good; got to be almost as good as Edward. Sometimes she would crawl up on my lap before bed and tell me stories. She imagined all kinds of happy things. She was sometimes a princess with a castle and a room filled with pretty dresses, sometimes she was an astronaut or a mountain climber. But every story she told and everything she imagined had a happy ending." Abuelo swallowed hard and his shoulders shook.

"I had all these hopes for Maria. For each of my children. But when your mother told me about your father and about you, something inside of me went dark. I was angry that your mothers' stories, that her dreams would not come true. I knew then that she wouldn't be the princess in the castle she had imagined or get a chance to climb a mountain. I was so angry. And I hated your father. I hated him for taking Maria's dreams. For taking MY dreams. And I was right about him. He was a very bad man. Selfish and bitter and terrible to Maria." Abuelo stopped suddenly and lifted his head, looking directly into Jimmy's eyes.

"And as I say this I know that I too have been that man." He paused. "I have made mistakes, Jimmy. When your mother needed me, I shut the door on her. I would not listen and I would not let her in. And you…. well, all I could think of was what you did to her. You were your father's son and because of you she would never get away from him." Jimmy felt these last words. The reality of them came like a blow to the stomach. They were some of the very things he had thought about himself and hearing them spoken now meant they must be so. He began to tremble.

Abuelo came to sit next to him then. Tenderly, he put his hand on the boy's arm. "But I was wrong Jimmy. You are NOT your father. You are your own person, and a loving, devoted son. Your mother's problems come from a lot of years of being left alone without the help of her family." Abuelo stopped and put his hand under Jimmy's chin, lifting his head to meet his own eyes. "That is mine to own, not yours. And finally this old, stubborn man understands he needs to take responsibility." He could see that he had upset his grandson and he reached over to put an arm around Jimmy, holding him tightly while Jimmy cried.

After a long minute Jimmy was able to speak. "I am so sorry abuelo. I think about everything you said all the time. I have tried to be good, to listen, and to talk to her about good things. I thought I could help her get better," Jimmy choked on desperate words.

"I know that. None of this is your fault, Jimmy. You have been a very good son. And since I have opened my eyes I see that your mother has needed more than I was willing to give. And right now she is where she needs to be. Your mother will get the help you tried to give her. The help I wouldn't give her," he waited. "Maybe now it's time for us to be a family. Maybe it's taken this hard thing to wake me up." Abuelo settled back onto the bed giving Jimmy some space. "We will take care of your mother however the doctors say is best. And I will listen to her and love her like I used to.

Jimmy nodded his head, letting these words of comfort and hope sink into him, warming the cold places he had hidden away for so long. He breathed deeply and shuddered and there was a little release of some of the pain he had carried.

"So now, my grandson, would you like to tell me a little more about your work and this young lady abuela tells me about?" Abuelo's tired smile brought a softness to his face that Jimmy had never seen.

Jimmy spent the next half hour filling his grandfather in on what it was like on the farm: how hard everyone worked and how much enjoyment he got from it. He talked about Donny and the friendships he had with the guys, how Bob and Donny had taught him how to drive the truck. And then he talked about Suzie and how they had met. About her family's bakery and how delicious everything was. Without realizing it he told abuelo that he was supposed to go out for pizza with Suzie on Friday night, but how now he didn't think he could.

Abuelo shook his head, his hand across his mouth. "You can't not go Jimmy. That wouldn't help you or your mother. I think you have to keep moving…like you always have. And you like this girl. Hearing you talk about her and your work is a good thing for all of us. So I for one hope you decide to go and that you have a good time."

And so with a five dollar bill and the blessing of his grandfather, Jimmy's date was on again.

***

Friday came with a mix of excitement and a good case of nerves. Jimmy was in his senior year of high school and thankfully he had a light class load. He only took what was required for graduation and so he had two study hall periods each day. Despite the fact that he wasn't interested in any of his subjects and was content with mediocre grades, Jimmy did do his homework. He didn't like the idea of not doing something his teachers had assigned and so he usually used his free periods to get his work done.

But today he didn't get beyond putting a heading and date on a piece of paper that was intended for English. A half hour before last bell he looked out onto the school parking lot. It was supposed to be cool, but for mid-September not unpleasant and no rain was forecasted. His plan was to get home quickly and check with abuela about anything that may be going on with his mother. Hoping all was okay, he wanted some time for a shower and a shave before taking the bus into the part of the city where Suzie lived. He planned to stop several blocks from her home where he heard there was a florist and walk from there.

Last night he had asked his grandfather about flowers and what girls thought of them. Abuelo chuckled and called abuela into the living room where he had been watching the news. "Margarette, do you remember the flowers I used to bring you when we first dated? Tell us, did you like getting them?" And then in unison his grandparents had laughed as abuela bent down to give her husband a soft kiss on the cheek. "Oh yes. I loved the flowers… maybe before I knew I loved you." She patted abuelo's head and went back into the kitchen. It was the most tender exchange he had ever seen between them.

Jimmy had laid out his shirt and freshly laundered jeans on the chair in his room. The shirt, he had bought only yesterday and abuela insisted on washing and then starching and ironing it. It looked better than when he took it from the store rack. And so this stream of daydreaming went on until the bell called him back into the present. A quick walk to his locker to grab his jacket and a book and he was following the crowd of noisy teens out the doors and into the bright afternoon chill.

Things went along just as he had rehearsed in his head. He had plenty of time to get ready and then a little time to pace the apartment before he needed to get the bus. Abuela hovered in the kitchen doorway trying to talk to him as he passed from room to room. He was nervous enough without her smiles and encouragements. But after all the years abuela had been covering her worry with strained smiles and small talk, he realized that today she smiled with her eyes and that her happiness was genuine.

Finally, with a last look in the mirror and pocketing his wallet that held half of his paycheck, Jimmy said a goodbye and walked out the door. The bus ride was uneventful and by 5:30 p.m. he walked out of the flower store with a small bunch of blue tipped daisies. The florist assured him that this selection was perfect for a nice young lady. She had wrapped them in some white paper and tied a thick, loopy blue bow around them.

He managed to move along while shielding the delicate bunch from the breeze and he made his way past the bakery and then to the street where she had printed her address for him. He hadn't called her since seeing her on Saturday, although he had almost canceled several times before he had talked to abuelo on Wednesday. He worried some about what he would say if conversation about his family came up. He had managed to keep to generalities anything pertaining to his mother over the summer when they had talked about themselves. Tonight he was going to hold to that.

Suzie's house was tall and narrow with grey siding and weathered shutters that were more pink than the red they had started out as. The porch wasn't deep but was the full width of the home and a white painted railing encased the entire area except for a narrow set of steps to the left that led to the front door. There was a painted metal glider with tan cushions to the right of the door and a folding lawn chair in the far corner that looked out to the street. The whole neighborhood was filled with houses of a similar style, set closely, most with narrow driveways between them and small patches of grass that met up to sidewalks that had expanded and contracted enough over the years to leave them quite uneven. To Jimmy this looked like what he imagined the suburbs to be.

He hesitated as he reached the first step of the porch and saw that the flowers in his hand were shaking. He took a deep breath, mumbled a short petition to God that it would go well and bounded up the steps, noticing some movement at the curtain in the porch window. As he reached for the doorbell, the door suddenly opened in front of him and there was Suzie all smiles and with her hair falling down around her shoulders. She looked so different to him without the bouncing ponytail, older and more beautiful than pretty. He couldn't find his words and he stammered a moment when she welcomed him inside.

But then her mother Nancy was in the hallway, full of energy and suggesting that they all come in and sit for a few minutes. Jimmy followed the two into the living room on the right. It was a cozy place and he immediately saw the school pictures of Suzie and her two older brothers on the wall. The room was simply decorated with a dark couch and a small TV that sat on a metal stand in one corner. To one side of the couch was an overstuffed chair with a large, dark-haired man folding up the newspaper in his hand. 'So this was Suzie's father,' Jimmy thought.

Suzie started by introducing him to her father using his first name, Art. But Jimmy, in good form, called him Mr. Anderson. He smiled and extended his hand to Jimmy who shook it, having quickly passed the flowers to his other hand. Nancy told them to sit on the couch and noticing the flowers she made a comment on how pretty they were.

"Oh yes, thanks. These are for you Suzie," Jimmy blushed and reached to hand them to Suzie, who sat some distance from him on the couch. Thanking him, Suzie returned his blush and asked her mother about a vase she might put them in. Nancy said she would go get one and offered to take them from her daughter. With Nancy out of the room Jimmy was afraid he would have to come up with something to say. Thankfully Suzie did a good job of telling her dad about Jimmy's work with the farm and how much Betty and Donny liked him. She was trying to paint him as a really nice, hardworking young man and he thought her all the more beautiful for doing it.

Suzie's dad asked Jimmy how they were making out on the farm and if he had any time on the tractor yet. Jimmy was grateful for these questions and began to relax as he told them what was happening at the farm and how he had gotten his driver permit, thanks to Donny recommending that Bob teach him. Nancy was back, setting the bouquet in the middle of the coffee table in front of them. Suzie bent forward to smell the flowers and touch a few of the tips with her impossibly tiny fingers. She thanked Jimmy again for them, noting that blue was her very favorite color.

Just as Jimmy wondered what would come next, Nancy brought up the time and how busy the pizza shop would be on a Friday evening. "We don't want to hold you kids up. Dad and I may go out for some groceries soon ourselves." Suzie understood that her mother was giving them an opening to leave for their date and she nodded in agreement.

"Yeah. Maybe we should start out. Are you ready, Jimmy?" She started to rise from the couch.

Following along, Jimmy got to his feet. "Yes. Sure. We can go whenever you're ready."

Her parents were on their feet now and Art put his hand back out for Jimmy. "Very good to meet you, Jimmy. I hope the weather keeps holding out for you to finish in the fields."

"Me too, thank you. And it was good to meet you, Mr. Anderson."

"Okay, you two, have a nice evening and mom and I are expecting you home by ten, Suzie." Art looked from Suzie to Jimmy and back.

"Yes, Dad. I'll be home." Suzie gave him a quick hug and her mother led them back out to the hallway where Suzie took a thick, blue sweater from a hook behind the door and put it on over her floral blouse. Nancy gave Jimmy a pat on the back and waited for them to leave.

Outside the wind had calmed to a soft cool breeze and there was light traffic on the street. Suzie pointed the way for them to turn and they walked along the sidewalk, careful not to trip on the many cracks. Jimmy asked Suzie if she was warm enough and she said that she was. She asked Jimmy if he had had any trouble finding her house and he said that he hadn't. They were each a little nervous and their conversation was short, but the walk helped and soon enough they had gotten to the little restaurant.

Once settled into a booth Jimmy asked Suzie what she would like and she laughed, "Pizza, of course." She made things easy that way and Jimmy finally relaxed enough to ease into conversation.

He went up to the counter to place their order and returned with a couple of pops and a handful of napkins. As they sat waiting Suzie thanked him again for the flowers and said she was glad that they had been able to get together. Jimmy considered for a moment what it would have been like to call and cancel the date, and he was all the more grateful for Wednesday night when abuelo had come to him.

Jimmy watched Suzie running her fingers through her soft, brown hair as she talked and he wanted to tell her that he thought she was beautiful and that he had never remembered being so happy to be with someone. The words seemed awkward to him and too big, but he did manage to tell her that her blouse was pretty and he liked the way she let her hair hang loose tonight. She smiled, happy for the compliment. They continued on with talk about school, work at the bakery and the farm until the pizza came.

Jimmy was surprised that he wasn't particularly hungry. He found he felt a little self-conscious to be eating with Suzie. He had eaten countless cookies she had given him this summer, yet tonight he had thoughts of the pizza's cheese sliding off the slice and onto his lap, the sauce dribbling down his chin. Suzie, on the other hand, was digging right in. She had managed several bites between talking and didn't appear to think anything of it. She finally commented about him needing to catch up or he was going to go hungry, so he did his best to stay clean with several napkins spread across his lap and one in his left hand.

Somewhere into his second slice Suzie stopped eating and looked at him thoughtfully. "Jimmy, I know I haven't asked you anything much about your family. And I don't know much really, but maybe a little. My mom being good friends with Betty and all, and I guess the guys have mentioned a few things to Donny." Her voice trailed off waiting for Jimmy to step in.

Jimmy felt heat rise in his face even as a chill ran down his spine. This was the stuff he had wanted to avoid. It wasn't realistic not to talk about his family, he knew, but he had dreaded it. Suzie looked at him with her brown eyes soft and listening. She was pulling at her bottom lip, just barely, with her teeth and she held one of her tiny hands in the other in her lap.

"You don't have to say anything, Jimmy. I just want you to know that there is nothing you could say that would scare me…I mean, scare me away." She drew in a deep breath. "I guess I'm just trying to say that I hope you feel you can talk to me. About anything. I care about you."

Jimmy tried to process what he was hearing. The sweet, beautiful girl that he sat across from, that he was silently crazy about, was saying she cared about him. As much as he didn't want to open the door into that room in his life where he kept his family, he was being encouraged to. And he knew that if there was anyone that he could talk to about his mother and his confused and lonely life, it was Suzie.

In a spontaneously bold move, Jimmy reached his open hands out across the table to Suzie. She immediately placed her hands in his, allowing him to feel how small and light they were. She squeezed his fingers and he closed his hands gently around hers. Words began first to stumble and then flow out of him. As Suzie listened with eyes warm and glistening, Jimmy told her the story of his life. From the early happy days in the apartment where Donna lived, through the pains of living with a broken mother and difficult grandparents, into the present where he wasn't sure where things would lead, but that there was some hope now for all of them.

For the first time Jimmy had told someone his story. He'd expressed his worries and his anger, his hopes and his fears. And as much as abuelo's confessions had helped, this helped so much more. Suzie listened in her gentle way. He knew she wasn't judging, but was feeling everything he told her with her good, kind soul. This girl whom he had known for just three months knew as much about him as he did and he knew he had laid his heart in her hands.

Finally, realizing the time, Jimmy suggested they get Suzie home.

On the street, now quiet and cool for September, Suzie found his hand and Jimmy moved closer to keep them both warm. They didn't say much until they arrived at Suzie's house where Jimmy knew he would need to prepare to leave her. He worried that he had gone too far with his story and began to apologize for what he had told her and how much he had said. She assured him with kind words of caring as she softly squeezed his hand. Without thinking, Jimmy bent forward to embrace Suzie. A hug that expressed both gratitude and fondness.

As he pulled away, Suzie found his cheek with her lips and lay the softest of kisses there. Startled with this pleasure, Jimmy smiled shamelessly. He asked if she would like to do this again, to go out on another date. She giggled, like a child, and said that she hoped to see him very soon and would he please call in the next few days.

With promises to talk again on Monday, Jimmy floated all the way home.

***

Monday came and of course Jimmy and Suzie talked and planned to see each other again. By the following week they had become something of a couple and were seeing each other regularly. They had pizza dates and nights by the TV at the Anderson's home with her family. It didn't take Jimmy long to fall in love with this girl. She was everything good that he could imagine in a person. She was strong, yet sensitive and independent, while still needing to love and be loved. Jimmy thought that maybe his mother had been like Suzie when she was young and before her battles.

Chapter 16

Uncle Edward had driven Jimmy and his grandparents to the treatment center to pick up Maria nearly a month after they had taken her to the hospital. It was an unusually warm day for early October and Edward pulled up to the main doors and let abuela and abuelo out while he and Jimmy parked the car in a small parking lot to the side of the building. Jimmy had wanted to wait outside, not wanting to see the place where his mother had gone. He didn't want any memories of it. But even in the car he couldn't help notice how some of the windows were decorated with construction paper cut outs of pumpkins and leaves, one of the larger windows (likely the cafeteria) had streamers hanging across it and the words "Happy Halloween" cut out in block letters. It looked like the artwork at an elementary school.

Just a few minutes later Maria stepped out of the door that abuelo held open for her and Jimmy's grandmother. Jimmy watched her walk down the short sidewalk to the parking lot, holding his breath. She saw him as she neared the car and she quickened her steps till she was at the back door, pulling it open. Jimmy didn't have time to wipe the tears from his face before she got to him.

"Jimmy!" she exclaimed and she drove her head into his chest, holding onto him as he wrapped his arms around her.

"I've missed you mom," he managed to whisper.

"I've missed you more," Maria choked. "I've missed you for a very long time." And the words hung there like a confession as they drove the streets towards home.

Maria had returned to them looking rested and stronger. Everyone made her comfortable and gave her space that first day. They didn't ask her any questions and they tried not to expect much from her. She slept on and off and watched TV when she was awake. On the second morning she appeared at the kitchen table for breakfast and helped abuela with the dishes. It was a school day but she asked Jimmy if he'd like an excuse to stay home this one day and he was more than happy that she asked.

She told them a little about her time in treatment. How she had met daily with a counselor privately and then in small groups where she had learned some things about her negative thinking. She told how they worked on teaching her strategies for getting out of these cycles and how to find new ways of thinking about herself and her life. She was given a schedule for continuing counseling and small group meetings to attend along with a medication to take. She even showed them the bottle, setting it out on kitchen table for them to see. This bottle, unlike what Jimmy had seen before, was clearly labeled with his mother's name and the type and amount of medication to be taken. It was doctor prescribed and selected specifically for Maria's needs.

But even with Maria's transparency and apparent determination, they each silently worried. For weeks they held their breath while watching for signs of Maria withdrawing from them. But day by day she continued to move forward bit by bit. And she was faithfully attending her group and private counseling sessions. When she decided after a month that she was ready for a job, Jimmy finally exhaled and his grandparents had the extended family for dinner. They had wanted to celebrate in some small way since Maria's coming home but had waited for a sign that their daughter, their mother, was really back.

And so winter came with the Vazquez family contentedly busy with their lives. Abuela was smiling and laughing with the neighbors and abuelo was walking with a lighter step. He came home from work and greeted his wife with a kiss. The farm had kept Jimmy on Saturdays through the winter, finding odd jobs for him. And of course, a good amount of his time was spent with Suzie.

As Christmas had approached, Jimmy had struggled with what to do about it. He'd been seeing Suzie for months and not once had he invited her to his home. He was still reluctant about her meeting his mother, even as she was doing so much better. It was Maria who brought the whole thing up one evening while they stood at the window watching a car spin out on the snowy street in front of their apartment.

"Jimmy. We hear so much about your girlfriend and we can see how happy she makes you. Don't you think it would be nice to have her over to meet us?" Maria turned from the window to look at him.

Jimmy felt himself blush. "I guess I've thought of it. But…well, I just wanted to wait till you were okay with it." He was surprised with his honesty.

"Well, I'm more than okay with it. And I know you've worried about me a lot and probably wondered how I would act. I sure don't blame you honey. But I'm doing okay now. I have to work at it, but I am. And I want you to move on with life, Jimmy. So, if you are comfortable with it, why don't you ask Suzie to join us the day before Christmas Eve? We could have a little dinner and dessert and celebrate without the whole, big family here." Maria bent close to Jimmy's ear then and said, "We wouldn't want to scare her off with some of those cousins of yours." He smiled then and hugged his mother as he promised to ask Suzie the next time he saw her.

Maria took the Thursday before Christmas off so she could shop and make dinner. The smell of lechon asado and guineos en escobeche con mollejas filled the apartment. His mother made sure to make arros con gandules, a dish they would be having again at the Vazquez family's Christmas dinner. Abuela helped clean the kitchen and his mother went into their room to change. Abuelo had on a new blue shirt, which abuela had washed and starched for him, and a green and blue striped tie.

His mother returned wearing a beautiful red silk blouse and her favorite navy blue skirt. She had tied a red scarf loosely around her waist and let the ends trail down her side. She had on a pair of heeled black shoes and black stockings. She wore a hint of red lipstick and a brush of pink blush across her cheeks. Her hair, which had been up in big rollers, fell long and loopy over her shoulders and onto her blouse. Jimmy thought she was as beautiful as he could ever remember her and he was suddenly overwhelmed with love and admiration for her. Abuelo put a record on the player and the sounds of guitar, mandolin, and trumpet danced in the air and filled the apartment with happiness.

And so finally they all met Suzie when her mother dropped her off that evening. The sweet girl carried two small bunches of flowers, one in each hand and gave one to Maria and then one to abuela. The women each hugged her, repeatedly thanking her as they scurried to find little vases to put them in, making a fuss about putting them where everyone could enjoy them. It made Jimmy think of his first date with Suzie when her mother had reacted similarly to his gift, and he smiled.

Suzie and Maria were so easy together that the hours went by quickly with laughter and stories being shared over dinner. "Did you know I worked in a bakery years ago?" Maria asked Suzie. "It was when Jimmy was just a baby. But I never made anything that was both delicious and beautiful like you and your mother do." Maria smiled at Suzie and she returned it with a blush.

And after dinner, with the music making merry, abuelo led abuela in a dance. Suzie clapped and tapped along and asked if Jimmy knew how to dance like that. Suddenly, abuelo was in front of them, taking Suzie by the hand and guiding her into the dance. And then Maria did the same with Jimmy and off they were in a dance with the music, abuela clapping and laughing. And anyone watching that night would have seen the little group was dancing to the rhythm of love.

***

The end of February brought an announcement from Maria. She had decided she was going to move out into an apartment of her own. An apartment of "their" own actually, since she had talked to Jimmy about it first and wanted him to move with her. He had been surprised that his mother wanted to make this change, that she said she had been feeling it was time to move on to a new stage of her life. He hadn't considered any other life for her beyond his grandparent's small apartment which had been their home for almost seven years and he was concerned that his mother might not be ready for something so new so soon after her breakdown.

But she assured him that she needed to gain back her independence. She tried to explain that she was feeling a little like a child being held back, even when it wasn't because of anything her parents were doing. She was grateful for the support they'd given her for so long. But, she said, she wanted to get back to being a real mom to Jimmy. She explained it as being similar to the expectations she had for him. She expected that the day would come when Jimmy would want to start a life for himself, hopefully marry and maybe have children of his own. Could he understand that his mom wanted a little of that for herself?

And in some way he did understand. It was true that her life had been on hold for years. Maybe this was the move she needed to be healthy and happy. Even with his reservations, there was no way he would ever say no to going with her and so they went to his grandparents about it together.

The conversation had been hard. Abuela began to cry and abuelo just sat there looking completely confused. He'd start to say something and then stop, thinking better of it. Maria assured her parents that this had always been part of the plan but that she had let her fears and her issues with low esteem stop her. "This is part of healing," she told them. If her moving meant a step forward in her process of healing, then neither of them dared to question her further on it.

***

On March 12th of Jimmy's senior year, he and his mother moved their meager belongings into a nice little apartment just three blocks away. Maria was committed to keeping Jimmy in his school district for the remaining months and a friend of hers had helped her find this place. Jimmy himself hadn't seen it until he and his uncle walked through the front door, carrying the new couch his mother had bought the day before. Suzie, along with the extended Vazquez family, had insisted on helping them get settled. Things were in place in a matter of a few hours.

His grandparents and Suzie stayed on for a short time after Edward's family left and abuela made a quick dinner for them from the refrigerator that she had filled with groceries. They ate huddled around a small table in the kitchen, sitting on a few folding chairs. It was a quiet meal and Jimmy was caught up in his own thoughts, as was everyone else. Only his mother and Suzie talked along about Maria's plans to paint the place and maybe save up for a new coffee table. She seemed most happy about the fact that the apartment had two bedrooms and Jimmy would finally have the room he deserved.

So began a period of trying to regain the blissful life they had had together those early years. But they both soon learned that it wasn't realistic to think that they would get back what they had. Jimmy was a young man now with a girlfriend and work to share his time. And his mother, he discovered, had found things of her own to do. Better said, she had found someone with which to do things. Ben showed up for the first time two weeks after they had moved in and he soon became a big part of their lives.

Jimmy could tell something was different with his mother a few days before Ben had knocked on their door. She was in a frenzied cleaning jag: vacuuming, dusting, and washing windows. She had asked Jimmy to help her paint the living room the first week they were in the place and things were immaculate. Maria had made a complicated dessert on Friday night and she told Jimmy to make sure he was home on Saturday for dinner. It wasn't a complete shock to see a man at the door when Maria ran to open it. She had come out of the bedroom wearing a dress he had never seen before and her hair and perfume gave the rest away.

Ben stepped in after giving Maria a kiss at the door. He was tall and clean shaven, with light hair and eyes.

He wore a bomber jacket and a buttoned shirt with jeans; typical looking guy but very clean. Hands that didn't work, Jimmy noticed. In them he held a bouquet of red roses and a rectangular, wrapped box. Jimmy couldn't help wondering if the flower thing mandatory for all first dates.

His mother blushed and remembered then that Jimmy was in the room. She turned to introduce her boyfriend to her son. Each of the men extended their hand to shake. 'Yup,' Jimmy thought. This guy has an office job.

Maria asked Ben to sit while she went to get a vase for the flowers he handed to her, another kiss gently placed on her cheek. He suggested she open the gift first, which she did while they went to sit. She opened a box and pulled out a beautiful glass vase. The colors melted as if naturally from one to another in swirls throughout the glass. Jimmy's eye was untrained to things like this, but he bet it was an expensive piece.

Maria gasped with surprise and joy. She remembered this vase! They had seen it in a glass museum he had taken her to a few weeks before. She thanked him with a warm hug and a kiss before excusing herself to get the flowers in water. Jimmy took note of the fact that Ben and his mother had been seeing each other for at least the last few weeks and he wondered if part of his mother's wanting to move had been because of this fact.

Ben carried the weight of the conversation for Jimmy as the two sat waiting for Maria. He asked him about school, was he looking forward to graduating in a few months? He knew about the farm and about Suzie and he seemed comfortable asking about them as well. Jimmy found out that Ben worked in real-estate. What that meant exactly Jimmy didn't know but he surmised that Ben sold properties and made a very good living doing it.

Maria returned with the flowers and set them proudly on the new coffee table. She found a seat on the couch close to Ben and he held her hand. The whole thing was very weird for Jimmy and he wondered if he and Suzie had looked like this. He decided that the weirdness was more from the fact that his mother was with a man. Though he guessed that she had been with a few different guys over the years, this was the first he had ever seen one. Maybe that was because this was the first guy that was worthy of being seen. At least Jimmy hoped that was the case.

Later, over dinner, Maria and Ben explained to Jimmy how they had met. Ben's grandmother was an eighty-eight-year-old woman who lived at the senior assist home where Maria worked. She regularly participated in the day programs that Maria helped with. His mother loved this new job of hers, helping with senior activities both at the home and excursions out around Buffalo. Since working there, she had come back with many stories about these seniors. She enjoyed all their little quirks. They were quick to tell you what they thought, both good and bad, and had plenty of advice for anyone who'd listen.

Around the holidays, Eleonore's grandson had come to visit while they were preparing for a bingo game. Maria invited him to stay and play along and surprisingly he said he would love to. Ben went on to tell how he couldn't take his eyes off of the beautiful, young woman who went from table to table, helping the players find their numbers. By the end of the game Eleonore had told her grandson to come back in a few days while she'd find out if Maria might be interested in him.

"And so, since then, I've been coming by to see my grandmother a lot more than usual," Ben grinned and reached out to squeeze Maria's hand.

A while after dinner Jimmy said he was going to hang out in his room, maybe give Suzie a call. He was there for hours before finally around midnight, he heard Ben's voice, low and deep at the door. Then it was quiet again for a few minutes before he heard the door open and close and his mother walk into her bedroom.

Chapter 17

It was a warm and partly sunny afternoon on June 25th, a great day to celebrate a graduation. Jimmy was honestly surprised he had made it to this day, considering the hard years with school and his social and family life. Up until last fall he couldn't have cared less about even attending the ceremony, but now with things moving in a good direction and with his mom and Suzie wanting to celebrate, he was happy he'd come this far.

There was limited seating in the auditorium so it was just Maria, Ben, Suzie, abuelo, and abuela that watched Jimmy cross the stage, shaking hands with the principal and superintendent while being handed a diploma in a black jacket. He stopped for just a second, looking out and spotting Suzie, who was snapping away on her camera.

Maria had organized a party with extended family and friends a few weeks later. Jimmy wasn't sure what he thought about the idea of having it at the golf club where Ben was a member. It sounded expensive and he was sure it wasn't on his mother's money that it was happening. Ben seemed to have a way of convincing his mother of what was best, always glad to be able to help. But Jimmy thought it was more of a quiet way of controlling the situation. Still, he shut his mouth and thanked his mother and Ben for their thoughtfulness.

Ben drove them in his car to the golf club's party house. The place was beautiful. The lawn was like nothing Jimmy had ever seen; several shades of green cut in perfect squares, acre upon acre. Clusters of large willow, oak, and maple trees dotted the expanse of green without obstructing the fairways. From a landscaping perspective, it was a magnificent sight.

They pulled into the parking lot where Jimmy could see many cars had parked already and upon getting out, he saw a banner congratulating him, James "Jimmy" Gregory, on his graduation. Ben led them up the wide, wooden stairs and onto a porch where huge flowering plants hung from hooks and several white wooden rockers sat looking out onto the property. Just inside a large group of cousins, aunts, and uncles, Donny, Betty, and Bob and the two other full time guys along with several of his grandparent's neighbors were standing in the vast entryway, talking and waiting for him to enter.

They saw him then, and a roll of clapping and shouts of congratulations filled the air. Jimmy could barely breathe, and the larger part of him wanted to turn around and go home. But because everyone was there for him, he did his best to appear happy about it.Suzie had come up to him and she hugged him. She walked alongside him as he made his way through the crowd, shaking hands and thanking them for coming. After a few minutes, Ben whispered in his ear and then called for everyone's attention. Jimmy stood near the entrance to the dining room and tried to talk over the murmuring crowd. He thanked them collectively for celebrating his graduation with him and told them that they should all follow him into the dining room. "Please everyone...come eat and have some fun."

Inside, more than a half dozen large round tables with white and purple linen brought color to a small area in the front section of the enormous room. The front wall was almost all glass, the windows easily ten feet high. A small makeshift stage had been setup in front of the windows and decorated with white and purple streamers and again another banner with Jimmy's name and graduating year. Suzie noted that the room was decorated in his school colors and that the mariachi band that was setting up was all for him. He turned to her and nodded his head, feeling it was all too much. Then he turned to his mother who stood by Ben, looking over the whole thing. She appeared a little overwhelmed and maybe more nervous than he was, if that were possible. He went to her and gave her a hug and a kiss. She smiled then, and kissed him warmly and wished him a beautiful first day of the rest of his life.

As the guests all settled, Suzie's family found a table next to where abuelo and abuela were sitting. Jimmy saw them and went around to each of them, hugging them and suggesting that they pull the two tables together so they could all sit as one large group. Abuelo liked the idea and set out with Mr. Anderson's help to combine the tables. Jimmy noticed that Ben and his mother were talking alone by the entrance to the dining room. After a few minutes, she went out into the hall. Ben returned to the group and told them that they should start a line for the food that had been set out on long banquet tables along a side wall.

Jimmy asked about his mother and Ben said that she went to the restroom. "She'll be back in a few minutes I'm sure," he assured.

But after a bit, with Maria still gone, abuela whispered to abuelo and she too went into the hallway. Jimmy was sure she was checking on his mother and he was grateful. After Jimmy and Suzie and her family filled their plates and sat down to eat, the rest of the guests filed into line at the buffet tables. Cold salads led the way into hot casseroles and then several trays of freshly carved meats.

Ben and abuelo were busy talking when Maria and abuela returned. Though his mother looked like she might have been upset, she came in all smiles, announcing that she was looking forward to getting some of the wonderful food. Ben gave Maria a little kiss and led her to the tables, followed by Jimmy's grandparents.

Part way into eating, the mariachi band started and some of the extended Vazquez family got up to dance. Ben held out his hand for Maria and she smiled reluctantly but then giggled at something he whispered to her. He swung her out onto the floor and into a dance. While this was happening and Jimmy and Suzie were talking with her family, abuela tapped him on the shoulder. "Jimmy. There is someone here who would like to congratulate you. Someone who hasn't seen you in a long time. Here, just for a few minutes, let me take you to them."

Abuela was pulling him to his feet but he managed to give Suzie a quick kiss on the cheek as he stepped away with his grandmother. They wound their way to a table near the back through the guests who stood around tables, who patted him on the shoulder and who sang and danced along with the band. There, with a few of abuela's neighbors, a man and a woman with a thick pile of red hair pinned to the top of her head sat with a small plate of half-eaten food in front them. The woman saw Jimmy coming to the table and quickly popped up to meet him. "Jimmy, you remember Donna, don't you dear?" Abuela asked.

One look at her and a familiar warmth, one he hadn't felt in years, came over him. He was surprised that when she reached her hand out to him that he wrapped his arms around her in a hug, feeling a bit choked up. "Jimmy, I am so very, very happy to see you. What a fine young man you have become…I always knew you would be, but you are so much more."

He pulled back to look at Donna then. He saw the porcelain face of the angel who had cared for him and had loved him the first years of his life; the angel who had been there on his bad days and on his good days and on those last terrible days. "Thank you. For coming. I guess I can't believe it really. That you are here," the words stuck in his throat and jumbled in his mouth.

"Congratulations, Jimmy. You've done very well for yourself." Jimmy hadn't noticed until then that Patrick had come as well. They shook hands and he motioned for Jimmy and abuela to sit down.

In no time stories of Jimmy's childhood were being told and Donna and abuela were laughing as they listened and as they shared. Apparently, Jimmy's grandmother had been writing Donna letters over the years, telling her things about Jimmy and Maria even after their early visits had faded away and all that was left was the annual birthday card from Donna. He was suddenly embarrassed to think of those birthday cards with their $10 and the little note wishing him well. He hadn't written a thank you since receiving the first one. But Donna was all smiles and full of questions about his work, his girlfriend, and all the many things abuela must have written about. Jimmy guessed she knew about the bad stuff as well, but of course Donna would never ask hard questions and Jimmy was glad to let those things stay between the women.

He learned that Liam was in the army, stationed in South Korea. His parents hadn't seen him in six months. Patty was finishing up her last year at Niagara University. She would graduate with a degree in secondary education and start teaching while finishing her masters. It was good having her close, Donna said. Then, "Do you remember how she was always playing teacher with you Jimmy? Gosh. She never gave you a minute's rest about your homework, did she?" and they laughed at the memory.

Just as he was wondering about his mother and what she knew about the Hennessey's being there, she and Ben approached the table. Donna embraced her warmly, as familiar as if it was just yesterday that they had taken the kids to swim or sat at the kitchen table over coffee. But Jimmy guessed that the two hadn't spoken since that last winter six years ago. Seeing his mother with her friend brought a tender longing for the old days he didn't think he'd ever feel. But he didn't imagine his mother felt the same way. The "old days" had almost ruined her.

The two talked along for a few minutes before the conversation started to stall. Jimmy knew when his mother was struggling. This would be an emotional day for a strong person, but for his mother to organize this event and to be interacting with so many people, then to see Donna after all these years… Jimmy knew it was taking everything she had. But before she said her goodbyes, she pulled on the chain that had hung around her neck for all those years and brought the Celtic knot cross out from under her blouse. Donna reached out to touch it, smiling before she felt for and held her own cross in her fingers. The two hugged again and wiped tears from their eyes.

"I'm so happy to see you still have it, Maria. I hope you always remember our friendship," and Donna gave her friend a kiss on the cheek. Before Maria left, Donna handed her a piece of paper with her address written on it. "We got that little place of our own finally. I would love to have you come by… anytime, Maria."

Several hours later, after the dancing and the eating and family and friends had wished Jimmy well one more time, Ben took them home. Jimmy had been tossing around new concerns he had about his mother after seeing her today and he was wondering how or if he should approach her about them. He decided he'd better wait and watch her a little more closely before jumping to any conclusions and upsetting her.

When Ben asked Maria if she would like to go back to his place for the night, she said she was tired and would rather stay home, maybe watch TV and go to bed early. Ben didn't seem to know how to take a hint and he ended up on the couch with Maria, the two of them lying wrapped around each other, the TV volume low and Ben nodding off while Maria looked at the screen without really watching.

Jimmy went to his room, taking with him the pile of cards and the few gifts that had been left on a table at the club for him. He spread them out on his bed, intending to open them. But as he sat there flipping them around, sorting them by size, he couldn't shake his concern for his mother… how she had acted today. He was going to go see abuela as soon as he could get away, talk to her about what she thought she might have seen when she went to the bathroom to find her daughter.

And then as he thought about the bathroom, he got up and went into theirs. He closed the door and took a deep breath as he opened the medicine cabinet. But he didn't see the prescription bottle he was looking for. He wondered if his mother had ever kept her medication there. He really hadn't bothered to ever look.

Tonight though, he wanted to find that bottle. He decided that she might be keeping it in her bedroom, maybe on the dresser. Quietly he peeked into the living room where he saw that Maria was now dozing off as well. 'Good,' he thought while he crept back down the hallway and into his mother's room. With the little light that was left from the waning day, he was able to poke his way around. No pill bottle on her dresser. No bottle in the drawers as far as he could see or feel. Her jewelry box held the few earrings and necklaces she owned and Jimmy noticed ironically, the note that Donna had written his mother the day they moved out of the apartment house.

Where did she keep it? He began to feel the panic of the reality of what he was becoming concerned about. Still he looked. He felt around between her mattress and box springs and then under the bed. Nothing. Then he thought of the most obvious place and he moved out into the kitchen where she always set her purse on a tiny shelf there. He opened it and felt around, then looked to make sure. Still he hadn't found it. He was upset, but determined.

He went back into her room and pulled open the door to her closet. He stepped into the narrow area not meant to be walked into. He closed the door behind him and turned on the light. As best as he could he stooped down and opened the few shoe boxes he saw but they only held keepsakes and shoes. But in one he found a thick envelope that ended up holding a copy of the divorce papers apparently his mother had been sent by his father many years ago. There was her signature and also the signature of James Gregory. He realized that that was as much as he had seen of his father since he was a baby.

And then there, under the envelope was a vial shaped orange bottle. As he turned it over to read the label he discovered that it was his mother's and had been prescribed by the psychiatrist she had first told her family about. Jimmy noticed that it had been filled on May 20th and that there were still maybe a dozen pills left in the bottom of it. Today was July 10th and so with a fearful feeling of dread he realized his mother hadn't been taking her medicine for over a month.

Flushed and upset, he tried to reorder the boxes. He pulled on the chain to the light before opening the door. He made his way back to his room, trying to consider why his mother had stopped her medication and what he was going to do about it. He fussed with the envelopes on his bed before finally grabbing them up and setting them on his dresser. He wasn't opening them tonight.

Several hours later Jimmy heard Ben leave and his mother pad down the hallway to her room. She closed the door behind her and he didn't hear anything from her when he got out of bed around 7:00 a.m. the next morning. The sleepless night had left him considering and then deciding that he would go to his grandparents today. Donny had given him the day off with pay as a graduation gift and Jimmy was glad for it. Depending on what he heard there, he might go to Ben as well.

Apparently his grandmother hadn't slept very well either and she was especially glad to see Jimmy at the door. She had been having dreams of a waterfall and the loud roar of its powerful waters on the rocks below had woken her for several nights. He didn't have to work his way into a conversation about his mother because abuela had been concerned herself and she explained to Jimmy that recurring dreams of water meant sadness and grief were coming.

Over a cup of black coffee, she told Jimmy that she had found his mother in the clubhouse bathroom in tears and trembling. She wasn't willing to talk and she pulled herself together as soon as abuela asked her what was upsetting her. But abuela was sure Maria had been struggling to keep herself together the rest of the day. And when Jimmy told them about his search and then the discovery of her hidden medicine, they all looked at each other with fear in their faces.

Their conclusion was that if Maria had recently stopped taking her medication, then she might not be going to counseling either. Even though she made Jimmy believe she was keeping her Friday afternoon appointments Jimmy had caught her once talking about Ben taking a Friday off so they could day trip along the wine trails. And if she wasn't doing either of these things, these things that had helped her manage her life, then she could be headed for trouble again. And the only reason for it that they could come up with was Ben, who had a way of sweeping people up in his plans and his expectations. Had he expected her to be able to navigate her new life without counseling or medication? Had he led Maria to believe that his love was all she should need?

Jimmy wasn't about to let any person take the life away that his mother had struggled to get back. He was going to Ben's apartment.

***

It was the Tuesday after when Jimmy was able to reach Ben without his mother knowing. She was at work and although Ben was as well, Jimmy called the real-estate office where he knew Ben worked and asked to be transferred to him. The secretary put him on hold for a minute but returned to the line and said that Ben would be glad to take his call. Before Jimmy had time to think, Ben answered.

Jimmy knew he couldn't blast a bunch of accusations, frustrations, and concerns about his mother over the phone. But as he tried to keep his voice controlled, he felt it lose strength and then strain as he choked back anger and fear. Ben must have heard it immediately because he asked what had happened. Was Maria okay? And then Jimmy began to cry and Ben said he was leaving work and would pick him up in an hour.

Ben began asking questions as soon as Jimmy opened the passenger door to get in. He looked pretty agitated and his hand shook as he shifted his sports car into its higher gears. It was pretty obvious he was worried about Maria, and Jimmy didn't have the patience to wait until they got to Ben's place before telling what he knew.

He started with the graduation party, his mother crying in the bathroom, his abuela with her there. He went on to explain how he looked for her medicine, how she had hidden the bottle away in a box, the old date, that she obviously hadn't been taking it. Then he mentioned the wine trail trip that would have been on his mother's counseling day. He asked Ben why he would plan something like that when Maria needed to be at those sessions and why would she stop taking the medicine that had been helping her.

In the silence that followed, Jimmy turned to Ben and asked him again, "Why, Ben? Why?" Ben didn't say a word, but drove with a fury through the side streets until they got to his house. He turned sharply into the driveway and cut the engine, sitting there with more silence hanging between them. Then he put his hands to his face and groaned. When he finally pulled them away, Jimmy saw in his face what he hadn't considered. Ben didn't know about this. He didn't know about Maria's fragile mental health, about the medication, the counseling.

And so for the next few hours Jimmy and Ben talked, Jimmy pouring over the story of his mother's life struggles and Ben, looking stricken, promising to talk to Maria, to give her his full support. Jimmy decided to let Ben have the first conversation with his mother. He hoped she would listen to this man she cared about so much.

When the two had talked until there was nothing else to be said, Jimmy got up to leave. He declined the offer of a ride saying he wanted to take the bus back, to pull himself together. Ben got up and followed him to the door, repeating his promise to take care of Maria. Then the soft-handed, suit and tie dressing, corporate real-estate agent reached out and hugged Jimmy, the blue-collar farm worker. And Jimmy knew then that Ben really loved his mother.

Knowing what he did, Ben called Maria that evening and asked her if she'd like a quiet date night at home when she was up for it. They agreed on Friday, planning to make their favorite shrimp dish together. Jimmy had plans of his own that night with Suzie.

Chapter 18

On Friday morning Jimmy got up and ready for work, which he recently started full time now that he had graduated. He dropped a few peanut butter sandwiches in a lunch bag before gently rapping on his mother's bedroom door to get her up. She had wanted to take him in to work the mornings she was off. She loved having her driver's license and the little Dodge Omni Ben had helped her find a few months ago. It was a new freedom and one that Jimmy appreciated as much as she did.

Jimmy was uneasy about how tonight would go but he couldn't bear the thought of letting things go and having his mother lose herself again. She had been doing so well. They drove quietly, each with their own thoughts. At the farm, Jimmy leaned over to give his mother a hug and kiss. He wished her a good appointment with the counselor and she nodded and smiled, dismissively he thought.

"Mom," he looked at her intensely, with love in his eyes, "Always remember how much I love you." He heard his words, the weight of them hanging in his own ears.

"I love you too. And I'm so proud of the man you have become. All on your own it seems."

"No, Mom. Not all on my own. You gave me life and your goodness runs through me." He looked at his mother until she could no longer hold his gaze. He closed the door and lingered as she waved and drove away.

***

That night, around ten, the Anderson's doorbell rang. Mr. Anderson moaned and rolled to his side in the recliner and Nancy came from the kitchen where she had been looking for recipes in magazines. She turned on the porch light and looked through the window. Quickly she opened the door, calling to Suzie and Jimmy who were watching TV. They heard the deep, quivering voice of Jimmy's grandfather and as they got to the hallway, they saw him stagger just inside the doorway.

"My God! Are you okay, Mr. Vazquez?" Nancy was at the man's side, holding his arm. Jimmy reached out to grab his grandfather whose legs had begun to buckle.

"Jimmy. Oh, Jimmy! My God. Your mother..." he paused and broke into tears.

"Abuelo! What? What's happened?" Jimmy hollered.

Abuelo held on to his grandson and wrapped his arms around him. "Jimmy. Your mother is dead." Abuelo fainted in Jimmy's arms.

***

Mr. Anderson was in the hallway with them, helping Nancy get Mr. Vazquez onto the couch. They revived the man with a cool cloth to the forehead. Jimmy couldn't find the strength to get off the floor where he had fallen with his grandfather in his arms. He was in shock and he couldn't make sense of what Suzie was saying. He vomited as she tried to help him stand.

Finally, Mr. Anderson came back for Jimmy and guided him into the living room where he sat him in the reclining chair. Nancy was bringing water to the two stricken men, her eyes spilling over with tears. Suzie was seated on the arm of the chair, holding Jimmy around the shoulders, crying softly.

When Mr. Vazquez found his voice again he tried to relay what had happened about an hour ago.

"We got a call at the house. It was the police. They asked if we knew Maria. I knew what that meant. My God, I knew what it meant, but still, I hoped."

"Abuelo, what did they say?"

"They said there had been an accident. Maria's car and another. The paramedics had not been able to save her. She was already gone by the time they got to her," abuelo broke into groans, and then began crying. "We need to go, Jimmy. Rosa rode with abuela to the hospital and I've come to get you."

Jimmy couldn't process this information. An accident? Her car? Where was she? Was Ben with her? He pulled himself out of the chair and went to his grandfather, both trying to move but quite disabled in their shock.

"Mr. Vazquez, if you would let me, I want to take you and Jimmy," Mr. Anderson held his hand out in front of the older man.

Abuelo looked up into the face of Suzie's father. "Yes. Please, Mr. Anderson, if you would."

The five of them made their way out to the car. Jimmy sat between his grandfather and Suzie, holding tightly to each of their hands as he silently yelled at the God who would let something like this happen.

***

At the hospital, they were led to a small room where grieving families could gather privately. The chairs and carpeting were warm beige and brown but the lighting was harsh and industrial and it burned Jimmy's eyes. He ran to his grandmother and held her in a long hug while they wept together. Suzie and her parents hugged her as well. The Anderson's said they would be out in the main waiting area, that they wanted the family to have this time alone. Jimmy asked Suzie to stay with him. Only then did he notice that Ben was there, leaning off in the far corner against a wall. Jimmy didn't want to make eye contact with him. He was struggling with a nagging conviction that he should have been the one to go to his mother. He should have been the one to speak to her.

Any real conversation didn't happen until after an ER doctor and a policeman came in to speak to the family. The doctor explained that while she couldn't determine the exact cause of death yet, Maria had suffered multiple rib fractures that penetrated deep into her chest. She also had severe head trauma and that alone, if Maria had survived, would have most likely left her in a vegetative state.

But it was the police report that left the greatest impact on Jimmy. Ms. Gregory had exited off a section of expressway on the south end of the city. She had gotten to the end of the exit ramp, but instead of stopping for the light, she had continued out into the street appearing to be trying to make a left turn. A car in the southbound lane hit Ms. Gregory's car on the driver's side at 50 mph, pushing her car into the north bound lane where it appeared to have originally been headed.

Ms. Gregory was pronounced dead at the scene by EMT's and brought by ambulance back here to the hospital while police contacted family. The doctor and the police officer each expressed their condolences. Before leaving, the doctor directed them where they could go to see Maria if they wanted, but warned that it might be difficult for them in her condition. The officer told them that they would have

Maria's personal effects at the station when they were ready to come pick them up.

Before anyone knew it, Jimmy was face to face with Ben, glaring at him. "What was my mother doing way over there? And why wasn't she with you?" The words were loud and full of accusation. Ben, who had been silent the whole time himself, wiped his eyes and then his mouth and asked Jimmy to sit down. He asked them all to sit and let him tell them what he knew.

For the next half hour or so he tearfully told how he and Maria had made dinner together, opened a bottle of wine, and shared a glass as they cooked. He said he was anxious to talk to her about what he had learned about her past. What Jimmy had shared and the concern they all had for her.

"Part way through dinner, I brought it up. Not sure what I said first, but I told her that I knew about her depression and her treatment. I told her that you and I had talked." Ben stopped and looked up at Jimmy just long enough for him to notice before staring back down at his hands. "And I told her I loved her and that I would never want to get in the way of her being well." He stopped again and waited, drew in a deep breath.

"And Maria got up then. She was crying and she picked up her dinner plate and set it on the counter. She was surprised and hurt, I could see. I thought, 'at least we have this out. Now she will know I want her to start taking care of herself.' But she started yelling at me. She said I was trying to get rid of her, that I wanted an out and that I had found it. I tried to tell her that NO, I did NOT want an out. But I did want her to do the things she needed to in order to stay well. I wanted her to be in counseling and to get back on her medication.

"And then she stopped. And she looked at me in horror. 'How do you know about my medication, if I am taking it or not?' All I could think to tell her then was that you had been worried about her. That she hadn't been acting herself and the family was noticing. I didn't know what else to do. What else to say."

Jimmy couldn't speak. He played what he was hearing over in his head. The implications of it were screaming at him. He was sickened to think of his part in this.

Abuelo's voice came softly, "What happened then Ben? What did she do?"

"I tried to keep her there," he pleaded with abuelo. "I tried to get her to sit with me and just talk through it. I begged her to. I told her I loved her. And she did sit for a little while, but she was upset. She kept saying that she needed to think about things. She wasn't sure if she trusted me.

"And then after maybe a half hour, she just got up and said she was going home. She would call me in a few days. I waited a while and then I called the house. Two times. Left messages. I wanted to talk to Jimmy." Ben directed his gaze at him again. "I wanted you to know what had happened."

Abuela was weeping loudly now and abuelo held her as he looked with concern to his grandson. Jimmy couldn't meet his eyes. He couldn't look at Suzie, who was holding his hand, or at Ben, who was waiting for him.

Finally, he got up, shaking and defeated. "I want to go get my mother's things. I want to go to the police station and get her things," he whispered while looking at Ben.

Chapter 19

*F*ive days later the Vazquez family held calling hours for their beloved daughter, mother, and sister. It was an especially sunny day because, in Jimmy's heart, God didn't care about his grief. This was the hardest thing Jimmy had ever had to do and he was visibly shaken. The director had suggested a receiving line with Naomi, Edward, and their spouses, followed by abuelo and abuela, and finally Jimmy, standing closest to his mother. She was closed in her casket, eerily the focal point of the room. Flowers were everywhere and the smell of them made him feel sick. He told his grandparents he wanted Suzie with him and they agreed that it should be that way.

The Vazquez's priest had come to be with the family for a short time before all the people coming to pay their respects overwhelmed them. Through Maria's death Jimmy's grandparents had held on to their faith like a person holds on to one of those metal bars on the shower wall. It held them up when they were too weak to carry their own weight and it steadied them and gave them comfort as if God were something tangible, solid and with arms, to embrace them. Jimmy had wanted to hold on in this way, but he couldn't quite get a grasp on God and instead of surrendering his pain, he pushed the angst he felt deep inside of himself.

The extended family, which always was overwhelmingly large at holiday parties, seemed to have grown even bigger as they poured into the funeral home. The murmuring of their voices, the mixed sounds of sadness and of laughter upset Jimmy and as he looked out at their staring faces he began to feel weak. He couldn't imagine standing like this for hours, shaking hands and thanking them, while they rambled on about his mother without really saying anything. Thank God Suzie was there to hold him up, both emotionally and physically.

Ben had walked in a few minutes after the doors had opened and he was painfully emotional. He was wearing a black suit, white shirt, and black tie, but somehow he didn't look put together. His shirt was not tucked as tight and wasn't as crisp as Jimmy had seen in the past. His tie didn't seem to be knotted quite right nor was it centered squarely at the neck. As he managed through the line, he kept his handkerchief in his hand, dabbing his eyes, his nose. When he got to abuelo, the older man embraced him with both arms, patting his back. As they separated, abuelo asked Ben if he'd stay on through the calling hours with the family. He knew that this was a very hard day for him as well as for them.

But Ben said he didn't think he could. He didn't feel right about it. Saying good-bye to abuelo and abuela, he came to Jimmy and waited there, not sure what to do. Suzie saw the awkwardness and she broke in, hugging Ben long enough for Jimmy to collect himself. Finally Jimmy extended his hand and as Ben shook it, the two reached their free arm around the other and hung on for some time. They were each feeling their own pain…each other's pain.

"I am so… so very sorry Jimmy," Ben whispered, broken voice. "I just wanted….to help her."

Jimmy didn't hear anything else for a heartbeat…only Ben's words. "So did I. So did I…," his voice trailing away.

Somewhere in the crowd of extended family, friends, and coworkers, a woman with a thick pile of red hair knotted up in a bun came into the room with her husband and daughter. She saw the crowd; she saw the flowers and the icons of Mary all about the casket; she saw the picture of her friend in a frame. And then she looked at the line she would go through. Sister, brother, father, mother, each trying to bear the pain. And then she saw the son. The boy who she had loved as one of her own. The boy who had seen so much sorrow and had been bruised, but not broken. She panicked then, afraid to face him. To hear his voice and see his tears. She felt her heart grow heavier and heavier and as she got closer, it finally burst in her chest. She pulled away from the line, from her husband and daughter, asking them to pay respects for her as she scurried for the doorway.

When Patty got to Jimmy, tearful and mascara smudged, she stammered to find her words. This was not the Patty of their childhood and Jimmy was touched by her sincerity. She held out her hand, a woman's hand, long and freckled. As she drew in a breath to speak, she began to cry and her arms opened to hug Jimmy. He drew her in and the two cried together for a moment, filling in lost years in the span of seconds.

They looked at each other and no words could express what was said there. Yet Patty uttered her deepest sadness for all that Jimmy had lost. She told him how she remembered fondly the fun they had all had and how grateful she was to his mother for helping her become a swimmer since her own mother hated the water. They parted with sad smiles and polite promises to see each other again. When Patrick got to Jimmy, he gave him the tender hug he knew Donna would have given him and he expressed the sorrow he knew she felt. And Jimmy didn't know that Donna had come for him. And that all she could manage in the end was to go home and pray for him every day for the rest of her life.

***

Maria's sudden death had taken a big toll on the whole family but Jimmy had kept trying to push his pain down into that dark unseeable place inside. He was still trying to appear strong when he returned to work a few days later. Donny had told him to take his time about returning but at least work gave Jimmy a small break from the weight he carried.

Mercifully his aunt Naomi had been the one to come and get Maria's things. She managed to fit her sister's life into a handful of boxes and bags and stuff them into her van where she dropped them at the local Salvation Army. She had talked with her nephew more in those few days than she had in his collective life. But after spending the week with her parents, she returned to her life and her family in Pennsylvania.

Jimmy wouldn't admit it to anyone, but he was struggling. The depression that had set in felt heavy, like a coat filled with rocks and every part of his life was taking exhausting effort. He loved Suzie with all of his heart but even being with her was hard. He hated the quiet of the apartment where images and thoughts of his mother flooded him, yet he hated the busyness of life at the same time.

It was abuelo who rescued his grandson. He knew staying in that apartment alone could not be good for Jimmy and after a few weeks he and abuela came by to talk to him.

"Jimmy, we've been thinking," he started. "Abuela and I miss you and we worry that this place is too much for you to manage on your salary. It's up to you, but we were hoping you might maybe consider coming back to live with us." His grandfather had managed to word it so that it wasn't as much about Jimmy's need as it was the practicality of the matter.

Jimmy tried not to cry, but he couldn't suppress a sigh, one of relief as he thought about getting out of the apartment that still carried his mother's life on the walls she had lovingly painted when she was happy and hopeful. It was killing him. He didn't wait to consider but thanked his grandparents and told them he would move in within the next week.

Suzie was an anchor, steady and supportive, and she held Jimmy in place as the two of them packed up his things. It was hard, touching things that had been part of his life with his mother. They placed an ad in the paper for a small apartment sale trusting they'd be able to get a few dollars for the furniture, the kitchen ware etc. Jimmy found all his graduation cards, still unopen in a shoebox under his bed. Was it just a month ago that the family had celebrated with him? He realized all over again that that was the day that his concern for his mother had led to the talk with Ben and that, to her death. He was overcome with grief as he thought about it, holding that box in his hands.

Suzie had come into the room and seen his stricken face. She held on to him as she sat with him on the edge of the bed. "I've got to open these. But the thought of that day. It's killing me, you know?" he looked into her eyes.

"I'll help you. I'll help you through it all," the little anchor said to the ship adrift at sea. She took the box from his hands and packed it with his other belongings going to abuelo's house.

***

Settling back in with his grandparents helped and strengthened him and after a few weeks he decided to finish the last painful task of opening his cards. He sat with them on his lap alone in his room one evening after Suzie had gone home. He immediately recognized his mother's writing on the front of one of them, her pretty hand somehow making the name "Jimmy" lovelier than it was. He set this aside, not ready to open the wound quite yet. Finding abuela's small neat printing, he put the envelope under his mothers, hoping for it to balance the pain he already felt.

One by one he was met with happy cards filled with congratulations and notes encouraging him to follow his dreams and wishing him well. Almost all of them had a monetary gift. These bills he set on his dresser not sure what to make of the money, knowing that he should write thank you cards but not feeling very grateful. He opened the Hennessey's card and read the thoughtful note from Donna. He became emotional but he managed to hold it together and he added the very generous $30 gift to the other bills.

Just as he was about to open his mother's card, abuela tapped softly on his door. He let her in and she immediately saw the cards piled on his bed and the envelopes tossed on the floor. "Oh," she said. "I'm sorry to be bothering you." She put a cup of cocoa and a few cookies on the dresser and walked out of the room. He closed the door behind her and drawing in a deep breath, tried to pick up his mother's card again. He heard muffled voices right before another knock on the door came and he opened it to both of his grandparents.

"Jimmy. I know this is not the best time. But abuela saw you opening your graduation cards and she wanted me to bring this to you. I didn't want you to have it. Maybe especially now. But…well here it is."

"Another card? Who's it from?" Jimmy reached out to take it.

"Jimmy, we had a visitor just before you moved back." Abuelo drew in a quick breath, "It was your father." Abuelo stopped to let the words register. "He said he knew that you'd graduated." Abuela was pulling a tissue from her housecoat.

"Jimmy, I don't know what his story is and I didn't ask. I hate the man. It was hard enough to have him at my door for all he put you and your mother through." Abuela had to leave the room at that point.

"What was he like?" Jimmy whispered. "I mean, did he look like he was well?"

Surprised by the question, abuelo said gruffly, "Oh, yes. He looked well all right. Fancy shirt, fancy car. Your father came from money and he was more spoiled than a rotten piece of meat." Abuelo's face had turned red and he left the room, closing the door.

The next day Jimmy left work a little early so he could go to the bank. He had opened all his cards and he kept his mother's out on his dresser, able to see her love radiating from it. Her note had been thoughtful and positive. He read no sadness or darkness in its words and he wanted to remember her like that.

The card from James Gregory was short in words, a "Congratulations and wishing you a happy and strong future," scrawled below the Hallmark verse. Enclosed was a check for $10,000; an incredible amount of money from a deadbeat dad. To Jimmy it felt like a payoff and he was pretty sure it was. But abuelo said to go and get that check to a bank. He said that at least Jimmy would have something from that son-of-a-bitch excuse for a father that he could use.

But abuelo hadn't told Jimmy everything about the morning that James Gregory had knocked on his door. While it was true that he had come with the graduation card for Jimmy, it was also true that he had come to say how sorry he was to have heard about Maria. And while abuelo stood there shaken by his phony condolences, James had the gall to ask about Jimmy and wondered if maybe he could come back to see him.

Abuelo stepped out into the hallway and closed the apartment door. "Don't come back here James," abuelo had warned. "EVER! You'll be lucky if I give this card to my grandson. Nice timing showing up now, after all these years. Now when my daughter is dead and my grandson is all grown." Abuelo spit out the words, his face red with anger.

James turned and started down the hallway. "I haven't forgotten my son, Mr. Vazquez," he looked back, his voice raised. "But you wouldn't know about that, now would you?" and he walked on down the hallway, down the stairs and out the front entrance. Abuelo watched him get in his shiny grey sports car and drive away. He walked into his apartment the envelope shaking in his hands. The encounter had upset him and he was afraid to think that James would ever come back. He thought about throwing the card away and with it the memory of the visit.

But instead, quickly and without thought he opened it. Inside he found a typical graduation card with a picture of a young man wearing a cap and gown. But when he opened it a piece of lined paper fell out on the floor along with a check. He picked up the check and was taken aback to see what it had been written for. He immediately put it in his trousers pocket.

He sat down in his chair to read the paper, handwriting on both sides when abuela came in from the kitchen. She looked at her husband, asked what was wrong, what was he reading. He looked up at her and his face warned that it was something he did not want to share with her. "Not now," he barked.

James had written a short letter and in it he expressed his sympathies at Maria's passing, how truly sorry he was for Jimmy's loss. He somehow knew how much she had loved and cared for Jimmy. He talked on then about how he had grown up and realized his mistakes over the years. He said he was married recently, that he had a young daughter, and that he felt bad for not having been a father to Jimmy. James and his family were moving to California soon, that's where his work was taking him.

He didn't expect anything from his son, he explained. But he did wonder if Jimmy would ever want to meet him, just to talk. At the end of the letter was a phone number, a way for Jimmy to reach his father if he ever so decided. It had been simply signed "James."

It upset abuelo to tears. His daughter had just died and God knew the part James Gregory had played in her collapse. And his grandson had been denied access to what should have been one of the most important people in his life. Again without thinking, abuelo refolded the paper before tearing it into tiny pieces. These he took to the kitchen sink and setting a match to them, burned them till they were ash. Abuela watched, somehow knowing that the whole thing was too big for her. Then he took the check and put it back in the card, setting it in his dresser till he got a new envelope for it.

But what abuelo didn't know was that his daughter had been receiving envelopes from James Gregory several times a year during the last six years. There was never a return address to flag where they had come from. Each one of them contained a large check and a short note from her ex-husband. And each one of them Maria had quickly torn into pieces, just as abuelo had James' letter, and stuffed them deep into the trash.

Chapter 20

Spring 2010

James waited until he saw Molly moving on her mattress before he spoke. It must have been sometime in the afternoon because the light had shifted and intensified and he was very hungry. But more than all that, after seeing the bathroom walls he wanted to learn more about this place from Molly.

She sat up finally and when she saw him in the chair she sighed. "Sorry about that, James. I tend to sleep a lot."

"No problem. I got the best sleep since I had to leave my truck over a month ago. I really appreciate all this." He paused but then continued. "And that bathroom is pretty amazing. There was enough light for me to see the mural there. Did you find it like that?"

Molly sighed again. She gathered her blanket around her shoulders. "No. That was one of the first things I did after finding this place. I hardly think of it now, it's probably been over a year." She became quiet again.

James was caught up in a memory, the thought of the last beautiful work of art he had seen and who had created it. A deep longing washed over him. Finally coming back to the present he said "Molly, I'm no art critic but I do know beauty when I see it and that is some beautiful work. How did you manage it?"

"Oh, well there's a guy that has a paint shop right off of Genesee Street. I went in there one day to look around a little. I've never been able to pass by a place where I might find something to paint with. Even though he's no supply shop I thought, hell, paint is an art supply so what's it gonna hurt to ask. Told him I played around with media…liked to paint and he ended up mixing me a few pints that day. And he offered to give me partial gallons from customers looking to get left over paint out of the house. So yeah, that's how I got the paint. The brushes were harder but again if you're willing to wait, you can usually find people tossing out what you are looking for."

James hesitated, thinking again. His past and this present coming together. Finally he moved the chair he was sitting in closer to Molly's mattress. "So you're an artist. Do anything else since you've been here? Would be hard with the very low lighting in this place, I'd imagine."

James thought he could see a faint smile cross Molly's lips, but he wasn't sure if he were imagining it. "A few things. But I can't just DO art you know. It takes inspiration and a certain energy and I don't have too many creative periods like that." Molly stared off into a corner of the room. "But my God I love it when they come over me.

"But enough of that for now. You're hungry I'm sure and I need to visit the ladies room." Molly stood up and waited expectantly.

"Didn't think we could go out till after dark."

"That's true. But because sometimes I stay here for days at a time, I've had to hoard a few provisions. Come on. I've probably got something to hold us till nightfall." She grabbed the candle and lit it before leaving the little room, closing the door behind her.

In the hallway they made their way back to the bathroom she had engineered and decorated. James waited with the candle and when Molly came out she was carrying one of the pails with a cloth draped over it. He understood that they would need to go to the dumping window. "You still okay? I mean. Do you need to contribute to the compost pile?" Molly asked matter-of-factly.

James shook his head and Molly moved on down the hall. Soon James could see better and he realized they were approaching some source of light. Molly walked right on by a huge room, probably the central work or warehouse area lined with long tables and strewn with old boxes. From it light was coming in through a long line of exposed windows that ran along the top of one wall. They worked like skylights and allowed for a bit of the outside to shine in.

"Wait Molly," James backed up to look in. "What is this?" He was gazing at the wall that was softly lit by the filtered light. Here again he could see that there was some sort of mural covering about a third of the wall. This one looked like something of a forest. He walked in and over to it. It was stunning. Among a dense growth of pines and spruce there were fox, rabbits a number of deer and several other woodland animals. The scene was as realistic as anything he could imagine and for a moment he felt himself outside the walls of the dark building and standing inside the shade of a wooded area. If he walked any deeper he would frighten the creatures living there. It was another beautiful work that Molly wasn't even going to show him.

"Just more paint," she dismissed it. "Come on. I want to get rid of this and go get a granola bar." She pointed to the pail she had just used.

As he turned to her he noticed the opposite wall. It was much harder to make out not being on the sunlit side, but he could tell part of it had been painted. Walking closer he saw specks of white paint glistening off the weak candle light he held in his hand. He brought the candle closer making out a starry night, a faint sliver of moon high in the sky. He walked along down the wall a ways finding more astronomical figures casting a glow from their black backdrop.

But then suddenly the picture changed and he was standing in front of a massive sort of web, like a spiders web but thick as cord. Holding his candle right up to the wall he could see something in the web. He realized then that caught up in its clutches, still alive were what looked to be people, each with tormented faces, some gnashing their teeth and others awash in tears. James drew in his breath.

"Yeah. I didn't want you to see that. At least not yet." She turned to the forest scene. "Stuff like this," she waved her hand. "Like the garden. They come to me in periods like you saw me in last week. Life is amazing and so am I. Can't hold me down and can't rain on my parade." She stared, seeming to admire her work. Then she turned to the dark wall. "And this? Kind of my flip side, I guess. That girl, in that corner up there," she pointed. "I think she's me. But then again, maybe that one is," she pointed to another figure.

James couldn't resist getting close and holding the candle up to see better, and moving from face to face he saw that they were all likely the same person. The young women were thin and had long dark hair. Anyone of those tormented faces could have been Molly's.

"Molly. I don't know what to say."

She started to get agitated, her voice suddenly high and thin. "Say I'm scary and dark. Say I'm sick, that I'm crazy. That I'm bipolar. That's what the professionals call it. What do you think? Ready to run for the door yet?" Molly broke out in tears and she ran out of the room as fast as she could with that stinking pail in her hand, leaving James with what he had just learned.

Chapter 21

The timing of Jimmy's return to his grandparent's apartment could not have been better for all of them. Several months after he settled back into his old room, with plenty of his mother's memory still alive in the space they shared, abuela had begun to have some problems with her own memory. It had crept in slowly. Little things like forgetting where she had put the basket of clean clothes or that Jimmy had told her he wasn't going to be home for dinner that night. For a while it was easy enough to excuse her lapses as part of the immense depression she felt after losing her youngest child. Everyone was struggling to continue on with some sort of day to day life when their hearts were all still so freshly broken.

But over time the issues went from understandable forgetfulness to abuela having problems completing everyday tasks. She would struggle to find where she had put her iron, the one she had kept on the top shelf of the closet for all the years Jimmy had been there and she could not remember dates, days of the week, or the few regular appointments she had. She'd start something then walk away from it and begin doing something entirely different only to find later that she had left the refrigerator door open and the bags of groceries half unpacked.

One day she left her closest friend Rosa's apartment, turned the wrong way in the hallway and ended up opening the door of another apartment, wondering where Carlos was before she realized what she had done. Abuelo hated what he was seeing but feared what a doctor would say. He hadn't yet come back from his own dark place after Maria's death and the thought of entering another one overwhelmed him.

Finally, frustrated and concerned for his grandmother's safety Jimmy ended up calling Edward to come over and talk with abuelo about his grandmother. Edward had been left unaware of the magnitude of his mother's problem and when it was finally explained to him he was firm in his conviction that they take her to a doctor. Abuelo finally relented, knowing that what he couldn't face was not the most loving thing for his wife.

After a physical and a few blood tests they were referred to a neurologist. It was a formality really; the doctor had all but told them that Mrs. Vazquez suffered from dementia so when the diagnosis of Alzheimer's was made, the family left the neurologists office with a handful of pamphlets on how to care for your loved one and pages of resources that could be called upon. The hardest part of the whole thing was the frank conversation the specialist had with them about their loved ones future. As gently as the doctor could be while still conveying the gravity of his message, he told them that Mrs. Vazquez's disease seemed to be advancing rapidly and that the reality was that she would need more care than they and their home could provide in the foreseeable future.

The family was more determined than ever to see their sweet abuela through this tragedy and they worked out a schedule to help abuelo with her care. With a lot of dedication and diligence they were able to keep her home for close to two years. Edward's wife, who cared for her own ailing mother, managed to come each week to clean and make a few meals while Edward and one of their sons still living close by took extended lunch breaks and turns on weekends staying with abuela while abuelo rested.

Jimmy and Suzie spent a large part of their time together at the Vazquez home and Suzie was a gentle caregiver as abeula became increasingly confused with her surroundings and the people in her apartment. She acted as a nursing aide, bathing and dressing abuela for bed, making sure she was comfortable, and talking her through her anxious paranoia. Jimmy had wanted to do more, but he was there every night in the apartment with his grandparents which was a great comfort to his grandfather.

When abuela began to wake and wander, confused in the apartment Jimmy made a sort of bell alarm that hung like a trap from their bedroom and apartment doors. If she opened a door the noise set off by the cowbell woke them and Jimmy was the first one to bolt from his bed and guide his grandmother back to the safety of her room. Having Jimmy living there was an invaluable help to his grandfather and the old man was humbled by his grandson's priority to them.

But by the second summer of abuela's diagnosis her agitation and confusion became increasingly concerning and the doctor had recommended to abuelo that it was time to make the hard decision to move his wife into a continuing care home. Naomi who had only sporadic contact with her mother, more by phone than in person, had been the most vocal about not moving her mother from their home. She had begged her father to come to Pennsylvania and stay with them, that she would see to her mother's care.

But abuelo refused to make such a change. It would have been too much for his wife, he told Naomi, and the idea of it was just too much for him as well. So she took an extended leave from work to stay with her parents that summer. After about three weeks of experiencing first hand her mother's decline and the amount of time and energy needed to care for her, she agreed to help them look for a facility for abuela. It took all of Edward, Naomi, and Jimmy to persuade abuelo, who struggled terribly with guilt feelings about leaving his wife of fifty-four years, that this move was necessary.

They settled her into half of a shared bedroom at a large nursing care facility. She was on the second floor, where the doors in and out were all locked for the safety of its residents who all suffered from dementia. A small keypad by the entrance allowed for family to access the floor with a four-digit code and to come and go during visiting hours.

She had a steady group of visitors but none more reliable than her husband Carlos, who was there six days a week from the resident's lunch hour until part way into the *Wheel of Fortune* show when his wife almost always fell to sleep listening to Pat Sajak and Vanna White. It was incredibly painful to find her always in her room, sitting in the rose-colored chair they had brought from home and begging him to take her out of there. She begged random visitors and the staff just as much as she did her own family, for she didn't know any one of them from the other. It broke abuelo's heart to look into her eyes and see no signs of recognition. She talked to him like he was the plumber, pleasant but having nothing to share.

Abuela continued to fade in the manner predictable to her disease. While she had never been a large woman, she had been strong and fit. But over time her body had become thin and frail. Abuelo and the staff encouraged her to walk but she had no desire to, she didn't understand what was happening to her and the hallways just confused and upset her. She became quite sedentary and eventually she stopped talking. It was the most painful thing Jimmy had seen abuelo suffer through because like with his mother he was utterly helpless. And this was his wife, the one he had loved longer than any other.

***

They lost her on a Sunday afternoon one year and two months after her move and three years after her diagnosis. Abuelo had been summoned in the early hours of that morning and with Jimmy and Suzie, Edward and his wife, and they sat around the bed of their incredibly gentle yet strong, loving, and devoted matriarch. Jimmy had gone out of the room to speak to his aunt Naomi and when he returned his grandfather had climbed up onto his wife's bed, sitting at her hip one last time and kissing her creased forehead as he cradled her in his arms.

Jimmy stayed with his grandfather in the Vazquez's apartment after his grandmother's death. He was in his early twenties and abuelo was in his early seventies and it was the best arrangement for both of them. Abuelo benefitted from the added safety and help that having a young, strong man around provided him as he had been feeling the effects of fifty years of physical labor. But more important it was the understanding and companionship of his grandson that, after all their shared losses, was a comfort beyond all value.

For Jimmy it was an obvious financial help living there, where he was only paying a small portion of what he would be responsible for in a place of his own. And abuelo's example had helped him grow to be a responsible and dependable adult. Abuelo understood that as a young man Jimmy didn't need his supervision and he was respectful to keep most of his opinions to himself. Jimmy came and went and did as any young adult with a roommate would. While abuelo was always respected as a grandfather and an elder, the two of them had developed a new kind of friendship during the years between Maria's and abuela's death. They were both men who had been through a series of very hard life experiences and they understood something about each other because of it.

Very slowly, without his realizing it, Jimmy was beginning to build a life for himself. It would never be complete in the way it was supposed to be. Losing his mother was like tearing off a lead branch on his tree of life. There would always be a large gap and a wound where she had been. And then with abuela's death, another branch, smaller but still important to the shape of his tree had been taken. But trees with deep, good roots are strong. And Jimmy, like a strong tree, was able to slowly heal even as the wounds would forever leave their mark on him.

He and Suzie had been dating since his senior year and the family all knew that it was a matter of time before they would marry. They had begun to talk about their future together as a matter of fact. They had their goals and they were both realistic about obtaining them. Suzie had finished a two-year business degree at the local community college and after a year back at the bakery she had returned to school for a second degree in culinary arts, hoping to graduate before they set a wedding date. Her dream was to help her mother grow the family bakery into something larger and possibly with several locations.

And Jimmy had gained confidence and purpose while working at Hope Grows under the encouragement of Donny and Betty. Chuck had retired shortly after Jimmy came on full time. Then Donny had begun to have some significant health problems and had to face the reality that he could no longer manage the day to day operation of the farm. He had no family that was interested in farming, his sister never married and his two daughters both left the simple life of their childhood for big jobs in big cities. His two grandsons never learned what it was like to work the land.

Bob liked working with the cows that made up the small 250-head dairy. He had no ambition to own or operate the farm, but was content to do what was asked of him and go home at the end of the day. It was Jimmy who instinctively understood the rhythm of the fields, when to grow and how to increase yield. He worked the soil and handled the crops with a reverence, like they were pieces of art in God's great gallery, so it was natural for Donny to approach Jimmy about taking on the general operation of the farm. Donny felt that, while no one could love his place quite like he did, Jimmy would care for the farm as if it were his own. And Jimmy had gained the respect of his few coworkers for being hard working and dedicated. They were truly happy to hear that Jimmy, at only twenty-four years old would become their manager.

Telling Suzie about his new role at the farm was about as satisfying a thing as he had remembered experiencing since she had said yes to their first date. He shared his news with her family over dinner that night and Suzie had hopped out of her chair, squealing with joy and jumping up and down on the new kitchen linoleum, stopping only to kiss him on the cheek. She made him feel proud and he knew then that he was ready to officially ask her to marry him.

A few evenings later Suzie made dinner at abuelo's and they sat down together to tell him about Jimmy's promotion and their plans to marry. Abeuelo was quiet for just a moment, struggling to swallow the bit of pork he had been chewing. Then his voice came soft and cracking, "I'm so proud of you son," and the tears in his eyes brought tears to Jimmy's eyes as well. The three of them sat there sharing the new joy of happy tears.

It was an exciting and amazing time for the two of them. With their income looking good and a wedding date set for the following October 20th, they decided to do the one thing they had dreamed together about since they had first talked about marrying. They began the process of looking for a home.

Jimmy had wanted to live outside of the city ever since, at seventeen, he first put his foot into the soil of a field on the farm. Looking out at the endless green land, the breeze swaying the leafy vegetation, and the quiet of it all changed him. He felt closer to finding peace there than he did anywhere else and he desperately hoped Suzie would see the beauty of living in the country that he did.

They had looked around the Anderson's neighborhood and some of the other middle-class dwellings just outside the heart of Buffalo. There were some nice homes in decent neighborhoods and any of them was better than the streets of the city, lined with crowded apartment housing and noisy neighbors. But Jimmy had also taken them on drives along the rural roads of some towns outside of Buffalo. These little cities were all within thirty minutes of Buffalo and each had their own school systems and a mix of agricultural and suburban areas. Hope Grows was located a few miles outside of one of them and Suzie had been there before of course. But now they were looking at the area with new eyes.

On their rides, they saw homes with acres of mowed grass and trees with kids hanging from their branches. They found basic conveniences and amenities in the small downtown centers and several beautiful horse farms added to the charm of these rural areas. But Jimmy realized it would be an enormous lifestyle change for Suzie and he was careful not to try to persuade her.

When on one of their drives Suzie saw two laughing boys come up out of a creek bed, pails in their hands, wet and covered with mud, she made Jimmy stop the truck.

"This is it, isn't it?" she looked at him with her beautiful smile, eyes crinkled up. "How could we ever give our kids less than that?" she pointed at the boys who had scampered across the road and up to one of the houses.

And because Suzie and Jimmy wanted children more than anything besides each other, they eagerly set out with the guidance of Nancy's realtor friend to find a home in the country for their future family.

Chapter 22

$\mathcal{I}$n May of 1990, with the wedding just months away, the family had attended Suzie's second college graduation. With her new knowledge, she would be able to expand the offerings of the family's bakery and, with time, grow the business. Jimmy had adjusted to his new responsibilities at the farm and attended seminars and read anything that might help him learn more and better faming processes.

The Anderson's had been very happy to be able to help the young couple with their wedding. Suzie was their only daughter and they had decided that her dress and reception would be theirs to cover. And Nancy Anderson had said repeatedly that they were not to cut corners on the guest list. "It's your day and you only get one of them," she intoned. But both Suzie and Jimmy had decided on a smaller wedding, keeping it simple more because of preference than out of need.

Jimmy's Aunt Naomi and Uncle Edward along with their families were all invited. Abuelo had one living brother and he would be coming as well. Of course the Eddinger's, Donny and Betty, along with a few close farm friends and two old buddies from the neighborhood were also part of Jimmy's guest list. Jimmy knew that if abuela were alive she would have loved to have had her sister and brother there but he wasn't sure what proper protocol was in these situations. And he didn't feel comfortable asking his future mother-in-law or in any way making the Anderson's feel obligated to take on any more expense. But when Jimmy talked to Suzie about it she laughed and chided him for potentially causing trouble with her mother if ever she found out they'd considered cutting any family. Nancy didn't let you forget things like that.

Bob would be one of Jimmy's groomsmen along with Steven, Suzie's brother, and Hector, a friend Jimmy had kept in touch with since high school. Bob had remained a big brother of sorts to Jimmy and he would have asked him to be his best man had it not been for the picture that came to mind whenever he said the words. Whenever he thought of the role of 'best man' he kept coming back to the best man he had ever known, and that was abuelo of course.

This thought stayed with him and about this one thing he looked to the Anderson's for advice. "About the wedding. I was wondering. Well is it, you know. Is it proper...for a guy to have his grandfather in the wedding?" He asked suddenly while sitting in the living room with Suzie's parents, watching the news one evening.

Nancy sat up straight and looked over to the couch where her daughter sat leaning into Jimmy's shoulder. "Do you mean you want abuelo? As your best man?"

"I think so if it's okay, you know," he blushed.

"Okay," Nancy got up and sat on a corner of the couch. "I think it would be amazing. There is no higher honor than to be asked to stand up in that place. And to have your grandfather. Well, it's just...."and Nancy began to cry.

"That's what I told him, Mom," Suzie added. She gave Jimmy a little pinch before she hugged him and kissed his cheek. Even Mr. Anderson smiled and shared his agreement on the matter.

Around this time they had put in an offer on an older, four bedroom home about twenty minutes southeast of Buffalo. The home was on the outskirts of a modest-sized city and only minutes from most conveniences and an elementary school which was said to be very good. Jimmy felt strongly that it would be a good fit for Suzie. And she was being so agreeable, willing to drive into Buffalo to the bakery.

The realtor had shown them a few homes in their price range with the property and room they were hoping for. But there was just something special about the third one she showed them. It was on a long stretch of road with a large dairy farm farther out from town and a small grouping of homes within a few miles of the downtown area. Almost like a stretched out neighborhood that had grown up out of the country, these homes each had large mowed yards and several acres of property.

The home she had taken them to had just come on the market. It was older and white with black shuttered windows. Its paint had begun to peel in a few areas and the black of the shutters was faded but otherwise it was neat and clean appearing. She told them it was built in the early 1930's and that the style was something close to a modern Victorian, whatever that meant. It looked to Jimmy like a modest farmhouse, solid and in good condition, a large front porch stretched most of the width and the front door was set to the left. The front yard was deep and a broad maple tree stood tall to one side, giving the porch a little afternoon shade.

Suzie lit up immediately. She stood in the front yard looking up at the porch with its swing and the black painted door with its brass knocker while the realtor talked them through the facts about the home. She pointed out the wide stoned driveway that they had parked in and that she'd take them to see the two-car, detached garage after they saw the house.

"And you've got a really nice space here. You're on about 1.7 acres."

Jimmy saw all the property and imagined the practicality of that garage and was encouraged while Suzie saw that big porch and the bikes on their kickstands in the driveway of the home across the road and was almost bouncing on her toes to get in the place.

They finally walked up onto the porch and entered a small foyer. It had been wallpapered some years ago and showed its age. But the stairway that ran up to their left was beautiful with its dark maple banister. A blue carpet covered the floor but you could see the rich grain of hardwoods from the exposed stairs. To their right, they walked into the living room. It was large and rectangular, with a fireplace in the center of its longer wall and two large windows looking out onto the front yard directly across from it. Again, the older wallpaper and blue carpet carried through into this room but it was clean and supported a lot of furniture.

Just beyond the living room was a small sitting room with one wall that was all windows. The owner had furnished it with a little white wicker set. The realtor called this a sunroom and Suzie smiled and squeezed Jimmy's hand. He knew she was falling in love with the place.

Behind the living room was the entrance to a small dining room, again with some flowery paper on its walls and to the left of that room you entered the kitchen. It had older style white painted, wooden top cabinets and some sort of huge metal cabinet/sink combination that took a large part of one wall. The metal cabinet piece was painted white enamel and had cut outs for your fingers to pull the doors open. The single sink in the center of this unit was large and deep and a dull stainless steel. The steel top work area had several deep grooves on each side for water to run off into the sink. Suzie noted that her grandmother had a sink and cabinet piece just like this one in her first house.

In following the 1950's style that the kitchen had been apparently last renovated in, there was a very large old enamel electric stove with a side cabinet built into it. "Period stuff," the realtor told them. It all works just fine. Notice the refrigerator is newer and there is a nice area here for the kitchen table, all of which the seller is willing to include," she smiled.

Jimmy looked around under the sink, at the plumbing, asking a few questions about the walls, the windows, and the electric, some things his future father-in-law and Donny had both said to watch for. Not surprised to hear that the house was on fuses and that the wiring was one upgrade they might eventually consider making, he was happy with what they had seen thus far.

"Now Suzie, I want you to open that door," her mother's friend had nodded to a door on the back wall of the kitchen.

With just a little hesitation and taking hold of Jimmy's hand, Suzie turned the glass knob. Jimmy had already guessed that there was another room behind it noting that the door was an interior one but he didn't let on to Suzie. They both walked into a small hallway that was pleasantly painted tan and had a slate-colored linoleum floor. Immediately to their left was a half bathroom with a nice-sized sink and bottom cabinet, matching wood-framed medicine cabinet, and toilet.

"Oh, this is really, really nice," Suzie said excitedly. Jimmy had to agree that a newer half bathroom was a luxury he didn't expect.

But also in this back part of the home there was what Nancy's friend called a mudroom. There was a washer and dryer against the wall behind the bathroom and a long row of oak cabinets above them, a world of storage. They were shown the back door that looked out onto the deep driveway and the garage there. Jimmy could feel himself smiling as he spoke.

"Laundry on the first floor? This is a great space. I could pop off my farm clothes in here and not make a mess. And this door?"

"Oh well, I think it's your turn to open one," the realtor smiled. "But this is it for surprises, I promise," she said.

The door opened into a square room, maybe 12' by 12'. The floors were a rich hardwood, dark cherry and pristine. The mossy green walls were warm and pleasant to the eye and the room still smelled of fresh paint. The two windows were new, with twelve pretty white panes dividing the glass into little rectangles. There was no furniture in the room but it was obvious this room had been recently remodeled for a purpose.

"So this whole back area of the home is a complete remodel. The owner was about to move office furniture into this room when he was asked to relocate for work. But gosh, I didn't want to show you my little surprise until we had seen the rest of the house." Jimmy and Suzie both looked around, touching the new floor and opening the new windows. They were both excited now and as long as there were no serious issues with the rest of the house Jimmy was prepared to call the Anderson's and abuelo to come and see the house, that day if possible.

The family had been equally excited about the place. Abuelo was almost reverent walking through the home, oohing and ahhhing, tears in his eyes. All the rooms and the expanse of property was an estate to this man who had lived all his life in a little box in the city. With big thumbs up from everyone and a promise from Mr. Anderson and Steven to help with some upgrades, the young couple put their offer in, praying for it to be accepted. The realtor was hopeful; knowing that the owners needed to move and a fast sell was to their advantage.

Chapter 23

The wedding had been a beautiful day in every way imaginable. The weather was seasonable and peaked at near sixty degrees and the sky was unclouded and as bright as the best days of fall allowing the ladies to be comfortable in sweaters and the men in their sport coats and suit jackets. Abuelo, dressed in a sharp black suit with a blue tie like the groomsmen, was given a large blue carnation and a white rose for his lapel.

"The rose is for abuela," Jimmy whispered in his grandfather's ear as he helped him pin it in place. Bob had pinned the same two flowers to Jimmy's lapel, the carnation being the flower of the wedding and his white rose he wore in memory of his mother. It had been Suzie's idea and from the tears those roses brought to the men's eyes it was a special addition to the day.

The bride was all smiles as she walked down the short aisle of the chapel in the Anderson family's church. She was a tiny fairy, floating in a cloud of white tulle. Her father, Ron, wasn't holding up as well and he kept wiping his eyes and nose with a small white handkerchief. But at the end there was Jimmy with wet eyes and a big grin holding out his hand to receive his bride. Nancy, her hair pinned up in a curly bun instead of the typical ponytail and wearing a loose-fitting, navy dress stood at the first pew and smiled at the couple adoringly.

Mr. Vazquez stood beside his grandson, straight and proud, appearing taller than his five-foot-seven frame. He considered it the highest of privileges to be there and his special responsibility to represent all of Jimmy's family, the ones that couldn't and the one that wouldn't be there for one of the most meaningful days of the young man's life. The ring was securely in his breast pocket and he kept his hand held up against it until it was time to give it to his grandson. He fought back tears as he placed it into Jimmy's big, strong hand.

And in a matter of little more than half an hour Susan Anderson and James Gregory, who had been two persons, became one flesh as they were declared husband and wife. The couple kissed excitedly, linked arms, and skipped up the aisle, unable to contain their joy in the moment. The rest of the day was a whirl of pictures, hugs and kisses from family and friends, eating, and dancing and the new Mr. and Mrs. Gregory loved every minute of it. Everyone went home that October 20th with a smile on their face and the memory of witnessing young love at its best.

***

Mr. James Gregory and his soon-to-be-wife had become the owners of the four-bedroom home they had fallen in love with two months before they married. Their offer had been accepted after one counter and papers had been signed that August. It had given Jimmy and his father in law some time to work on some things before the couple moved in. A riding lawn mower had been an early wedding present from the Anderson's and Nancy had put a big, blue bow on it and parked it in the garage for them to find. You wouldn't think it possible to love a gift so much but Suzie wanted to learn to drive it immediately and she made it her job to mow the lawn every week. Jimmy found her all the more irresistible riding that tractor, sunscreen half rubbed into her face and her ponytail bobbing up and down.

Jimmy was satisfied to get the old paper off of the bedroom walls and the sheetrock smoothed out and painted before the couple moved in. They had found a nice used bedroom set at an estate sale and with a mattress ordered they were excited to move it into a finished bedroom. But Mr. and Mrs. Anderson made themselves available to help those first months before the wedding. Occasionally for a few hours on a week night and a good part of the weekend the two, along with Suzie, scraped and cleaned the walls of the house. With the harvest season moving towards peak, Jimmy needed to spend a lot of his time at the farm, so he was very grateful for the eagerness of Suzie's parents to do so much of the dirty work.

Abuelo had not said anything specific about feeling left out of the projects and he had been to the house a number of times, getting into a little plumbing work with Jimmy and painting some window trim. But he had bemoaned his age several times, the troubles with his old hips and back and the knees that didn't bend like they used to. Jimmy knew abuelo struggled with the limitations of his aging body more than he'd admit especially with his grandson having a bit of a fixer upper to work on. Suzie, who always knew how to draw out the strengths of a person while diminishing their weaknesses, talked with abuelo about a little project she had wanted to work on after the wedding.

It was the kitchen which was dark and plain. She wanted to "brighten it up" as she put it and wondered if maybe he would like to help her as she looked for paint for the walls and a table and chair set that they could paint or clean up. She told him she had come to love the beautiful colors of his own kitchen and the one that Maria had decorated in her apartment. Could abuelo help bring some of that color and light to their dated little kitchen?

The older man was on to his soon to be granddaughter, but he played along with her enthusiastic appeal for help. He realized sadly that this would have been his daughter's favorite project and something the two ladies would have done together. But abuelo, who didn't know anything more about decorating than most men his age, eagerly accepted the challenge. He set about asking the neighborhood women how they had transformed their places, knowing that a bright, inviting kitchen was one of the prides of a Latino home.

He took notes about paint colors and the fabrics used for window curtains. He asked where they found some of their decorative accents, the little roosters, the mosaics on some of the walls, and the colorful plates on painted shelves. He brought his camera along and took pictures, developing them for Suzie to see. He decided to do this one small thing well, in doing so he would be honoring his wife and daughter while Suzie was honoring him.

It ended up being far more satisfying than he expected. With the wedding getting close, everyone had been busy with last minute details but abuelo took this time to attend yard sales, garage sales, and estate sales by the dozen. What he found in the little barrio's around him was a plethora of household items from the little kitchen accents he was hunting for to bigger pieces of furniture and housewares. For a few dollars he had a nice collection of things that he thought Suzie might like. He set them all aside for after the wedding when they would begin on the kitchen.

He took the bus to a few estate sales out in the suburbs and at one he happened upon a beautiful table with a leaf and six chairs, immaculately cared for. He was so excited about buying it that he forgot to note what the owners were asking for it, and he was a bit taken back by the price.

A kindly woman noticed his surprise at the cost and whispered to him that he might want to counter with a reasonable offer. He didn't understand how these sales worked and she helped him by evaluating the dining sets value and what he might be able to get it for. With her suggestion he was able to buy the seven pieces of furniture for $75 less than originally asked for and he was giddy with the purchase. He prayed they would like the gift as he watched Edward load it onto his truck. They took it directly to Jimmy's country home and while no one was there they left it in the garage setting a note on it just as Nancy had done with the lawn tractor.

Jimmy and Suzie had found it when they were at the house a week before the wedding to move Suzie's clothes and personal items into the house. They were shocked to open the garage and find the set there. Suzie rubbed the top of the long table gently with her palm noticing the beauty of the wood, its ornate details, and dark rich color. They knew that this piece belonged in their dining room and they couldn't get it in there fast enough. The two went to abuelo's that evening and they thanked him for his thoughtfulness, promising to have a large family dinner at the table right after the wedding.

The couple had decided to apply any honeymoon money to their home, telling each other that they would wait and have an extra special getaway for their first anniversary. So they held true to their promise and had a few dinners at their new home in those first weeks after they married. But the first one was just for the Anderson's and abuelo. It was a time for Jimmy and Suzie to thank them for the love and support they had provided and to celebrate their new home. Suzie raised a glass to abuelo.

"This table," she said, "will be a table for eating and celebrating, for family and friends to come together. Maybe soon we will fill these chairs with children and then…. wow, won't that be something." She said blushing and laughing. Nancy liked the idea and raised her glass of wine to the new couple, the new home, and her future new little grandchildren.

Chapter 24

Spring 2010

It took James a few minutes to catch up with Molly more because of the dark halls than because of her speed. She was back in her room but left the dirty pail just outside the doorway like some crude address plaque. The door was open and James could make out her frame curled on the mattress her head turned toward the wall. He knocked and tentatively walked into the entrance of the room.

"It's probably best I leave." He spoke in barely a whisper.

He could hear her muffled crying suddenly stop and her tone became harsh. She raised her head and turned toward him. "That's what everyone says at some point. Wouldn't expect anything different from you." She put her head back down with her hands over her face and lay motionless.

Not knowing what to do and certainly not knowing what to say James went out into the hallway and into the room where he had slept. He began putting his few belongings into his backpack and he folded the little blanket Molly had given him and set it on the lonely table that was the only furniture in the room. He was feeling really bad about what had transpired with Molly and he sat down in the corner of the room to wait until dark when it was safe to leave Molly and the hurt he had caused behind him.

At some point he woke from a light sleep with the uncomfortable sensation to use the bathroom and he realized he would have to dirty a bucket soon. He fished around in his backpack for his old watch to try to see what time it was, but he knew he wouldn't be able to wait for nightfall.

"What are you looking for?" Molly's voice was soft and low but still it startled James. He dropped the bag and sat up straight. "Scared you, didn't I? I mean, just now by talking to you when you didn't know I was here."

"Um. Yeah, I guess a little." James spoke to the silhouette seated on the opposite wall.

Molly got up and walked over to where James was. She sat down heavily beside him. "Listen James. I guess I shouldn't have gotten all mad and defensive earlier. It's just that I'm not one to let people in on my personal stuff. And I was hoping, you know, that it would be different this time. With you."

"Molly. Don't…"

"Don't what, James? Don't get into it? Don't try to make you feel guilty? Well, I'm not here to do that or to try to hang on to you or anything. But I did want to tell you I'm sorry for making you uncomfortable. And I wanted to thank you for waiting here till dark and not just bolting."

"I wouldn't do that. You stuck your neck out for me. And I hurt you. And I'm leaving because I can't handle that. I don't want to hurt any more people, Molly." James drew in a deep breath and it caught and he shuddered a moment. But then he reached out with his hand, barely touching Molly's arm. "Like I told you, you're not the only one with a past you want to forget."

Molly got up then, pulling James by the hand until he stood up next to her. Tentatively she put her arms around him and gave him a squeeze, holding on just long enough to assure him that he hadn't hurt her. At least not more than she could handle. Molly hadn't hugged another person in so long that she silently wondered if she had been appropriate with it. "Maybe I can tell you some of my story and you can tell me some of yours. You know, sometime, maybe.

It relieved James somewhat that Molly had responded in the way she had. "I don't want to pry and I don't want to upset you so it's on your terms. The only thing stopping me right now is my bladder and if I can go empty it that it will make the time till nightfall a whole lot more comfortable."

He could hear the smile in Molly's voice. "Um, well, of course! Let's go take care of that then." And Molly walked out into the hallway, picking up her pail and waiting for James to follow down the hall.

Minutes later the two had taken their buckets and emptied them out through the chamber pot window, leaving their mark on Mother Nature. James noticed that the light in the sky was dim and he guessed it was the dinner hour. His stomach confirmed, growling rather loudly as they walked back through the building toward the bedrooms.

With another three hours yet before Molly felt comfortable leaving, she handed James a protein bar and invited him to wait it out in the large factory floor room where the whole thing had started.

"There's at least a little light there. Sometimes you can make out a few stars if it's a super clear night and enough rain has cleaned some of the grime off the skylights."

The two settled onto one of a few remaining benches left behind when the factory was left to die its slow death. They wordlessly chewed their dinner and handed a bottle of water back and forth between them, James wondering if Molly would choose this time to tell her story. After a while of just sitting there, Molly got up.

"So like I was telling you. The doctors decided I have some sort of bipolar disorder." She looked at James and waited a beat. He looked up at her but said nothing. "I was a pretty regular kid, I think. Like I hung out with friends at school and went to sleepovers, that kind of thing. I didn't have a lot of motivation but what middle schooler wants to clean their room or do homework?" She stopped and giggled awkwardly and James made sure to laugh as well.

"Then it just started creeping up on me, I guess. Sometime in high school. I'd get so sad. And my mother'd be like, 'What's wrong with you Molls? How many times are you gonna tell your friends no you don't feel like it?' And the thing is I didn't have any reason for it. People liked me. I'd been drawing and painting a lot and people liked that too." Molly sat back down on the bench and took the nearly empty bottle from James's hand. She took a long drink and handed it back.

"And then more and more I just closed up. I hated all the things I used to like and I couldn't paint except to move the brush around a little, feeling nothing. Of course my parents freaked out and I ended up in counseling for depression. And somewhere in that period of time while they were filling me up with positive thoughts and happy pills I had this incredible light switch flip on. All of a sudden, after months of dreaded living, I became the most excited and motivated in all my life.

It was senior year and all in one day I re-signed into art club and added yearbook and masterminds to my schedule. Now, me in masterminds…THAT was crazy." She laughed for real this time and it made James smile. "I spent maybe a week calling friends, hanging out. Just doing anything and everything I wanted. Oh, and my art? I was up for nights at a time working on a brainstorm idea. It turned out to be my first work that made it to a gallery. But by that time I couldn't have given a shit. My joy had run out again."

James sat and thought about this. It depressed him on several levels. His own mother came to mind, and he couldn't shake the idea that she had suffered alone for years. Molly broke through his thoughts. Very quietly she asked. "So what do you think James?"

Not knowing where to start he said what he felt. "It must have been so terrible for you."

And then Molly's lips quivered. "I haven't been understood for a long time. But you got it, James. It was terrible. More doctors. The bipolar diagnosis. New meds. Good loving protective parents who drove me crazy with the trying to fix it when I just wanted them to understand that they couldn't and it wasn't their fault."

James felt the fires of conviction burn and he fought the urge to get up. But he waited there with Molly and let her tell more about the empty hole of depression and the blessed, blessed misery of mania. The mania she wasn't willing to give over to the soul-dulling medications even when it destroyed her relationships. The mania she called her artist form.

PART 3

Chapter 25

S omehow nearly five years had gone by as the Gregory's worked, celebrated holidays with their families, and made new friendships with neighbors while keeping old ones with friends from the farm and their childhood. They went to an occasional football game and they met friends for drinks on many Friday nights, often sharing a pizza back at one of their homes.

Jimmy had grown comfortable with his work and the farm was doing very well under his supervision. Donny had recently died after a long battle with cancer and Betty let Jimmy know that she hoped he might be able to buy the place from her someday. Donny had told his wife to make a deal that made it possible for Jimmy. With this hope planted Jimmy was driving hard toward that goal. He and Suzie were saving what they could and were thinking they might be able to manage a serious talk with Betty in the next year or two.

Suzie had opened that second bakery she had dreamed of just inside their town's limits in 1993 and called it Little City Bakery. Although her parents had taken the loan it was understood this was only to get Suzie established and that she was responsible for half of the debt. But the business took off and the profit margins were good. Suzie was well-known by the residents of town for her amazing decorating skills and delicious cakes and cookies. She loved her work and the people as much as they loved her.

In the middle of all of this success was one big gaping hole in their life that the Gregory's tried to walk around for fear of falling in to its dark sadness. They had not been blessed with any children. Every day the reality of what they missed woke with them in the morning and went to sleep with them in bed at night. Worst was the one pregnancy and then the miscarriage in December of 1992. Every Christmas brought the sting of a baby lost and the babies that had not come to fill the bedrooms, the chairs at the table, the hearts of the young couple.

They made one appointment with a fertility doctor late in 1993 and were assured that they had been doing nothing wrong. Sperm counts were okay and Suzie's reproductive system looked healthy. "Stress can make it harder to conceive," they were told and it was suggested that they just get on with their lives and give it all another year. That was almost two years ago and neither one of them wanted to go back and face the possibility that they were one of those few couples that just never were able to have children. They discussed adoption as an option and they held on to the possibility as a last resort but Suzie still held out for the hope of a pregnancy. Jimmy didn't want to admit that he had begun to wonder if maybe a biological child would come with some of the imprints of depression or anxiety that his mother had carried or that his child might be distant or lack empathy like his own biological father. Did this come from nature, nurture, or a combination of these things? He would never tell Suzie these thoughts. Her dream to mother a child was his as well.

Because of this longing and the anguish of waiting, work, family, and friends were all magnified in Jimmy's life.

With their work lives full of successes and their network of friends well established Jimmy turned to his wife and his elderly grandfather who he loved and protected with new fervor.

When he could, Jimmy would ride into the city with Aaron who he had recently hired, and they'd meet up with some friends who routinely joined him for a few beers after a long workweek. They had found a small, busy neighborhood bar in south Buffalo where they had come to gather on Fridays, talking loudly about their week, sharing stories and slapping each other on the back for no good reason. The wives and girlfriends would join them there, usually after the boys had gotten settled and knocked down a beer or two. Suzie tried to end her workday at the big bakery in Buffalo so she could meet Jimmy there.

On one of these late-summer evenings Suzie came in around 7:30 p.m. She had changed into one of her cute little floral cotton sundresses at the shop and had pulled her ponytail out, letting her wavy brown hair fall over her narrow shoulders. She bounced on her toes as tried to see her way to the back of the bar where the group usually congregated. Noticing her was a man in a dress shirt and loosened tie who was drinking with a few similarly dressed guys. He raised his eye brows to one of his buddies and smiled like the Cheshire cat. He watched the little fairy of a girl land in the arms of the wide shouldered farmer who kissed her on the forehead before releasing her to the group of girls around them.

As the music played loudly some of the ladies swayed their bodies to the beat, a sort of crowded dancing, trying to get the men to join them. Suzie was laughing and bumping hips with one of her friends when the guy who had noticed her made his way towards the group in the back. He watched Suzie as he squeezed into a spot at the bar and several times he smiled at her and held his drink up in the air approvingly. Sheila had noticed him first and she whispered to Suzie, who looked up to see him looking at her with his foolish drunken grin. She turned away in the other direction but continued to dance with her friends.

Jimmy hadn't noticed the gawker until Hector nudged him and pointed his chin in the man's direction. By this time Jimmy had had a few beers himself and wasn't in the clearest frame of mind. He drew in his breath and waited, watching Suzie swinging her little hips to the music, her hair bouncing…and the creep who was bobbing his head and holding his hands up in the air in a stupid looking attempt to dance while keeping his eyes on Suzie.

Swallowing down his beer, Jimmy bolted from the back corner of the bar to the spot where the onlooker was fixed on his wife. He grabbed hold of the guys arm hard, pulling at him and making him spill his drink down his arm.

"What the hell man!" the Cheshire cat man said.

"What's your problem, idiot? That's my wife you got your dirty eyes on." And Jimmy gave him a little elbow to the side.

"Whoa there, farm boy. It's a free country and who says I can't look at that cute, little, brown-haired one if I want to. She's got the moves… bet she knows how to use them," he laughed at Jimmy, showing his big white teeth.

In an instant Jimmy was on the guy, knocking him to the floor with a fist to his left cheek. The two were swinging and swearing, Jimmy landing more punches than the drunker guy. He could hear Suzie crying out for him to stop but he was seeing red. He landed a few blows to the guy's head and abdomen before a bouncer from the bar wrapped his sausage arm around his neck and pulled him away.

"That's it. You're out of here. Don't try to fight it cause then I call the cops and let them take you." The 300-pound bouncer dragged Jimmy to the door. Jimmy turned to see Suzie coming up next to him with her makeup smudged with tears.

He thought about attempting to explain that he was trying to protect his wife from the stalking Cheshire cat guy but instead he said, "Screw it, this place sucks anyway." Outside the door he caught his breath and put his arm out to Suzie. She pulled away and watched him with a look of disbelief.

"Baby, I'm sorry. But that guy." He began to yell. "That guy wanted you. No one's gonna talk about you like he did while I'm alive." A few of their friends had come out of the bar and were standing around Jimmy and Suzie. They began talking then, a few to Jimmy and some of the girls to Suzie.

"Damn. You schooled him! He's got some blood on his nice white shirt to prove it," Aaron slapped Jimmy on the back.

"Yeah. He was pretty wrecked when you got your hands on him but I think he's gonna remember tonight," another said.

Suzie came over to the guys just as Jimmy was tucking in his polo shirt. "I'm ready to go home."

"Yeah, me too." Jimmy looked into the tear stained eyes of his little fairy and he saw a disappointment he had never seen before. He followed her to where her car was parked and silently got in the passenger door.

For a few days that followed the bar fight Suzie put up a cold shoulder around Jimmy. He wasn't used to her anger towards him and it hurt. Jimmy knew she was upset about his fighting and he wondered how she couldn't understand that he had been trying to protect her. But eventually she came around again, Jimmy having to say that he had been wrong to choose fighting as the way to set that idiot straight even though he thought that was exactly what needed to be done.

***

Abuelo had increasingly become a concern to his family. The seventy-nine-year-old man had been having some trouble walking, the pain from his hips keeping him up at night. The stairs to his apartment had become difficult enough that he tried to avoid using them any more than absolutely necessary. He had begun to sit in a kitchen chair that he had moved in front of the living room window instead of going down to the stoop in the evenings to watch people pass by. Rosa had noticed and was bringing his mail up to him most days.

He had not complained to anyone about it but it was easy to see his pain. His movements were slow and intentional and he had taken to using a cane at times, resting his weight on his better hip. His face wore the strain he was feeling and the apartment showed signs of a tenant struggling to keep up with the household chores.

Discussions had been going on between family members for some time. Edward finally confronted his father about their concerns, insisting that he allow them to take him to an orthopedic doctor to discuss his mobility issues. Not surprisingly abuelo argued and insisted that it was no more than normal aging and told his son to leave him alone about it. Edward argued back and told his father that either he see a doctor or Edward would tell the rest of the family that he was taking abuelo to live at his house. He warned that he had the blessing of the family on the subject even though they had not talked that far yet.

Feeling pressured, abuelo ended up making and going to one appointment where he was told that an X-ray and MRI were likely to reveal significant arthritis and joint breakdown. Surgery, as long as he was healthy enough, was likely to greatly improve his pain and mobility. "A new hip is like a new lease on life. You won't believe how much better you can feel," the doctor enthused.

But abuelo wasn't having any of it. He argued that he hadn't known a single family member or a friend for that matter that had had a hip replacement and he didn't like the idea of the cutting out of bone and the long weeks of recovery. And he had a good dose of unspoken fear about surgery in general, not knowing if he would ever wake up again. He'd take pain over the possibility of death any day.

"Well… until you decide to listen to the doctor and get your hip replaced we all think it's best you come live with me and Kate," Edward was back at it days after the appointment. "What if you fall? You'll need more than a hip if that happens." Edward carried on with his father about it for several weeks, each conversation ending in a heated argument with abuelo yelling in frustration for Edward to leave. Jimmy knew Edward's house was not the right place for his grandfather. His Aunt Kate's mother was still living with them and she was a nasty woman. Abuelo would die on the street before he'd share a home with Edward's mother-in-law.

And Aunt Naomi had gotten in on it. She implored her father to come live with her in Pennsylvania. She tried to sell him on the nice big room and private bath he would have. "You can have surgery when you're ready and I'll hire the best nurses to care for you." But her tone was always pretentious and she never understood abuelo's stubbornness about staying in Buffalo where his family was. She actually was offended when he first said it, asking him who he thought she and Uncle Joey were.

Even before abuelo's mobility had become concerning, Jimmy and Suzie had talked about the possibility of eventually having Jimmy's grandfather live with them. He was essentially Jimmy's father and neither of them was going to let a parent struggle to live alone when they had a big house in the country.

They went to abuelo only after talking to Jimmy's uncle and aunt. Edward knew immediately that it was the one solution his father might actually consider, at least if given some time. But he cautioned his nephew to think it through, consider the changes it would make for them, especially if they had children. The word "if" had been a painful sting for Suzie. And Aunt Naomi didn't understand any of it. "My father is being completely unreasonable. You too kids are just starting out. He will be a burden to you."

Jimmy prepared himself for abuelo's arguments. "He won't come easy," he told Suzie. They went together on a Sunday morning, bringing croissants and cookies from the bakery as they often did. While they all sat at the kitchen table sipping their coffee Jimmy got right to it. "Abuelo, Suzie and I want you to come live with us. We're barely half an hour from here, still close to the family. And we've got that room downstairs behind the kitchen."

Abuelo stared at his coffee cup. "You mean your little office? The one that will be a playroom when the kids come?" Suzie looked at abuelo with a faint smile. She could have kissed him for saying it so matter-of-factly.

Jimmy paused. "Yes, abuelo. That one." Rather than go into a long explanation he continued. "When I needed you, you were there. Don't deny me the chance to do the same."

Abuelo was silent for a long time, his coffee growing cold.

"But it's up to you, of course," Suzie finally added.

Abuelo looked at her, his eyes sad. "I know your uncle has pushed this whole thing. If it were up to me we wouldn't be having this conversation."

Suzie stammered, tears welling up in her eyes. "I know, abuelo. I'm sorry. I didn't mean it like it sounded."

"Oh, sweetheart. Don't cry. Please don't. I know what you meant. You're trying to be respectful to an angry old man who doesn't deserve it." Abuelo reached over to Suzie, patting her hand with his own. "You are so good. So sweet." He patted her hand some more. "And you too, Jimmy. So good to look after me like you do."

"So, what do you think, abuelo? It wouldn't be the first time we've lived together." Jimmy laughed as he looked at his grandfather.

"But it would be different. I am old now and you two are married. A couple with a family of your own yet to come. I don't want to say it, but I'd be…."

"Then don't say it, abuelo. Because you wouldn't be anything other than a wonderful addition to our home." Jimmy felt himself getting upset, angry to think his grandfather might not agree to move. He struggled to stay calm, knowing it would only be worse to make the old man feel guilty.

Another silence as the two men sat with their thoughts. Then abuelo said, "Could we all maybe agree to try it for a few weeks? I keep the rent on the apartment and not move all in."

"Yeah. Maybe just come for an extended visit, like you would if you lived out of state or something," Suzie helped the idea along.

Jimmy looked at the both of them, he felt his frustration draining.

"I might like that. A vacation in the country. But you have to let me help out around the place." They watched as abuelo slowly rose from his chair, shuffled over to a drawer where he pulled out a thick notebook spotted with food from its years in the kitchen.

"Abuela's cookbook," Jimmy remembered.

"Yup. It's all her bests. I've still got two good hands and a good appetite."

They picked abuelo up the following weekend for his extended vacation with family. He brought one suitcase of clothing and personal items, the cookbook resting on top. Four weeks later they were all back at the apartment to get the rest of abuelo's things, what he would take for his room at his new residence. Edward organized a moving sale.

Chapter 26

Abuelo accepted the move for the most part, doing the little things he could and insisting on writing a small check to his grandson every month. "I don't want this! I didn't ask you to live with us so I could collect rent from you," Jimmy was upset when abuelo handed him the first check. He crinkled it up and threw it in the trash.

"Your memory is short, Jimmy. Have you forgotten doing the same thing when you lived with me?" Abuelo hobbled back to his room, red with anger. He got his checkbook and scribbled out another check, giving himself time to calm down before he hobbled back into the kitchen and quietly set it on the table so he wouldn't embarrass Jimmy any further. Abuelo understood he needed to respect his grandson as head of the household and other than the money issue he kept most of his thoughts to himself.

The two men eventually picked up where they left off when Jimmy had moved out to live in his own home, only their roles had reversed. With his wife's cookbook Abuelo began to plan and cook some of their meals, something he never did in all his years as a working husband and father. But Suzie was very grateful, coming home to food in the oven and the old man sitting on a tall stool at the sink, washing the dishes he had dirtied.

And the young couple didn't change much of their routine. They still went out more Friday's than not with the few friends left that were not home taking care of children and they even began playing coed volleyball on a winter league. It was enough to let abuelo know they still had their own life. In this way most of the first year went by without incident.

But new decisions were being made, ones that would hopefully shape and grow the family. Hope Grows was still in Betty's hands and while she had held out for Jimmy to buy it, he knew she wouldn't much longer. She was almost seventy and only the farm held her to the area. She had begun to talk about moving to Arizona where her daughter lived.

That summer Jimmy and Suzie had gotten serious about it. They revisited the farm loan officer at their bank to have another look at their finances and had taken abuelo and the Andersons out for a drive around the place. Everything and everyone was leading them towards taking the opportunity. The bakery was more than paying its owners back and the Gregory's had a nice savings going. And the family all knew how much of Jimmy's heart and soul was in the fields of the farm. Aside from Suzie, it was the one thing he showed unabashed pride in.

The two had talked for a while about moving. The farm was ten minutes from their home. The distance had never been an issue in the years Jimmy acted as general manager but being the owner was different. Most farmers lived on the property they owned and worked. Would it be wise to be so far from it? It was a hard decision and had almost stopped Jimmy from moving forward.

Suzie was his voice of reason as usual. She suggested they continue on for now as things were and see how it went over time. Jimmy thought he'd offer the farmhouse, Betty and Donny's place, to Ken. He spent a great deal of time alongside Jimmy and had learned a lot in the last few years. He was in his early forties and a bit of a loner with no family other than his nephew Aaron, who also worked for the farm. He would be a good fit to oversee the property and it would give the couple time to evaluate what was best for them and for the farm.

***

The big day came, and they had an 11:00 a.m. appointment at the bank. It was September and a beautiful day. Abuelo had ridden along sitting in the back seat watching the traffic as they neared the city. He was a quiet but steadying presence for the couple.

"By acreage this farm may be smaller than some of the big ones around here but from a financial standpoint it's very healthy. And the owner practically gave it away. I think you're making a sound investment kids." The loan officer looked up from the pile of papers they had begun to go through.

An hour later they walked out of the bank with a folder of papers for their safe, the coveted deed boldly declaring James and Susan Gregory owners of the 700-acre farm know as Hope Grows. Jimmy undid his tie and loosened his collar while Suzie kicked off her pumps inside the car. They pulled up to the front of the bank, where they had left abuelo leaning on his walker. Suzie got out in her stockinged feet and opened the passenger door helping abuelo get in to the back seat. She folded his walker and dropped it in the trunk.

Jimmy stopped home just long enough to put the bank papers in the couple's safe. He gave the documents another look, still surprised to see his name next to that of the farms. Carefully he tucked them in between the deed to their house and their birth certificates. He returned to the car to find

Suzie sitting next to abuelo in the back, the two contentedly listening to Dean Martin sing *Sway* from a CD Suzie had recently picked up.

He smiled at Suzie, who winked at him. She rested her feet on the back of the front seat. Abuelo had closed his eyes but his lips were upturned and Jimmy knew he was happy. The three of them drove the half hour to the Anderson's. As soon as the car turned into the driveway abuelo straightened up as best he could and wiggled further over towards the door, making room for Nancy to join them in the back.

The couple got out to give and receive hugs and congratulations from the Anderson's. Nancy slid in next to abuelo, who was patting the seat. She gave him an energetic side hug and kiss on the cheek. Ron Anderson sat in front with his son-in-law and Nancy led them all in conversation. By the time they arrived at the restaurant they were to have lunch at, they were all talked out except for Nancy who somehow still found more questions to squeeze from them. But her excitement made Jimmy feel good about their decision.

The group took a table in the back of the restaurant where Suzie's brother Paul and his girlfriend Melony had just sat down. There was more hand shaking and congratulations before everyone sat down and the wine was poured. Abuelo was biting his lip and there was sweat shining his forehead from the pain he experienced in getting from the car to his seat in the restaurant, but he did everything to keep it from registering on his face. He knew he would have to make a hard decision about his failing hips soon. But that would be for another day.

Part way into their dinner Suzie gave Jimmy's hand a squeeze before quieting the group so she could talk. "So you think you all came to celebrate our new venture as owners of Hope Grows. Well, that's true. I'm proud of Jimmy for going after what he's wanted since…well…. since he wanted me." Everyone laughed. "It's great for me to know he actually owns the land that he loves so much. But there's always been that one other thing that the both of us have wanted even more…"

"Oh my God! She's going to have a baby," and Nancy flew up from her chair and started for Suzie. Everyone started clapping and even Mr. Anderson appeared emotional.

Suzie was startled and with tears in her eyes she looked at Jimmy, who got up and put his arm around his mother-in-law.

"It's not quite what you think," he said quietly. And suddenly you could hear a pin drop at the table. "But it is about a baby."

Jimmy waited a beat and even Mrs. Anderson stood with him, silent and waiting. "So what Suzie is trying to say is, we made an appointment with an adoption agency and well… I guess that speaks for itself. We want to have a family. We've decided to begin the work towards adopting a child."

Abuelo was the first one to offer his congratulations and raise his glass of wine. The others fumbled to get to their glasses and loud congratulations were heard from around the table. Mrs. Anderson gave Jimmy a hug and kissed his cheek before reaching over to her daughter and doing the same. "I'm sorry I got that wrong, honey. But I'm just as happy for you…really, I am," she whispered.

"I need this, Mom," Suzie pulled away so her mother could see her face. "We both need this," and she looked at Jimmy before returning to her seat next to him.

"Well, I think it's great," Paul raised his glass of wine before taking a long drink.

Mr. Anderson was quiet but he reached across his son to take Suzie's hand. "It's one lucky child that's going to get to call you Mommy." He smiled and patted her hand in reassurance.

Tears brimmed and then fell from Suzie's eyes. No one could tell they were tears of joy mixed with sorrow. Hope mixed with fear. Questions lingered about whether they'd be deemed a good fit and how long it would take. Could Suzie manage motherhood and her work at the bakery? Would owning a business be a deterrent to their being considered?

Going home that night the Gregory's held each other in bed. They talked about the day, hardly believing they had actually bought a farm. And at the same time they felt their excitement tempered by the confusion at lunch. They both knew they wanted a baby. They knew, as they held each other there in the quiet of their room, that they were desperate for a family and they recommitted themselves to loving a baby, no matter how that baby came to them.

***

The initial adoption appointment was a month out and the days of waiting slowly ticked by. Jimmy kept his mind focused on the farm. While there were no real changes to his work, as its owner he took renewed interest in all its working parts. He checked in with the few employees and drove the perimeter of the property every evening. Ken was settling in at the house and seemed to be pleased to be able to live "on site." He was prepared to see to any issues that may happen after work hours until Jimmy could get out there himself.

The excitement about starting their family grew and the couple found themselves spending their nights walking through the baby departments of the local stores. Suzie couldn't resist pulling out the drawers of the little dressers and touching the infant sleepers. Jimmy lingered over the cribs, telling his wife he was interested in their safety record while secretly he was imagining himself looking over its rails to find his infant child looking back at him, tiny face smiling.

For several weeks Suzie had been waking to butterflies, feeling nervous about things. Two different afternoons she had left work and went home where she crawled into bed, waking up several hours later. The excitement was getting to her and she willed herself to settle down, trust that it would all work out. Abuelo quietly watched her at dinner pushing more of her food around the plate than putting it in her mouth.

Thursday morning Suzie had come in to the kitchen where abuelo was standing at the counter with some toast and a cup of coffee. She got out a quick "good morning" before putting her hand to her mouth and running for the bathroom. It was several minutes before she returned, taking a few tentative bites of the toast abuelo had put out for her. She gave up and tossed it in the garbage while grabbing her apron and jacket. As she headed towards the back door, abuelo stopped her.

"Suzie. Do you really think it's your nerves that have you feeling this way?" he questioned.

She stopped and stood there silent for a minute before answering. "I don't know?" her voice cracked with emotion.

"Oh Suzie, what are you afraid of? Really?" Abuelo seemed to already know.

"I'm afraid. I'm afraid I may be pregnant." She began to cry.

Abuelo did his best to shuffle himself to the table where he asked her to sit for a minute.

"And why are you afraid? Because of what has happened before?"

Suzie looked up at him where he stood leaning on his walker. "I want a baby more than anything. But I'm afraid to hope, you know? All these years. Not getting pregnant. Then the miscarriage. The hope taken. I don't think I can handle another hope lost."

"Do you know if you are pregnant this time?" he whispered.

"I haven't confirmed it, but I think it's likely."

Abuelo put his head down and said a quick prayer before answering. "Then you know what you have to do Suzie. And you know you can't do it alone. And you shouldn't. This is about the both of you. No matter what happens."

Suzie hugged abuelo and thanked him. She got in the car and drove to the drugstore where she picked up a pregnancy test before going to work. She waited for Jimmy that evening. When he came in the door she took him aside and told him what she thought might be happening. The two of them went upstairs, Suzie carrying the drugstore bag. Jimmy waited while his wife went into the bathroom. She called him in where the two of them waited out the minutes sitting on the edge of the bathtub.

When they checked the little white stick it confirmed what Suzie suspected. It didn't seem possible after all these years. They looked at it, at each other in disbelief. They both laughed and hugged and went downstairs to tell abuelo, but the memory of that one other stick from years ago hung there between them. It would be months before either one of them would allow themselves to completely breathe, to appreciate the providence of that moment.

The couple went to see Suzie's gynecologist just to confirm the pregnancy before telling the rest of the family. They remained cautious and closed-mouthed about it for well after the first trimester when Suzie was showing and friends and coworkers were talking. They had cancelled the appointment with the adoption agency. While Suzie wasn't sure they should stop learning about adoption altogether,

Jimmy was adamant that all their thoughts and their energy should go towards seeing the pregnancy through to full term.

Hearing the baby's heartbeat at their ten-week appointment left them both in tears and while they were happy and hopeful they each remained sober, aware of all the possible things that could happen and leave them heartbroken yet again. And as the weeks slowly came and went Jimmy became increasingly obsessed with Suzie's health and the baby's well-being. He asked her to cut her hours at the bakery and he wouldn't let her carry laundry up and down the stairs. While she protested and told her husband that she was healthy and capable she secretly was grateful for his over protection. She herself had wanted to step her schedule down and give herself every chance possible to deliver a healthy baby.

***

Abuelo had made an important decision regarding his own life around the time the couple had announced that they were looking to adopt a child. With both of his hips in bad shape, the pain unbearable at times and his right knee beginning to give him trouble he finally asked Edward to take him to an orthopedic surgeon, the same one he had been badgered to go see over a year ago. He had been avoiding surgery all that time, telling himself he was managing well enough as he was.

But now he faced the reality that with the kids finally starting the family they had always wanted he was only going to be a burden in the condition he was in. It was time for him to face his limitations and to do whatever it took to get mobile again. He knew Jimmy would not let his grandfather move out without one hell of an argument but with two new hips that's exactly what he planned to do.

So while the Gregory's were busy with their work and consumed with the pregnancy, abuelo was secretly going to appointments and finding out what his options were regarding his hips. Edward for all the arguing he had done to get his father to this point did not gloat about his father's decision. It had to come to this, he knew, and he was ready to do anything he could to help his father from his years of pain. It was ironically good timing on Edward's end, his mother-in-law had just died and he felt that he and Kate could care for abuelo, at least while he recovered. He would wait to see how things went before getting into the possibility again of having his father come live with them permanently.

The initial consultation with the orthopedist had upset abuelo. Apparently his hips were pretty far gone and the doctor was amazed that he was still mobile with the help of the walker. And while he would need both replaced, the doctor felt the left one should be first and it would be six to nine months after that before he'd consider doing the right one. "You are an eighty-one-year-old man and while you appear strong and in good health, all surgery has risks. You will have to go through a number of physical exams to see that you are reasonably fit for surgery. And the recovery period can be difficult and long. There are many factors that play into how well this will go for you. I am optimistic. But I need to be realistic with you. It's going to take time and patience on your part."

Abuelo, who had not wanted his son in the consult with him, took a few minutes to collect himself before returning to the waiting room. When Edward asked about the appointment on the way home, abuelo had simply said that the doctor was optimistic and while it would take a while to recover, he should do fine.

Several weeks later, even before Suzie and Jimmy had heard their baby's heartbeat, abuelo had gone to the hospital for the series of bloodwork and exams that were needed in order to schedule his first surgery. He was anxious to get things moving now, angry at himself for having waited until things had gotten to this point. The two weeks until he followed up with the doctor about drove him mad.

When Jimmy would try to help him up from his chair after dinner or Suzie would come in to his room with his mail or a snack he got upset. "Don't do things for me. I don't want your help," he'd bark. They weren't doing anything more for abuelo than they had been for some time and they wondered if his attitude had something to do with the baby coming. Jimmy realized he might want to talk with his grandfather, to reassure him about his place in their lives.

Abuelo never told Edward and certainly not the kids what had been said at his follow up appointment but the doctor had some reservations about the operation. "Your bloodwork is very good except for an elevated cholesterol level. And most all your organ systems are functioning as expected for your age. But you've got a valve in the heart. It's called a mitral valve and it's leaking. It isn't that uncommon at your age and I'm told it's not to the point of needing surgery right yet, but it adds more risk to your hip replacement." The doctor went on to list his concerns and the possible complications.

Abuelo emotionally checked out of much of what the doctor said at that point until he heard, "While these are the risks, I've had similar patients whose lives are so compromised by their pain and loss of mobility that they choose surgery. All things considered, I will not tell you I won't do your surgery. I'm giving you my best assessment and I recommend you talk with family, get a second opinion if you want. But if you decide to proceed I would want you to be comfortable with your decision."

Edward, who was reading a magazine when his father came out into the waiting room looked up, trying to read the old man's face. Abuelo managed a smile and told his son to go pull the car up to the door. He was tired and looking forward to a nap. The ride back was quiet and abuelo had no intention of talking the matter over with family. He was going to have the surgery. He would schedule it by the end of the week.

"Just one thing, Edward," his father looked at his hands. They were full of wrinkles and veins and dotted with age spots. He was surprised to see just how old they had gotten. "I'm going to need to stay with you while I recover. And it's going to be months, not weeks." Edward had brought this up to his father as a possibility when abuelo first came to him about the surgery and now abuelo was glad for it. Jimmy and Suzie would not have to try to care for him while they were trying to care for themselves. And with new hips he would be able to get a little place of his own. He couldn't imagine being away from Jimmy, the thought made him surprisingly emotional. But it would be the best thing. It was the right thing.

Chapter 27

Spring 2010-Spring 2011

ames and Molly talked well into the dark hours before finally stepping out from the factory walls and into the night. The two of them had decided to remain street friends. They would look out for each other, share food when they could, and spend time together as they were comfortable. It was best, they both thought, that they give each other space. Molly had the factory and she offered it to James as he may need it. It would always be a place that James could get in to, to sleep in, and get out of the cold and rain.

But he said he would not stay there all the time. The two of them were homeless for a reason. Their own reasons. And for either of them to feel beholden to the other wouldn't be good for either one of them. James liked the outdoors. He felt a peace and a calm come over him when he nestled in among the trees of the park. As long as he was safe and warm he felt he would do best sleeping under the stars.

And so that night was the beginning of a new friendship, a safe place for each of them while they lived their lives as homeless people. They ended up talking and napping through those first dark morning hours, Molly laying on one of the park benches while James stretched out his sleeping bag on the dewy ground. At dawn they made their way to the diner that Molly had shown James on her manic tour weeks ago. It was early and quiet and the owner saw them outside the door, waiting. He motioned for them to come in and poured them each a cup of coffee, toasted a few slices of day old bread, and they feasted on his generosity.

They walked for some of the morning, stopping to sit and to let the sun soak in through their clothes and warm their faces. After a few hours Molly grew quiet and James sensed it was time for her to go off. He would let her be for a while. Wait until she was ready to connect with him again. She reminded him that the factory was always open to him and that his coming in to get some rest would not upset her. And he knew she meant it, he would end up spending a good many nights and some bad weather days in the dark little room she had set for him.

For much of that summer James managed the depressing monotony of his homelessness by staying close to nature. He found it helped to stay busy, have something to do. He began taking walks, creating a regular route, learning where food could be found without embarrassment, even stopping to return a hello from some of the town's people who seemed to know about him but passed no judgement.

And he was always looking out for little things for Molly. He'd happen upon a notebook, some colored pens, or occasionally the much beloved can of paint. He'd carry them back in a cloth bag he had pulled out of a dumpster, one with zippered compartments, one he had neatly painted MOLLY on in red lettering. When Molly was reasonably stable she expressed her gratitude. She would tell him how she intended to use each thing. But, he learned that there were times when she just couldn't muster the emotional strength to express herself. She'd take the bag then and it would sit in the dark of her room, unopened until her temperament changed.

A number of times, when Molly was up for it the two would journey to the lake which was on the south end of the city. They would bathe by dusk in the warm waters, keeping a towel reasonably clean for this purpose.

And James tried to keep himself presentable. Soap was easy to find and soft summer rains made cleaning up pretty easy. He hated being out and looking for food with dirty hair and beard; it just drew unwanted attention. Molly had scissors and cut James' hair often, keeping it tight and close to his head. Once she asked James to cut her bangs, but it cost him some nights of sleep thinking of Suzie. While he had always gone to a barber regularly for haircuts, his wife rarely made appointments at a beauty shop. More often she'd come downstairs after a shower on a Sunday evening and pull a stool out into the middle of the kitchen floor. Handing Jimmy a pair of scissors she'd tell him to take a half-inch off her bangs and 'clean up the dead ends'. The memory of it, of her smelling of soap and beautiful without any makeup swelled up in his heart and stayed there.

As the months of summer moved along and the weather turned from gentle and warm to harsh and cold, James was grateful for Molly's factory. The protection it afforded could not be appreciated enough. It was during these inside times, when bad weather kept him in for several days at a time that James and Molly became closer, even as they tried to respect each other's space and allow each other to feel how they were going to feel at any given time.

Because of their proximity to each other James would learn more about Molly. She panhandled sporadically, kept a little money stashed away. He discovered later what she used most of it for. Occasionally when she was very depressed for long periods, she somehow managed to get hold of some drugs. She called them "mood elevators" and, while she only took them sporadically and when she could afford them, he hated them. It was the thought of them really, thinking of his mother all those years ago when he was a boy and she had that orange vial sitting around the apartment, taking them to dull her senses when her life began to unravel.

He remembered though that it was another vial, one with his mother's name printed on it that had helped her for a short time before her death. He realized even then as a kid that this vial was different… and in the way it was used and handled it was not bad. Jimmy wished that for Molly. That there was a medication out there, one that would target her problem and not just numb her or cover it up. One that would have her name printed on the bottle and a doctor prescribing it, monitoring it. One that would give her some stability without having to give up her gifts.

James couldn't understand why yet again he was with a person struggling with issues of mental illness. Was it supposed to mean something? Was it providence? Was it a cruel reminder of how poorly he had handled his mother when she had stumbled away from treatment? The thought of that, of his part in her accident tormented him. And then he would think again of his own little family. Suzie and their child, the one he was supposed to be there for, to protect. How it had all gone so bad so fast. How one strong wave could sink an overloaded boat. There were days when all he wanted was a beer and a bed. But he knew better. What good had that ever gotten him?

Chapter 28

Jimmy woke with a start, his heart beating fast and hard. These dreams had been going on for a while now and he was tired of being reminded, even in his sleep, of all that had happened in the last few months. He got up quietly and walked over to Suzie's side of the bed, looked down into the bassinet and placed his fingers gently on the tiny form of his daughter. He could feel her little belly moving as she breathed and he was relieved. He bent down and placed his lips on Suzie's forehead, barely a touch so she wouldn't wake. Then he did the same with his daughter, noticing the smell of her baby powder and smiling at the wonder of her. He grabbed his jeans and walked out of the room and downstairs. It was 4:00 a.m. and while he could have stayed in bed for another hour there was no sense in laying there in the dark, thinking.

Since Mia had been born Jimmy had found it easier to use the downstairs bathroom. He could turn on the light, shave, and brush his teeth without disturbing the sleep of his tired wife and baby. It was still hard to look at abuelo's bedroom, door ajar, and know he wasn't on the other side sleeping. It had been almost four months since the last time they spoke. The memory of that day in the hospital fresh again, abuelo so fragile from the heart attack he suffered while in rehab.

***

The doctors said it happened sometimes. Older patients had more risk factors and while everything was done to minimize those risks it was likely that abuelo had developed a blood clot which had ultimately caused his cardiac arrest. Jimmy had gotten the call at work: his grandfather was critical and not expected to survive. He could not believe what he was hearing. It was all too much déjà vu for him and he was frantically determined to get to abuelo.

The family ended up sitting together in a dimly lit waiting room, one dedicated to situations like this. They were allowed short visits, a few at a time with abuelo in his room in the ICU. Everyone that could be there was there: Edward and Aunt Kate, one of their sons and his wife; Aunt Naomi and Uncle Joey were on their way from Pennsylvania. Everyone prayed they'd make it to see him. Jimmy had called Suzie and told her to be calm, not to stress herself but to stay home. He would update her when he knew more, but she had come anyway. Nancy had driven them, and Jimmy, when he saw her in the hall fell apart in her arms.

Edward and Kate had gone in first. They returned to the group, eyes red rimmed. "He's sleeping. He looks peaceful," was all they reported.

"You go next, Jimmy," Uncle Edward said. He understood the place in his father's life that his nephew held. It was a good thing, he thought, that Naomi had not been there. Edward would still have said the same thing.

Suzie grabbed hold of Jimmy's hand, a fistful of tissue in the other and they walked through the double doors of the ICU. The front wall of each room was glass and you could see in to each one as you passed. Monitors and machines peeped and hummed above and around the beds, IV bags hung from polls and lines went in to patient's arms, others attached to their fingers, to their feet. Nurses stood at a main center station where they could see around them into each room. More peeping came from a bank of monitors that the nurses gathered information from.

They found abuelo's room. He was lying on his back; one hand under the covers, the other, with a clip on his finger was on top of the blanket. A heart monitor was situated to one side above his head. Not much else, no IV that they could see. His head was raised slightly and, like uncle Edward had said, he looked to be sleeping.

Jimmy began to cry at the sight of him, but he made sure that Suzie was sitting in a chair before he went to his grandfather, bent over him, and gave his forehead a kiss. His tears were streaming and falling on the blanket and on abuelo's face. He knelt down at the side of the bed, his head on the blanket and wept. Suzie handed him some of her tissues even as she held one up to her own face. Neither spoke for several minutes. They just looked at their grandfather, touched his face.

His creases were deep but soft and Jimmy traced one with his finger. Maybe he was stronger than the doctor thought. Maybe he'd survive this and be able to go home with nursing aides and bedrest. At the thought of it Jimmy raised his head, looked at his grandfather, and told him that he and Suzie were there. He told him to stay strong, that Jimmy needed him.

"I'm going to be a father in a few months and I want you to see that day. I want you to see that day, abuelo."

His grandfather moaned then. His hand moved and Jimmy reached for it, squeezing gently. Another moan and his eyes fluttered. Suzie got up nervously and went out into the hall to get a nurse. Seeing that his grandfather was trying to open his eyes Jimmy continued to talk softly to him, to hold his hand. And then there he was, his eyes looking into Jimmy's.

"Abuelo. I'm here. You're going to be all right now. Just rest. You need to rest." Jimmy stroked his grandfather's head, his soft white hair.

He saw the tears before he heard him speak. "Jimmy. Oh, Jimmy," his voice was thick and heavy with sleep.

"I'm here. Rest now. It's going to be all right."

The nurse had come in with Suzie. They saw that abuelo was conscious and the nurse whispered to Suzie that it was ok. "I'm glad you have this time," she said and added they would watch Mr. Vazquez's monitor from out at the station but that there wasn't anything they should do.

"Jimmy. Your father."

"Yes, abuelo, I'm going to be a father. And you will be a great-grandfather again."

Abuelo fought to open his eyes more. He squeezed Jimmy's hand suddenly. "Your father…the paper."

Jimmy didn't understand. "Rest now abuelo. We'll talk when you're stronger."

Again, but weakly abuelo said, "Your father. The paper… I'm sorry." His eyes began to close and a tear ran down his cheek.

"Abuelo, I love you so much," Jimmy whispered in his grandfather's ear. "I love you so much."

"Love you. I'm sorry…" abuelo mumbled a bit more, his voice trailing off.

Suzie waited with Jimmy several more minutes before touching his shoulder tenderly. "I think he's going to sleep for a while."

"I want to stay with him."

"Honey, I know," Suzie kissed her husband's arm. "But the others. They're waiting. We can stay and come back in later."

Jimmy reached down for one last hug, a kiss on his grandfather's cheek. "You rest and we can talk later." Abuelo was quiet, his eyes closed.

The Gregory's walked out of the ICU but neither of them would walk back in to see abuelo again. His heart would give out later that evening. Thankfully Naomi had gotten to the hospital and was able to hold her father's hand while it was still warm.

***

Jimmy was still hurting from the loss of his much loved grandfather. He wished abuelo hadn't insisted on the surgery. Would he have done it if Suzie wasn't pregnant? And Jimmy hadn't been able to understand what abuelo was trying to say to him that last night. Were the words just random thoughts like Suzie believed; the utterances of a man whose brain wasn't putting anything concrete together? But he had said them twice. The same words. What could the paper mean? Why was he sorry? Jimmy mulled it all over and stewed about abuelo's death and those words every day. They were with him in the truck and on the farm and they woke him at night, the possibility of a message not understood and what it meant to him.

For the last two months of Suzie's pregnancy she had been told to go on bed rest. She had high blood pressure and there was concern for both mother and child. She might deliver the baby too early and there was a small risk for Suzie having a stroke. This put the fear into both of the parents to be. It was their worst nightmare and after losing abuelo Jimmy could not possibly imagine losing his wife.

This period until the baby was born was one of the longest, most anxious times of the couple's lives. Jimmy had obsessed over what Suzie was and was not doing. If she got up to use the bathroom while he was there he went with her, holding her arm, half carrying her. He had propped her pillows and got her books to read. He had given her a bell so that she could ring him from downstairs, and he drove her crazy with his pampering and fussing. But he would not relent even though the doctor told them Suzie was not that fragile and walking for necessity about the house was fine.

Suzie had tried to assure Jimmy, to calm his excessive worrying. And he knew he needed to show her a strong exterior even while he continued to fuss and brood over her. It was during these months that Jimmy found himself unwinding with a drink in the evening after Suzie had settled down for bed. He had always enjoyed the social aspects of a cold beer shared with friends on Friday nights after a long week of work. Now he began enjoying the beer at home, alone in front of the TV in the dark, trying to settle his thoughts so he could sleep.

Thankfully, for all their stress and worry, the couple had been blessed with a beautiful and healthy daughter, born to them on May 7, 1997. Their little brown-haired, blue eyed wonder was a tiny six pound, six ounce beauty and they had named her Mia Carla for both her grandmother and her great grandfather. She was the joy of their lives and the hope of better times to come. No child could possibly be more loved.

Chapter 29

"Do you like it Daddy?" Mia was at the side door when her father walked in; her big blue eyes looking up at him as she held out a drawing done in colored pencils.

Jimmy got down on a knee and held the drawing up, "I love it sweetie," he enthused. "This is me on the farm, right? I can see the barn and the tractor. Oh, and there's Bubba out in the field." He pointed at the dog. "It's beautiful!"

Mia smiled broadly and giggled as her father tickled her. She wiggled away from his fingers. "Silly Daddy!" She scolded. "Here, take the picture for your office."

"Lucky me to have one of the early works of a famous artist." He got up and put the picture on the refrigerator with a magnet. Satisfied, Mia left the kitchen; Jimmy went over to where Suzie was washing lettuce in the sink. Giving her a kiss he said, "She really is good, isn't she? It's not just us being proud parents."

Suzie laughed. "Well, we are pretty proud parents. But no, Mia's good. When they told us at open house that the art teacher saw something special, I think they meant it."

"I wonder if we should get her into some classes or something. I mean for art."

"She's only six, Jimmy. Let's say we wait a few more years to see if she keeps on with her drawing like she has been. But I do think Santa might want to consider a nice art set this year. You know pencils and chalks and charcoal. Maybe even paints."

Jimmy smiled then, "Got it, Mrs. Claus." Suzie always knew how and when to do things. She was a fantastic mother and Jimmy loved watching his two girls together.

He went upstairs to change, the smell of the farm heavy on his clothes. He popped his head in to his daughter's room and reminded her to follow him down for dinner which was almost ready.

The two of them came down the stairs together, the dog right behind. Suzie pulled a bubbling casserole from the oven and set it in the middle of the table. Jimmy grabbed the tossed salad from the counter and asked Mia to get some dressing from the refrigerator. The three of them sat down for dinner, Bubba the dog laying under the table, waiting for any morsel that should fall his way.

The dog had been added to the family the Christmas when Mia had turned two. They set the sleeping puppy with its little black collar in a basket under the tree for Mia to find.

She had been so excited to find the retriever pup, all soft and fluffy. She kissed the poor dog over and over while trying to get her arms around it to pick it up. Mia loved it like a child loves a doll and named her Baby. She asked for a pink collar and bow to be put on her little dog and they let the name go until a few years later when their then five-year-old came to them in frustration about her dog.

"Steven said Baby is a boy, not a girl. And he told me how to tell. He's right, he's a boy."

"That's true, honey. Baby is a boy. Do you want to change his collar or his bow?" Suzie had asked her.

Exasperated, Mia had said "Yes! I'd like a blue collar and no bow at all. And his name, well, that's not good. Baby is a girl's name. He has to have a new name."

"It might be too late for that, Mia," Suzie suggested. "He's always been called Baby and he answers to that name."

"No way," she argued. "I'm naming him Bubba now. It's almost like Baby but it's a boy name. Steven said so."

Steven, their neighbor, was seven and one of Mia's forever friends. Certainly he was right about these things. And just like that it had been decided and the dog had been renamed. Luckily Baby adjusted to being called Bubba and Mia had loved him just as much without his pink bow.

***

The Gregory's had decided to stay in their house after they had purchased the farm. Ken proved to be a dependable employee and tenant at the farm house. And in the few years since Mia was born the population of children in their neighborhood had increased greatly and being an only child she benefitted from having many nearby playmates and best friends.

And as Mia made friends her parents did too. As is often the case, the parents of a child's friend become friends as well. The Gregory's gravitated towards relationships with some of Mia's friends, many who lived within a mile or two of their home.

They had grown happy and content in their little cul-de-sac in the country. Campfires were shared and parties were held across several back yards. In the winter, card parties were common and kids came along to play together for a while under the supervision of a hired babysitter. When they got tired they'd lay on blankets on bedroom floors until their parents were done with their adult games.

People in town looked out for each other too. Jimmy had first witnessed this when Suzie was on bedrest with the pregnancy. Having their friend's church arrange for dinners to see them through was just one example. The fire department after fighting to save the occupants from a house that was totally lost to fire organized a benefit for the family. Hundreds of people showed up and many helped to cook, to organize games for the kids and to entertain the crowd with their various talents.

Suzie ended up making an appointment to see about baptizing Mia with the priest of that little Episcopal Church that had fed them when they were scared and in need. Neither of the Gregory's had even talked about church before their child was born. But even without their being religious they understood the meaning of bringing their child before God for His blessings and guidance over her life. And somehow in the years after her baptism, Mia's parents found themselves still bringing their little girl to the friendly church, filling up the same pew near the right back corner first with a car seat and baby toys and later with books and puzzles, paper and crayons.

Mia continued to amaze and amuse her parents every day. She charmed everyone who met her with her big smile and personality and she found something amusing in whatever surrounding she was placed in. If they took her to a park she ran from slide to seesaw to swings talking to any child that might share her interest in conversation. If at a museum she politely listened to guides as they walked through the displays. If something didn't interest her she would find something that did whether it be staring at the earrings of the woman ahead of her or making tiny braids in her mother's hair. At church she was quiet, drawing her pictures; looking up occasionally to watch the people fidget and whisper in the pews ahead.

And their dear little girl was strong of will even as she seemed so demure. She delighted in debate and could go toe to toe with her parents, defending and reasoning everything from her thoughts about bedtimes and appropriate clothes to wear to the color of the sky which was not ever simply "blue." Even so, she did this with an interest in the other person's opinion, patiently listening to their thoughts even though they were more often wrong than right.

There was the time she announced to her parents one evening that she would not be going back to school the following day even though it was only her third week of second grade.

"What's going on that you don't think you can go back to school tomorrow?" Jimmy asked the question, preparing himself mentally for a paragraph answer.

"There's no way, Daddy. You have no idea what it's like. First there's Simon. I told you about him. He keeps touching my ponytail. And, yes, Mommy. I DID tell him to quit it please," she began. "And also there are lots of problems with the cafeteria line. The bagged lunch kids get to go through first. They get to buy their milk before the buying kids can get their lunch. So then there is like… maybe five minutes for us to eat before we have to take our trays up."

"Hmmm. I don't know about five minutes, Suzie. I've never heard about this problem from anyone else before."

"It's maybe ten minutes." Mia drew in a deep breath. "Maybe. But it's not fair. The bagged lunch kids get to sit and talk and have all that extra time. I have to sit down and eat so fast my stomach hurts and I can't even drink all my milk.

They knew well their daughter's tendency for the dramatic and were learning to pick up on underlying issues that may be Mia's real reason for upset. "Do you feel like you don't get enough time to talk to your friends?" her father asked.

"Well, I don't. Its lunch time and we are supposed to have thirty minutes. It's the only time Sabrina, Becca, and I can talk all day. And they both *bring their* lunch. The people in the cafeteria are not being organized, Daddy. I'm pretty mad about it." She sat at the kitchen table obviously upset.

They would have to finish reasoning this through with their daughter. "Well, Mia, I guess it would be upsetting to have to hurry to eat. And having your two best friends both bringing their lunches and having all that time to talk… maybe mommy can make a call to the school tomorrow and ask them about the problem with the line. See if other kids are complaining. But you'll have to go to school until we figure this out."

Mia put her finger to her lips, tapped them a few times thinking. "I'm thinking maybe I can pack my lunch; try that for a while and see if they work out the slow line problem. Maybe you won't have to call."

"Packing your lunch? We stopped that last year when you started sneaking junk into your lunch box, remember?" Suzie stared at her.

"Yeah, I know, Mommy. I was thinking that. And this time I would have to always have a fruit and some carrots or celery. I could get up a little early and pack it so you could see. No junk."

"What do you think, Mommy?" Jimmy looked at his wife, his hand over his mouth while he winked his eye.

"Well, maybe if you follow the rules about the food. I don't know. Do you think you can be patient and try packing again while the school works on the problem?" Suzie knew the answer.

"Yes."

"Okay then. We'll try it again. The way you suggested. Now, what do you think we should do about Simon and your ponytail?" Jimmy had returned the conversation volley.

"I think I will remind him that if he does it again I will have to talk to the teacher. Also I think I will be careful not to tip my head back on his desk."

Jimmy guessed it had been something like that. "It's probably best you sit up straighter then. Maybe he's just been frustrated and he's pushing your hair away."

"I don't think so. But I guess I'll give him one more chance." And in this way they had settled many little upsets, Mia thinking she had come up with all the answers herself.

Chapter 30

*I*t happened so fast that Jimmy was unable to recall the sequence of events. He had decided to clear a dense line of trees that for years had created a natural boundary between two fields. Why he hadn't done it years ago he didn't know, but Donny had kept them there saying that if ever the land was turned residential, the treed lot would be an asset when selling out parcels.

But as Jimmy's farm, he had no intention of ever seeing it be anything other than the high-yielding agricultural property it had become. He had taken out loans for better equipment and implemented more efficient farming techniques and Hope Grows had benefitted from his progressive approach. The wooded area was just a hassle to work around and Jimmy finally decided to begin opening up the field that spring day.

He, Ken, and Ken's nephew Aaron had taken two of the older tractors and a chain saw out to the northeast corner of the land where they'd begun to cut back a few of the pines and smaller maples, leaving the trunks for pulling out later. This day they had decided to cut and tow back as many cut logs as they could get.

From the way Ken and Aaron told it, Jimmy was up on one of the tractors pulling a larger pine log out from deeper into the grove where it had been felled. For some reason Jimmy had been standing up, looking behind him as he moved forward with the tow.

Somewhere in the next moments Jimmy's tractor found a small ditch, the front tires falling down into it suddenly. The tractor bounced and pitched slightly, just enough to send its driver over the left side where he was immediately run over by 500-pounds of the left rear tire plus the weight of the tractor it supported.

Aaron got to him first, finding a still conscious Jimmy splayed out on his back on the ground, his left leg bent at an angle that made it obvious that it was broken and blood beginning to seep through his jeans. His left forearm and hand were still pinned under the tractor tire where it had stopped moving. Getting up on the tractor; Aaron moved it forward out of the small ditch and off of the arm of his boss. Ken was already on his cell phone calling for an ambulance.

They could see that Jimmy had broken several bones and his forearm had been crushed as it had landed alongside a rock before the tractor ran over it and stopped there. As bad off as Jimmy's left extremities appeared to be, his head had just been inches from the tire when it had stopped in the ditch and his life had been spared.

Responders got to the scene of the accident as quickly as was possible, but it was too long for Ken, who was falling apart while watching his nephew bent down over Jimmy, trying to reassure him as he moved from shock to unconsciousness. While he was conscious he moaned pitifully, in horrible pain more from his back and leg than from the bloody arm that had little resemblance to what it had been. It took some time for the EMT's to get Jimmy stable enough to load into the ambulance, his jeans and shirt were both cut away so they could examine him and an IV bag was started. It was Aaron who called Suzie.

Suzie dropped her work, quite literally, on the floor of the bakery in Buffalo when she took the call from Aaron. Nancy was sick with a stomach bug and Suzie had needed to come in to decorate a large wedding cake. Luckily she was within fifteen minutes of the hospital where they were taking her husband. Suzie barked out an order to have one of the girls call her other decorator Christine who was working at the Little City Bakery and tell her to come finish the cake sometime tonight.

During the drive Suzie had the where with all to call Steven's mother, Debbie, and ask her to keep Mia. She didn't know what to expect when she got to Jimmy and she couldn't be worrying about her eleven-year old's safety if at home alone.

Jimmy was in surgery when she got there. Aaron had followed the ambulance to the hospital and then stayed, prepared to fill Suzie in while Ken had stayed at the farm, telling the staff what had happened and then, feeling sick, had taken the rest of the day off.

It was nearly six hours before an orthopedic surgeon came into the waiting room to talk with Suzie. He was short and slim and looked much too young to be a doctor, even to a woman who was only forty-two. He was thorough enough with his explanation but he delivered it in monotone, making it seem very impersonal.

"Mrs. Gregory. I'm Doctor Weston and I've been in surgery with your husband. He has a number of broken bones and torn ligaments and muscle in his left leg. I have pinned what I could. We will be watching for tissue and muscle death over the next few days. I anticipate more surgery. Scaring and some loss of muscle are expected but with time I expect it to heal well enough for Mr. Gregory to have use of the leg again. He has two fractured vertebrae in his lower back. These will need time and rest, but again healing is expected."

He drew in a quick breath before continuing. "Mr. Gregory's left forearm and hand suffered serious crush injuries. Bones in his forearm, his wrist, and fingers were broken and muscle, ligaments, and other tissue were badly torn as well. A vascular surgeon is with him working to restore blood flow. More surgery is inevitable. I am realistic about this. We will be watching for the possibility of amputation but our hope is that we will save enough tissue that that will not be necessary. But your husband will likely have a compromised forearm and hand. We will have to wait and see."

"Oh my God," was all Suzie could find to say.

"He was very lucky. No injury to head or chest. Nothing life threatening. For now, that's all I have. We will know more in the days and weeks to come." Doctor Weston turned abruptly and walked out.

An older, smiling nurse walked in as the doctor left. She told Suzie that they were preparing a room for her husband on the third-floor trauma wing. "He's going to be a while yet dear. If you need to go home, get some things, take a warm shower this might be a good time. When they do get him to his room he's going to be a while coming out of sedation. And they'll be keeping him as comfortable as they can with medication tonight. He might not even know you're here."

Aaron had gone on back after the doctor spoke to them and Suzie was all alone. She didn't feel comfortable leaving, the chance that Jimmy would be there awake wondering about her. "Could I maybe go and just get my daughter. She will be pretty upset about this."

"Hmmmm; she's young, I'm guessing," the nurse considered.

"Yes. She's almost eleven."

"Well, honey. I don't recommend it. Not for a day or two maybe. It might be a lot for her." She saw that Suzie was getting upset and gave her a little side hug. "Why don't you go home for just a little bit? Talk to your daughter. You can assure her that her dad is going to be all right but that for a few days he's going to be sleepy and needs the rest."

Suzie was grateful for the nurse's tenderness. "Yeah, I guess I'll do that. Will you please tell my husband that I will be back shortly…if he wakes up?"

"You bet. I'll pass that message on personally to the nurse that will be with him. Mr. Gregory will be in room 348. Just come up the main elevators from the entrance and turn right. Take care, dear." The nurse walked out and back through the double doors of the surgical department.

***

Jimmy left the hospital two weeks later to a home that had been prepared for him. Volunteers from the church constructed a wheel chair ramp off the front porch, winding down into the front yard and ending at the driveway. Again, meals for the family were being organized and everyone there was ready to help when and where they could. The Anderson's helped their daughter clear out the back office and with the help of a medical supply agency they refurnished it with a hospital bed and lift chair. The same agency provided a wheelchair and various other home supplies that would help Jimmy with some of the things he would have taken for granted a few weeks ago.

Mia had done her part. Her grandmother had taken her to one of her favorite art and craft stores where she found unpainted picture frames and she had painted them in vibrant colors and filled them with beautiful paintings of wild grasses and flowers, barns and birds in trees and sunny blue skies. She stapled ribbons to their backs, making loopy bows and handily hung them from nails all around her father's new bedroom. She had cut out huge block letters from poster board and strung a "Welcome Home" sign across the porch railing for her father to read as he was wheeled up the front ramp.

The in hospital social worker had made arrangements for a visiting nursing service as well as an in-home health care aide and occupational therapist to come to the Gregory home three times a week for several hours. Needing help with moving from position was one thing but help with the basics of bathing and toileting troubled and embarrassed Jimmy. In the hospital he had tried to wait for Suzie or a male nurse for these things and when that didn't work out he got short-tempered and irritable, mostly with Suzie who he had wanted to be more available to him.

While at the hospital Jimmy had come out of a second surgery with some muscle and dead tissue taken from his forearm and leg and two fingers amputated. He would be followed by both vascular and orthopedic surgeons for months of his recovery.

Suzie had gone alone to the hospital to get Jimmy. Mia had wanted to come but she wasn't sure how he would handle the ride; his pain being barely managed in the hospital. Suzie filled the prescriptions that she had been given the day before Jimmy came home and had them ready for him even though she knew he wouldn't take most of them. He had been gutting it out on the bare minimum required by the doctor while he was in the hospital. He told Suzie that he had no intention of getting addicted to pain killers.

As the van turned in to their driveway Jimmy let out a sigh of relief. He had struggled with the ride, every little bump and turn sending pain down his leg and through his back. "I'm sorry honey," she said. "I know that was hard.

Michael and Dad are here and they'll help get you in the house as smoothly as possible." Michael was one of the visiting nurses that would be helping him. Jimmy hadn't met him but he was a male and Jimmy had requested as many of them as he could get.

Suzie opened the sliding door of the van where Michael and Art were waiting for him with a wheelchair. Michael pulled him from the back while Art held his legs, the left one in a full cast from mid-thigh to ankle. Slowly they were able to situate him in the chair with the left leg and footrest already up.

Mia yelled out and came running from the porch. Jimmy put on his best face for her as she reached out her arms to hug him.

"Hold on, Mia," Suzie grabbed her, catching her before she made contact with her father. "We need to get Daddy in the house and comfortable first. He's had a long ride."

"Okay. Sorry, Daddy." She followed behind her grandfather who was pushing him up the driveway toward the ramp. "See what I made?"

Only then did Jimmy take in the scene in front of him. There was his home. The one he had bought with his loving wife and the "Welcome Home" sign his sweet daughter had made and hung from its big front porch. His mother-in-law was at the door, smiling and waving. But what he had seen first and what had soured the scene for him was the huge wheelchair ramp serpentine through his yard and on to his porch. He could see it was of sound construction and craftsmanship and, while he should have been grateful for it, all he could think of was what it represented and how ugly it was.

Chapter 31

Suzie had a quiet little family party for Mia the weekend of her eleventh birthday. She wanted to have a celebration where Jimmy was included but with him barely home a week she knew better than to have a houseful of kids over. So she scheduled a roller skating party for Mia's friends at the end of the month when she hoped she's feel comfortable leaving Jimmy alone for a few hours.

Mia's grandparents, her Uncle Paul and Aunt Melony, and Uncle Edward and Aunt Kate were all invited for dinner and cake. In hindsight having dinner might have been a little too much. For almost two hours Jimmy did his best to sit through the noisy chatter of the family dinner gathering. Nancy didn't realize just how loud she could be when she was laughing, which was most of the time. The sound of her high-pitched, happy voice grated on Jimmy like fingernails on a chalkboard.

He knew everyone was trying hard to make the evening about Mia and they all did their best to hide their stares and minimize their questions about how Jimmy was managing. But he was tired, exhausted actually, both in body and in spirit, and after dinner and a few beers he asked Suzie to take him back to his bedroom where he could rest for a bit. He gave Mia a kiss on the cheek and told her to make sure they came back to get him for cake and presents. Jimmy'd have to be next to dead to miss his little girl's Happy Birthday song and see her face when she opened her gifts.

***

"Can you please just sign the check? I'll make sure to set up automatic deposits from now on," Suzie was standing over Jimmy who was reclining in his lift chair, the TV turned to a soccer game. He never liked the sport and had never watched a televised game of it.

Jimmy was studying the piece of paper. "Huh. This is it then. I'm officially on the dole. Oh, and do you see that? JAMES GREGORY." He held it up to Suzie, pointing to his name. "I haven't been JAMES GREGORY since I was what… three days old? It's my father's name. That son of a bitch would probably take this in a minute, no regrets."

"You paid into this plan for years. That's the point of the whole thing. It's there for you if you ever need it. And it's just for now, Jimmy." She stood in front of him trying to make eye contact.

"I'll sign it for you, Suzie. It's for you and Mia since I'm contributing damn little to this household." Money had already been significantly less since most of the farm's recent profits were used to pay down new farm loan debt. And since the accident Jimmy wasn't taking a regular paycheck from the farm. He just couldn't do it. He was sitting at home while the guys were running his farm for him, Bob and Ken acting as general managers together. He scribbled his name on the back of the check with his right hand, remembering all the times he had tried to use this non-dominant hand to write in school like all the other kids. Frustrated, he handed it to his wife, who had her coat on and her apron over an arm. "I hate it you know," he looked up at her then, his voice thick.

Suzie got down on her knees in front of her husband and kissed him softly on the cheek. He had on a button-down denim shirt and sweatpants, both loose for the weight he had lost. Scratchy, grey and brown stubble ran along his jaw and chin, filling in the hollows of his face. "I know you do. I do too. But you're here. And I'm here and our daughter is here and we're still a family. I could have had that taken from me two months ago, so I still walk in to church on Sunday being thankful."

Jimmy gave his wife a kiss in return, smiling at her weakly. She needed to get to work. He knew that.

Suzie got up to go, smiling back at Jimmy. "Give yourself time. It's going to be all right."

He heard her close the door to the kitchen. "It's the time, Suzie," he whispered to himself. "I'm afraid of being left with nothing but it."

***

Over the months of summer and into the fall, Jimmy faithfully worked with doctors and therapists and endured two more painful surgeries to help repair more bone and tissue. It was very slow going and he wasn't where he had wanted to be at that point. He had finally gone from a hard cast of the leg to a soft one. He was putting weight on it and taking a few painful steps with the help of a walker. Walking would come, but again, it was a matter of time.

What was left of his forearm was disfigured and it was still too fragile to use. He wondered how much strength it would ever get back. His hand with its middle and ring fingers gone troubled him to look at but to everyone's surprise he had some use of the remaining digits. His wrist hurt like hell but he was able to move it somewhat and with his three remaining fingers he was able to grip small, lightweight objects. Doctors were very pleased with his progress in the area.

Calls came from the farm to their boss regularly for a while. He was given updates and asked questions as he always had been. But it was hard, not being there. He tried to answer questions, to ask about things as he always had done. But he didn't feel effective or capable away from the farm. Bob, Ken, Aaron, and the few other employees he had hired had come to see Jimmy at home a few times. They came in with their work boots and smells of the farm. They shared stories about work over a beer, as if nothing had ever changed. Jimmy did his best to banter with them then but each time they left he seemed to go deeper into a little dark place he had found to hide out in.

Jimmy wasn't able to work. And that's what he wanted. That was a long way off and the doctors didn't even pretend to suggest that he would be able to go back to do all of what he had done on the farm. The thought of being compromised for life, of not being able to easily climb on the tractor to plow and to plant, to bend down and pick all day if he wanted to, or to walk in the field without stumbling over the furrows… Well, there were days when it overwhelmed him.

But just when he didn't think he had the emotional energy to keep moving forward, there would be his effervescent daughter Mia. She spent a lot of time with her father, insisting he sit out on the front porch while she played in the yard with friends or peddled her bike up and down the road. He couldn't help but smile at her spunk.

At the beginning of the summer Mia had announced that she was going to play lacrosse at school in the spring. They knew that two of her best friends played and that that was likely her reasoning, but it was the first sport she had picked without them. Her parents signed her up for the popular T-ball when she was six and she managed a month with soccer when she was eight but Suzie was not destined to be a soccer mom.

Mia shopped with her mother for a stick, helmet, shin pads, and mouth guard. She came home to show them to her father, who made a big deal about them. He held up the stick and spun it around in his good hand. "Nice. Very nice. Not surprised by the color choice," he gave her a little jab with the pocket end before handing it back.

"Pink's still my color, Dad," she said. "And don't you just love the shiny, metallic finish? You're gonna coach me, right?" she looked at her dad seriously.

It caught him up short. "Honey. You know I'd love to but…"

"But you don't know the sport, never played it a day in your life. I know. I know," she smiled. "But," she said, "I need you to learn it with me. To teach me the rules. To watch me…you know…for form."

Jimmy didn't know what to say. His eleven-year-old was years beyond her age.

"Oh. And Becca and Alex will be here tomorrow for our first practice." Mia gave her dad a kiss on the cheek and headed out the front door.

***

Winter had been long and tedious but, while Jimmy made good progress and by March was walking unaided, he wanted more from himself. Somehow he had expected to be as able-bodied as he had been the spring before. He was left with a limp and chronic pain in his back and leg. While his left forearm would always be smaller and weaker, he had been relentless in exercising the arm and its bicep was huge by comparison. Although he could grasp and lift some weight in his hand, it hurt when he tried to use it for any real period of time.

Suzie had taken Jimmy out to the farm on a few spring mornings after the ground had thawed and was ready for disking. They met up at the main barn where Ken had gathered the employees together. It was painful for Jimmy, who stood there in his jeans and work coat trying to look strong and capable, as he talked to the guys while they tried to hide their staring.

He rode out to the fields, Suzie staying back while Jimmy got in the truck with Ken. They stopped to watch a tractor out in the distance, its movement slow and graceful. A few men were seen talking as they walked among the furrows of freshly turned soil. Jimmy wanted to be out there walking in the fields too; watching from the window of a truck driven by a guy who was acting as the general manager was soul crushing.

Jimmy went back out to the farm a handful of times on his own since he had been given the okay to drive. He poked around in one of the barns for a while, organizing some of the smaller tools and cleaning off a few pieces of equipment with an air compressor. He went to see the cows, some of the girls stopped and turned to look at him as he spoke to them, but soon enough they turned back to their eating. He drove down to the fields being planted to see if there was anything that he could do.

***

It had been a week and he hadn't gone back. He made a call to Ken, asking how things were, knowing that everything was being taken care of. Frustrated, he knew he needed to talk to Suzie about some of his recent feelings.

He waited until Monday night when he knew she would have had a shorter day at work. They had gone up to say goodnight prayers with Mia and Suzie had gone in to take a shower. She came downstairs in her much worn fuzzy blue bathrobe and a pair of grip bottom socks. She looked exhausted and it hurt him to see the toll that his accident had taken on her. But she smiled as always and wrapped her legs up under herself next to him on the couch while she turned through the channels on the TV.

"Suzie, I want to talk to you," Jimmy reached to take the remote from his wife's fingers. He turned the TV off; leaving the room dark except for a small light that glowed from the kitchen. "Listen, honey, this is all so hard for me…"

"I know it's been." She continued to look at the TV, its screen black.

"It's been hard for me because of how hard it's been on you. And on Mia." He stopped to consider. "You've been working way too much and too hard while I spend most of my time sitting here watching the world go by."

Suzie turned to her husband, her whole body pivoting. "Jimmy. You would do the same if it had been the other way around. And just look how far you've come. You've gone out to the farm a few times now and you're doing better than the doctors expected."

"But it's not enough. God, Suzie, I can't even put in a full day of work…like every other man does." He heard the agitation in his voice.

"Maybe not yet. And maybe not exactly like you had done before, but you will. You will. You know that, Jimmy."

He felt his eyes moisten and he choked back his emotion. "But I don't want it if I can't have what I had before." He hesitated while Suzie put her hand on his left arm. It felt like a touch of pity.

"You can't understand. I drive to the farm, talk to the guys, we laugh. I ride around in the truck and watch. They are busy doing what they know to do. They don't need me driving around and watching, directing traffic."

"Well, I disagree. You know every part of that farm. And as you get stronger there will be more you can do. So what if it's part time and so what if you're not on the tractor every day?"

Jimmy stopped her. He lifted her face with the fingers of his frail hand, until she looked in his eyes. "Suzie," he whispered. "I want to sell the farm."

Suzie pulled away from her husband, looking shocked by what he had just said. Finally she answered, "But, Jimmy. The farm? It's everything you ever wanted. And it belongs to you."

"That's just it, Suzie. It's not that the farm doesn't belong to me, but that I don't belong to it. Not now. Not anymore."

In exasperation, not understanding that her husband was grieving a great loss and that he still had a lot to work through, Suzie got up and stood above him. "You are NOT selling the farm! I haven't been working so hard to pay the bills for you to do that! I'm on the deed too and I won't let it happen." She walked upstairs and closed the door to their bedroom, leaving Jimmy alone in the dark.

Chapter 32

Summer 2009-Spring 2010

It was a Saturday afternoon in June, one that was warm but rainy, and Jimmy sat in the living room staring at the TV that was tuned in to one of the action movies he had seen many times. Suzie had gone in to Buffalo, to the bakery, to finish decorating and helping to deliver a very large wedding cake. She told Jimmy that the parents of this particular client were paying for a reception for 500 people. The cake would be the most ornate cakes she had ever done and it had to be perfect, the family was paying her big money. When she met with them and gave them her quote the bride's father had not batted an eye, but scribbled out a check that day.

Mia had come in after being dropped off by Becca's dad, the weather having shortened their plans. She gave her father a quick hello and a kiss on the cheek before she bounded the stairs to her room to change and do a little homework. Jimmy watched his daughter as she walked out of the room. She had grown taller this year and, at twelve, she had a few inches on her mother. And she was lanky, all arms and legs but graceful and delicate like her mother had always been.

Jimmy was tired and before he dozed off he was thinking that he should get up and try to fix the drain to the bathroom sink. It had been a few weeks since Suzie mentioned the slow leak. But he would take a little nap, just for a few minutes. His nights were still mostly restless and he seemed to do his best sleeping in the afternoon after a few beers and with the TV on.

Mia had come back downstairs and he awoke briefly to hear her clanging around in the kitchen. She was hungry and she had decided to make something for the both of them knowing that it was unlikely that her father had eaten lunch. She found an old standby, macaroni and cheese from a box, and she set a pot of water on the burner to boil.

Ten minutes later she stirred a little milk and the package of bright orange dried 'cheese' into the macaroni, scooping out a little butter from the plastic container in the fridge. She kept the finished product on the stove as she went to answer the phone.

While she talked along to one of her classmates about the last weeks of their sixth-grade year, laughing and planning for the summer, the pot of macaroni and cheese was bubbling away on the burner where she had left it, having forgotten to turn it off when she went to drain the macaroni at the sink. As the minutes went by her lunch went from bubbly, to sticky, then to hard and dry and finally to a burning mess. Jimmy remained asleep, dreaming about something stinking but being unable to find it.

By the time the smoke alarm went off the downstairs was full of thick grey smoke and the pot on the stove was black and fiery hot. Mia ran down the stairs, her eyes burning. It took Jimmy a few moments to wake up and realize what he was hearing. By that time Mia had grabbed the pot with her bare hands, the handle burning her. She reacted by dropping the pot on the floor. Quickly she got a pot holder and with it she managed to get the pot into the sink and run cold water into it.

Jimmy had come in, seen what was going on and turned the gas to the burner off.

"Oh, honey, are you all right?" Jimmy went to his daughter who had her hand under the cold water. "Let me see that," he grabbed her hand from the stream of water.

Mia pulled it back, returning it to the comfort of the cold. "I'm okay, Dad. I just must have forgotten to turn the mac-n-cheese off." She nodded to the pan in the sink, too burned to be salvaged.

"I don't care about that," Jimmy had gotten ice from the freezer and was wrapping it in a kitchen cloth. "I want to see your hand though. We can keep it cold with this," he held out the makeshift ice pack.

She turned off the water and held her right hand out to him. It was very red and shiny from the heat it had absorbed but it was not blistering except for a small half circle in her palm. It would hurt and Jimmy would have her keep it cool and uncovered, but he could see it would be fine.

"Thank goodness you're alright, sweetie," Jimmy hugged Mia.

"Daddy, look." She pointed with her other hand to the spot on the floor where she had dropped the pot. The linoleum had an ugly brown burn mark in the shape of a crescent moon.

"Oh, well. So what? Now your mother will have a reason to get the new floor she's been wanting." He smiled at her and kissed her forehead, sending her in to the living room to sit with the ice for a while.

But when Suzie came home a half hour later to find a burnt pot sitting out on the front porch, the horrible smell in the house and the burn mark on the floor, she was not so easy to dismiss it.

"What the hell happened here?" she looked at her husband, who was in the kitchen making sandwiches.

"I'm sorry, Suzie. It was an accident. Just some burnt macaroni. I may be able to do something about the linoleum without replacing it, but I doubt it." Jimmy looked away feeling his wife's eyes burning into him.

"Where's Mia?" Suzie moved toward the living room.

"It's okay, Mom. It's fine," Mia had her hand lying across the cloth of ice.

"How did this happen? Jimmy, how did this happen?" Suzie was yelling even as she held her daughters hand.

"It's my fault, Suzie." Jimmy was standing in the doorway. "I didn't realize the pot was burning…"

And then Suzie saw the beer cans, empty on the coffee table. "Mia, go up to your room would you?" Suzie's fists were clenched and her words were clipped.

"Mom, it's my fault. I was the one making the food." Mia tried to intervene in a fight she knew was about to take place.

"Oh, I bet you were. I have no doubt. Go up to your room for now, Mia."

Mia walked past her parents, looking each of them in the eye, seeing her father's sadness and her mother's anger. When she had closed the door to her room, Suzie began.

"My God, Jimmy, the house could have burned down with our daughter in it!" She yelled. "And this…" she went over to the cans of beer and pushed them to the floor with the back of her hand. "This is what I blame! This is what you do, day after day. Drink and sulk, sulk and drink."

Jimmy had his head down, looking like a dog that had just peed on the carpet.

"You're not the only one who's hurting you know. But the rest of us have to keep moving. It wouldn't matter if you were here or not." She drew in a breath. "Because you left us a year ago, as far as I can see." Suzie stopped then, having spent all her anger.

That night Jimmy stayed on the couch. He wouldn't make Suzie lay in bed next to him. He knew she was angry and, while what she said she said in frustration, the words had gone deep. Deeper and more cutting than any injury Jimmy had endured. Jimmy decided that night that the best thing he could do for his family was to follow through on what his wife said he had already done anyway.

***

The morning came too quickly for Jimmy. As the sun came up in the sky the dread in Jimmy's heart grew and he felt sick with the pain of what he was about to do. He could hear Suzie moving about upstairs and soon she would call Mia to wake and get ready for church.

Somehow he raised himself from the couch and made his way to the kitchen where he put on a pot of coffee and got some bagels out of the refrigerator. He went in to the bathroom to clean up and shave, just as he had always done.

Finally he heard the two come down the stairs and in to the kitchen, Suzie asking Mia to get her breakfast and go into the living room to watch a little TV before they left. Jimmy drew in a deep breath and wiped his eyes before walking in to the kitchen. Immediately Suzie came to him and put her arms around him.

"I'm sorry for last night," she whispered in his ear. "I'm just overwhelmed, I guess, and the whole thing pushed me over."

Feeling tears coming Jimmy broke from his wife's embrace and turned to the coffee pot. "I know," he stammered. "Things will have to change, I understand that." Jimmy turned back and walked over to Suzie, holding a cup of coffee out to her and kissed her softly on the cheek.

The three of them went to church, Jimmy finding it excruciating to sit there and smile, to visit with their friends in the little lounge over coffee and cookies after the service. He watched his beautiful wife and amazing daughter with the others, interacting as though it were just any Sunday. But Jimmy was seeing the whole thing through the eyes of a man that was living out the last day of his life. And in a way, he was.

That night the Gregory's went together into Mia's room to say prayers. Jimmy found the ritual heartbreaking this night, yet he managed through them, giving his daughter a long hug and a kiss on her cheek where he lingered, a tear from her father landing on Mia's cheek and mixing with the water left from her freshly showered hair. As they said their goodnights Jimmy leaned back over the bed to kiss her once more, whispering, "I love you so much Mia," before walking out of the room.

He would have an hour more with his wife, his soulmate and best friend for twenty-six years. She would sit in her blue summer pajama set, some popcorn between them, not knowing that her husband wouldn't be there to sit with her the next night. When she was tired she told Jimmy she was heading for bed and asked him to come up with her. His decline was no surprise: he often sat up late, the TV numbing him until he could find rest.

Suzie reached over to kiss her husband good night and he pulled her close and held her there, his face in her hair.

"Are we okay?" She pulled away to look at him.

His eyes glistened and he stared into the brown doe eyes that had drawn him in all those years ago. He noticed her soft brown hair, long and wavy as it had always been, but with a few streaks of grey running through it all these years later. He closed his eyes and he saw the two of them on their first date, Suzie's tiny hands holding his in a gesture of comfort. Jimmy opened his eyes when Suzie asked again, "Are we okay?"

"We will be," he whispered, trying to convince the both of them. "I love you."

Trying to stay calm he looked back to the TV and began flipping through the channels. Suzie hesitated only a minute but had she known what her husband was about to do, she never would have walked upstairs.

***

Sometime after 1:00 a.m., when the house was silent except for the snoring of dear old Bubba, Jimmy, with a filled duffle bag and backpack, a rolled up sleeping bag and $300 in his pocket walked out the back door of their house, got in his old blue Chevy and drove out of town.

Back at the house he left his cell phone on the kitchen table along with two letters blotched with his tears, one for each of his girls. And he had written a formal letter for the bank that held their home and farm loans. The letter stated that it was his intention that Mrs. Susan Gregory be made sole owner of both home and farm and with an unnatural right-handed signature, he, James Gregory, signed over the last of everything he had to her.

James drove aimlessly for hours that night. Eventually he made his way east, into the Finger Lakes region of the state. There were quaint towns and small cities just waking up and he saw that they were far enough from home and just large enough, he thought, to get lost in.

He drove in to the downtown area of one of the cities where he got a large cup of coffee at a diner and sipped it in the cab of his truck overlooking one of the many beautiful lakes in the area. For the next several weeks he felt his way around the little city trying to forget his old life and imagine a new one.

He realized that it would never work; the forgetting. But he did manage to create a routine of sorts, sleeping in his truck by night and spending his days by the lake and walking along the blocks of downtown where he found he went largely unnoticed in the summers busy tourist hub.

But eventually his money dwindled; the meals and occasional hot showers at a cheap motel left him realizing he would have to do something if he wanted to stay fed and clean and largely unnoticed. He had vowed never to touch a penny that went into the joint account from his disability payouts and he knew the last one would be deposited in September. He was due for review at that time and likely would be cleared for work after that point; he had no plans of seeing his doctor about it. That little money was all he had contributed to provide for the family he had abandoned. Even the other James Gregory, the one he despised, the one he would never have imagined he'd be like, even that James Gregory hadn't taken any money from his family when he left them.

And so James found his way into a little cash by working a few nights a week at a family-owned farm supply store just outside of town. They hadn't advertised any need but James had come in one day, poking around the shelves of animal feed, work clothes, and farm supplies. One of the guys asked if he needed help with anything and without thinking he said, "Yeah, a job would be nice."

The older man, tall and lean looked James over for a minute. He saw his limp, the hand and forearm under his wrinkled shirtsleeve and his tired eyes. Something knowing crossed his face and with a sympathetic voice he said. "Tough times?"

James didn't know what to say, and the old man quickly put his hand up to stop him from trying to find words.

"Listen. I don't need to know your story. I've helped a few guys out over the years. You someone willing to work at night, maybe under the table for no more than ten-twelve hours a week?"

James listened, nodding. "You'd be checking inventory and stocking shelves. The only requirements I have are honesty, dependability, and reliable transportation."

"But this," James extended his left arm, showing him the three digit hand and pulling his sleeve up so the kind man could see his forearm. "

"Well, it looks like you can still use it good enough. I don't need you for anything heavy or delicate if that's what you're thinking."

Two days later the owner had James come in and he showed him what he expected. It was easy work; stuff that James hardly thought couldn't be done during business hours by one of the clerks. But he was glad for the work and grateful for the money paid out in an envelope the old man handed him every Friday when he came in.

For seven months James worked for Mr. Millerd. With the money, he ate at fast food restaurants and kept himself clean and gas in his tank. But all good things come to an end and one day in the spring of 2010, while driving down the main route in town, white smoke started pouring out from the truck's exhaust as the engine was overheating. He knew right away what it was and what he needed to do. He had seen the signs of a leaky head gasket in the old truck and had bought some sealant, trying to limp it along, but on that day there was no more limping, at least not for the truck.

He got it into a parking lot at a shopping center where upon inspection he knew there was nothing he could do. Well aware of the cost of repairs and that the truck was months past its New York State inspection anyway, he emptied it of its few personal items. He stuffed his duffle and rolled a plastic tarp around his sleeping bag and slung it over his back. Leaving the truck, he carried its plates to the police station to report that he would have to abandon his shelter for lack of funds. He relinquished the plates to the DMV and in doing so took his mobile home off the road.

James never showed up for work the next day and Mr. Millerd never heard from him again. He had walked aimlessly for days, trying to collect himself and consider what the next chapter of his life might be. He made his way into a neighboring town where he ended up finding a small, overgrown park tucked away on its sleepy edge, the edge of town that had once been industrial and productive. Ironic, he thought, and he settled down under a picnic table in the trees to sleep.

Chapter 33

Spring 2011

Almost a year had passed. It hardly mattered to James that it was still daylight at this point. Sure, Molly might give him a hard time about the possibility of being seen but James knew that the cops had figured them out a long time ago and that, especially in the cold months, they turned a blind eye to such things.

He hoped that the medicine he brought to her last night would have started to take effect. Molly's cough had been getting worse for days and, as cold as it was, she was still too warm to the touch. James was grateful for the woman he had met at the doughnut shop. He had been worried when he didn't find the weekly bag of day old baked goods in the dumpster. It was the one thing that Molly looked forward to when she was depressed. And with her being sick now, she was lower than usual.

She had been resting when he headed out and he had left the stool propped up against the old building where he had used it to get out of the window. He was too tired to follow Molly's protocol on the matter. The winter had been long and hard and he didn't think even she had the energy to worry about it.

He managed his way back up and through the broken out window that led in to the room where he had been sleeping since Molly became ill. Every part of him ached and he looked at his cold little bedroll longingly. But first he would check on Molly in the room next to him, give her another cold pill and see if she would eat something.

She was awake but groggy and she began to argue halfheartedly about James's daytime entrance. But he held out the waxy bag of doughnuts to her and she quieted except for her rattling cough which came on in a fit. He fumbled in his pack, pulling out the thermos and sitting beside her while he poured out a small amount of warm coffee.

She managed a feeble smile as she sipped the warm drink and ate, swallowing down a few pills that James handed her. After a few minutes she set down the empty thermos top and lay back down, her head nearly on James's outstretched leg. "I guess taking a chance on you was worth it after all," she sighed and she closed her eyes to sleep.

Slowly James rose from the mattress. He covered Molly with all the blankets she owned, tucking them tightly around her. She let out a little moan but he could tell she was already asleep. He walked out into the hallway and made his way down to the brightest area in the dingy old factory.

Sitting there on a bench, his back to the little rays of sunlight that made their way through the dirty glass, he stared at Molly's beautiful mural. The forest was warm and green and the animals were at peace in their home there on the wall. James was wondering again about home, about the people that lived there. Had they found peace?

He touched the center pocket of his overalls and then slipped his hand in and pulled out the envelope he had found in the bag of doughnuts the woman from the van had given him, suddenly realizing how foolish it was to make any big matter about it. It was when he began to unfold it that he felt something shift inside. He held it up to the bit of light, trying to see through it, savoring the unknown for a moment.

Finally he opened it, tipping it carefully in his cupped hand. A small silver object fell out, attached to a length of silver chain. He looked at it for a few long moments. And then suddenly he drew in a sharp breath as he held the tiny silver cross out in front of him; it swayed from the chain in his shaking hand. "My God," he whispered. And he reached down under his layers to his neck where he pulled out a gold chain with his wedding band and a tiny cross hanging from it.

"It can't be." He said. But he was looking at the cross that had just come from the envelope, its Trinity knots on each of the four corners. It looked identical in every way to the one he had worn against his chest since the day his mother had died and he had found it at the police station with her personal effects.

James was stricken. For several minutes he held the two crosses in his hand turning them each over, measuring them side by side before he decided they were indeed the same. He had spotted a note when the necklace had poured out into his hand, so he laid each necklace carefully out on the bench next to him before reaching for the envelope on his lap.

As he was pulling out the paper to read he noticed a smaller card in the corner of the envelope. It had not come out with the note paper. Reaching in, he carefully withdrew it and held it out in front of him reading the name that was printed on it. Taking a minute to consider what he saw he whispered again, "It can't be."

With hands trembling and tears in his eyes James slowly unfolded the note. Immediately he noticed the pretty little line of hearts that had been drawn in red pencil down the right border. He knew immediately then who had written it and memories from a lifetime ago flooded his mind.

He discovered that the woman, who he had met at the doughnut shop, was Patty Fowler. Patty Hennessey Fowler, the Patty of his childhood, the daughter of his mother's best friend. It was her name that was printed on the index paper. And the letter? It had not been written by Patty but by her mother Donna and it was dated September 30, 1983, the day of Jimmy's eighteenth birthday.

Donna, the woman he called Aunt. Donna, who had fed him and held him when he was sick, who had walked him to school when he was afraid and whose kisses had always felt like little drops of dew on his forehead. He was holding a note from her and it was twenty-seven years old.

She wanted him to know how sorry she was. How she had regretted the things she couldn't do for him when he was a boy and regretted what she didn't do for him when he was a young man grieving the loss of his mother. She hoped that someday their paths might cross, that she might be able to give him the hug she had so wanted to on that terrible day in July when they both lost someone they loved.

"The cross," she said. "I want you to have it now. I've worn it close to my heart every day and I want you to know that I've carried you there too."

Jimmy held the paper in his hands long after he had read the words. He ran his finger along the little hearts that had been drawn there all those years ago, trying to feel their shape and the colors of the pencil.

As he thought on it, he began to wonder why it was Patty whose card and phone number were in the envelope. Donna would be in her 70's now and he wondered if maybe she had died. Maybe she had written the note and then died before getting it to him. He had seen fate deal many hands like that and he felt a sudden anger come over him at the thought of it.

"Patty," he whispered. "I didn't even recognize her standing right in front of me. How could she have possibly recognized me, the mess that I am?" Patty, he considered. Not just another kind person in the sea of people he'd seen in the last few years. Patty…she was real. There was her name, on a plain piece of index card and her phone number both written boldly in black marker along with the words, "Jimmy, call me."

***

It took four days for James to decide to leave. He sat vigil over Molly as she rested and took the medicine he handed her faithfully every six hours. He had gone so far as to go to the Friday community lunch program, a place he had hated to walk in to and bring back warm soup and tea for Molly which she thirstily slurped in the periods when she woke.

Finally her fever broke and he felt the sweat on her face. She was awake more and coughing less. Still, he thought, she had a ways to go but he didn't think he'd have to take her to the free clinic like he had threatened to do.

He sat down with Molly on her thin mattress after he had dragged it to the broken window in his room and had beat it with his hand into the cold air trying to clean it of sickness. It was something he remembered abuela doing with blankets from time to time.

It was hard for him to find the words to begin. He was unsure himself of what might happen if he made the call to the number Patty had left. But in the days while he sat with Molly watching the light filter in through the cracks in the wall and feeling the cold darkness of night descend he considered. Had fate been any part of their meeting after all these years? He could not thumb his nose at an old friend, if just out of respect for Donna.

James showed Molly the two crosses and the note that had been left for him. He explained to her who these people were, what they had meant to him and to his mother: telling her more about his past than he had ever shared with her.

"I have to make the call, Molly," he said tenderly. "I don't know what it might mean or if it is even a good idea. But I have to find out."

"Yes, you do, James," she looked at him with firm determination.

"I may be gone for a few days. I don't know. But I'll be back, Molly. I will. You know that."

"I do know that, James." Molly took his hand and held it in the softness of her new mittens, the ones Patty had given James when he told her he'd like an extra coffee for a friend. Molly had her head down, patting James's hand. "I do know that."

James cleaned up that day the best he could. He used a little water from their snow bucket and a bit of soap to wash his face and his hair. Shivering, he took off his shirt and scrubbed his underarms with his wet soapy hands. He took a pair of scissors and cut away at his beard until it was close around his jaw.

He waited until just before daybreak to leave. His backpack over his shoulder but his sleeping bag and blanket he left on the floor as he had for much of the winter. He had a few dollars to make the call at a pay phone but the rest of his pockets he emptied, leaving Molly with $6.28 and a note scribbled on a napkin saying, "See you when I figure this whole thing out. Take care of yourself and get some hot food."

Two hours later Patty Fowler rolled down the window to her van in the parking lot at the doughnut shop where she had found James the week before. "Good to see you, she smiled. "Come on, get in. It's cold out there."

He looked at her for the first time. She was Patty all right. Though her hair was short and tucked up under a beanie, it was as red as it had ever been and freckles still dotted her nose and cheeks. Bashfully, James opened the passenger door and lifted himself into the seat. He closed the door, keeping his left hand tucked up under his coat sleeve.

"I'm glad you called." She smiled at him. "I still can't believe I saw you the other morning. I've had my eye out for you for nearly a year."

He was surprised to hear this. How had she possibly known to be watching for him? Before he could ask, she explained.

"Jimmy. I hadn't heard anything about you since seeing your marriage announcement in the paper. But Mom was so happy to hear that you had gotten married."

"So, your mother, she knew that?" James was confused. "But the letter she wrote," he began. "It's dated from my eighteenth birthday. I assumed maybe she died before sending it to me."

Patty smiled. "Oh no. Mom's very much alive, thank God. And she lives here in town in a little apartment we converted from an outbuilding behind my house."

James waited for her to continue.

"My family moved out here about five years ago. I loved it immediately. Nice and quiet but friendly and better work for Dennis, my husband, and me. Then Mom had a stroke about three years ago and I convinced her to move out here, to be close to us."

"Aunt Donna? Oh no. Is she ok?"

"She's doing well, but I look after her." Patty turned the van on and heat started making its way from the engine into the cab, warming them both.

"I read about your accident Jimmy," Patty said suddenly. "You probably knew it made the paper and the local news.

And I'm sorry for what you've had to go through." She stopped and turned to Jimmy, putting her hand on his shoulder. "Listen. I can't begin to understand what you've been through and I'm not here to council you. But we are like family still."

He nodded, not able to speak.

"And then I thought I saw you. Just a few miles west of here, coming out of the DMV. You looked up at me as I was going in and I thought, 'My God. I think that was Jimmy Gregory.' But I told myself, no. What are the chances? By the time I considered finding out, you were gone. But from that day on, I've been watching for you. Somehow I knew I had found you and that maybe I would again." This time Patty had the tears in her eyes.

"You are good, like your mother," James whispered.

"Well, yeah, you think?" she smiled. "I'd be happy to be half of who she is." Patty cleared her voice. "Jimmy, I don't want to put you on the spot here. But I want to take you to see mom. I told her I found you"

James looked stricken. "Patty. I don't think so. I don't think I could do it. I don't want her to see me like this." He lowered his eyes like a repentant puppy.

Jimmy," Patty stared at him until he met her gaze. "My mother will see you as she always did. I can promise you that."

***

An hour later James was in Patty's house, washing up in her bathroom. Coming down the stairs he noticed pictures of children in various stages of life along the wall. Then he saw a portrait of Liam in dress blues, his face stoic and that of a man. "Must have stayed in the military," he thought.

He walked into the kitchen to find that Patty had made him breakfast. But his nerves only allowed him a few bites of toast and some orange juice.

"So did you go over…to tell her that I am here? You sure she still wants to see me?" James was overwhelmed.

"She does. And she needs to. It's for her maybe more than it's for you Jimmy." Patty walked to the back door, motioning for him to follow. They walked across the wet grass making light tracks in a thawing dust of snow. The door to Donna's apartment was painted red and had a pine cone wreath on it. There were two large windows one to each side of the door, but Jimmy couldn't see anyone inside. Patty knocked on the door before opening it and called out to her mother. From the brightness of the sun Jimmy had to adjust his eyes to the low lighting inside.

He heard Donna before he saw her. "Jimmy! Oh my God, Jimmy." The sweet honey of her voice made him feel like a little boy again. She walked with the help of a cane from the kitchen to where he stood inside the door. She reached out her hand, carefully, until she touched him. Then she put her long thin arms around him and hugged him with the intensity he remembered from so many years ago.

"Oh, Jimmy. All the years I've wanted to see you. I can't believe you're here after all these years." She finally broke her embrace and reached for his hand. He looked at her then and she held her tear streaked face up to him and in that moment he could see that Donna could not. She was blind.

Patty had turned on a lamp and asked them both to sit down. There was no awkwardness at that moment for Jimmy. But instead, a peace and a comfort, like being home descended upon him. And the conversation between them moved along as it would have if Jimmy were sitting at the kitchen table forty years ago, telling them about his day at school.

He learned more about the letter. How Donna had written it and then set it in her dresser. Waiting, she didn't know what for but she waited to send it and then she had heard about abuela and then, well. Then she had just not been able to send it at all. "All the hurt," her voice quivered. "And all the pain. I couldn't imagine. And I didn't want to open up a wound…your mother. I felt I needed to leave it to heal. Leave you to heal…" she broke off.

"And then I found the letter when I moved mom out," Patty continued. "I told her I would hold on to it. But I never did tell her about your accident or about seeing you last year. That's when I started carrying mom's letter around in my purse."

"She didn't want to upset me," Donna interjected. "Again, trying to not open up wounds. But thank God she told me she found you last week." Donna squeezed Jimmy's hand, the one that was not whole.

And as they talked on they learned more about Jimmy: the man, the husband, and father. What he had been and what he had been through and what he had walked away from. They shared tears. For people lost: Maria and Patrick and Jimmy's grandparents and for things not said and things not done.

"And that's why you've got to go back. To find out. I can't pretend to know what your wife will do, what she may or may not want at this point, but from what you've said she is a good woman and she loved you. But, Jimmy, regardless… you have a little girl." Donna spoke tenderly.

"And that's the thing Donna. My little girl. What does she think of me now? Her father abandoned her and her mother. And I wasn't a good man when I left. I'm not strong anymore. And I don't even understand myself. What came over me? And if I don't understand myself how can I expect them to understand?" Jimmy's voice was thick with emotion.

"Oh my dear boy," Donna whispered. Do you remember when you were little, how you looked at your mother. How you loved her …even when she had disappointed you? Isn't it true that that little boy always knew that his mother had done the best that she could and that she had loved him? And didn't that little boy love her for it?" Tears ran from Donna's sightless eyes and in that moment Jimmy knew that she could see better than he ever had.

Chapter 34

Spring 2011

Jimmy had spent two days with Donna, agonizing over the call he would make to Suzie. It had been a year and nine months since they had last spoken and when she picked up the phone and heard his voice she had begun to wail, relieved that he was alive and that he had called. They agreed to meet at a diner in a city not far from home.

When he saw her step out of the car, Jimmy's heart pounded in his chest. There was the little fairy that had mesmerized him all those years ago. Her brown hair was cut a little shorter and though it was a little grayer, it still lay in soft waves around her pretty little face. He saw her eyes, gentle and warm as always, the crinkles around them more pronounced as she approached him with a tearful smile.

As she reached for him with her delicate little hands he knew for sure that he had never, not for one minute, stopped loving Suzie and he realized just how very broken he must have been to ever walk out on her. They held each other in a long embrace and Jimmy wondered what she might be feeling at this moment.

There was so much to tell, so much to be said, but it wasn't all so easy to say. No, she wasn't remarried or seeing anyone for that matter. And yes, she and the family had gone out many times looking for him. But she had been cautious and hadn't contacted anyone to search for him. His letter to her had been so emphatic about his not wanting to be found and about her need to move on, she was afraid that she had broken him beyond the ability to heal and she worried for what he might do if he were found. She carried an incredible amount of guilt for what she had said to him that day and what it had resulted in…for all of them.

But it was Mia. Because of Mia, Suzie knew that there would always be reason to hope. She prayed every day that if not for her, that Jimmy would find his way back for his daughter. Oh how Mia had cried when he left. The letter he wrote she carried around like a child would a stuffed animal. She read and read it and tucked it under her pillow at night, not understanding what could have been so bad to make her father feel that he had needed to leave.

And as he had told Donna, he told Suzie. He was weighed down by guilt and anguish for having left his family. The Jimmy before the accident would have never done such a thing. But the Jimmy that he was now was different. He had changed. He didn't feel strong and in control and there were things about himself he just didn't understand.

Suzie seemed to understand this. She had been to a counselor, she told him. She had been working on the guilt but had found in the process that there were other things she needed to work through: anger was one, but also feelings of abandonment.

They both understood that as much as each of them wished to be together, to pick up where they had left off, that it wasn't realistic. At least not yet. Jimmy knew that he couldn't give his wife and daughter what they deserved until he addressed the issues that had brought him to where he was.

So neither of them promised more to each other than to try to work their lives out. Some of that work they would do alone and some of it they would do together. Suzie's only expectation was that Jimmy would get good counseling and do his best to try to rebuild himself. It was her hope that in the rebuilding he would be able to find his way back to Mia and her, but she put no heavy burden on him.

Jimmy had decided that for a little while, while the two worked on their future, he would stay with Donna in her apartment. It was a safe place for him and he knew he needed that if he was ever really going to heal.

Suzie had taken Jimmy home to see Mia. She had tried to hold back, to protect herself, to keep some emotional and physical distance between herself and her father. But when she saw him walking up the steps the façade fell away and she landed in her father's arms. He had wept at the sight of his daughter, more a little woman than a big girl. He lavished her with a years' worth of hugs and kisses and promised her many regular visits while he did everything he could to earn back her trust.

Before he left he reached around his neck and unhooked one of the crosses he was wearing, the one that had been there for twenty-seven years. He held it out to Mia and he told her whose it had been and how he had come to have another one just like it.

"This is yours now Mia," he whispered. "I know your grandmother would be so proud of the beautiful young woman that you are."

***

It had been eight days and Patty had come with Jimmy to the overgrown park on the east side of town. The part of town that had once been industrial and productive but over the years had, except for a sleepy old neighborhood, been largely left to itself. He was grateful for all that she and Donna had done and were doing for him.

It was late afternoon when they arrived and they walked around the area for a little while. There was a possibility that Molly was out today and Jimmy wanted to keep an eye out for her. Finally though, they came back and sat on one of the old picnic tables, the one at the edge of the treed lot where Jimmy often tucked in for the night. They waited and they watched in case Molly was to walk through the park as it got dark.

He told Patty more stories as they sat there. Stories about those first weeks sleeping there: how Molly had scared the kids away and how she had taught him how to navigate his new life, where to find food and how he had panhandled on a few desperate occasions.

She learned Molly's history, at least as much as Jimmy could tell. And she had wanted to come along. Patty had experience with troubled youth and was willing to talk with Molly, open a door for her and help her if she ever wanted to walk through it.

They waited there, talking until it grew dark. Jimmy would go to Molly alone as he always had. He would never betray her trust in him by bringing someone to her home. He had his backpack with him and he slung it over his shoulder noticing it felt heavier than the week before when he had last carried it.

"I have my doubts about it, but keep your fingers crossed. She needs this as much as I do." Jimmy gave Patty a one-armed hug before walking off into the wooded lot and through to the other side where the abandoned factory and warehouses were. There was little light from the moon and Jimmy felt the darkness and cold wrap around him.

Quickly he made his way to the back of building B and to the window that served as a secret door to Molly's home. Instinctively, he found the step stool and with some effort he pulled himself up and into the open section of window. He landed quietly near the sleeping bag and blanket that still lay on the floor, his bed for many nights.

"Molly," he whispered. "Molly, I don't want to scare you." He moved out into the hallway. It was so dark, there wasn't anything that could be seen but he knew where to turn, like a mouse in a maze.

He held out his hands in front of him and he found surprisingly that her door was open. He whispered again, "Molly. I'm back." Slowly like a cat he walked inside the room. He could hear nothing and he began to worry. Had he left her too soon? Was she sick again?

He reached down to her mattress where he began to feel around. Nothing. He felt nothing. Not even her blanket. He felt around the floor for her pack. He could not find it. He reached toward the little table that she had used. There was always a candle there. He would light it, he thought. Fumbling for it, he knocked it over and he heard the glass break.

"Molly," he spoke in full voice now. He reached into his backpack and pulled out a flashlight, something he had thought to bring but would have never expected to use. He snapped it on and turned it toward the mattress, finding it empty. Then around the room. Everything that Molly had ever had there, her bedding, her clothes, her blanket, were all gone. All he saw were the shattered pieces of glass on the floor by the table, shining eerily in the light.

He began to panic and he yelled out her name. Had he left her there, still sick? Had she been forced to go find help for herself? He should have waited longer, he thought. He should have waited until the coughing had stopped. He should have taken her to the clinic.

But then he caught glimpse of something that the edge of his flashlight beam had fallen on. It was on the floor, under the table. A piece of paper. He scrambled to pick it up. He set it out on the table and held the light over it. Immediately he recognized the scribbled writing of his friend.

Dear James,

I knew you would come back for me. Because that's who you are and that's what you do. And I thank you James. I thank you for all the times you saw me through. When you tried to lift my spirits and the times when you couldn't, when you just sat beside me. I'm not sorry I took a chance on you when I found you in the park and I would do it again. I'm grateful for what I learned because of you.

But things change. I guess they have to, don't they? You and I are different and we were out here for different reasons. We knew that from the beginning. And so I leave here for the both of us. You have things to take care of and I guess I do too.

Please take care of yourself and find your way back to your family. They are who you are and why I knew we would only share this little time at this little point in our lives.

All my love,
Molly

It took Jimmy a few minutes to collect himself. He took the note and tucked it carefully into his shirt pocket. Using his flashlight, he moved back out and down the hallway until he had made his way into the central room where once many women had been busy sewing and packing clothing.

He stopped in front of the huge wall and shown his light on it. He took his time taking in the scene that had been so lovingly painted there, by so lovely a person. "Beautiful," he whispered. "So beautiful."

Epilogue

Jimmy would never forget his friend and he often wondered what ever became of her. For some time he found himself driving around old, abandoned buildings, looking to see if he might spot a disheveled young woman slinking around in the dark; a step stool propped up against a wall.

His own healing would be slow, and there would be setbacks. But eventually, when he was able, he would pray for Molly as the people who loved him had faithfully done; the people that understood that everyone was a sojourner in this life. That one's journey could be complicated and for some there would be times of great pain. There would be messes and mistakes, a need to forgive and to be forgiven.

Jimmy knew that he and his friend had not been very different in this way. That they sojourned together *for this little time* had been no mistake and his hope was that Molly's journey would lead her home.

Acknowledgements

I am especially grateful to my son Joe DeRaddo. It is because of him that this story became more than ideas on my computer. He encouraged me to make something of it and was the first person to read my manuscript. I want to thank my daughter Katie DeRaddo for using her computer and communication skills to share the story through social media.

A special thank you to Casey Kunes for talking with me and answering my questions on matters of farming. Also thank you to Rafael Diaz for feeding me while we talked about Latino food and culture. For dinner, hospitality, and conversation about publishing, and for getting me connected with a publisher I thank John and Cheryl Avanzato.

Lastly, I want to thank my publisher, Michael Fabiano, who walked me through each step of publishing with his positive, encouraging attitude.

About the Author

Pam DeRaddo is a wife and mother of two grown children. She and her husband, Sully, live in upstate New York.

Pam grew up in Geneva, New York in a close knit community where much of her extended family were her neighbors. She enjoys nature, gardening, quiet campfires, and conversations with friends and strangers.

Pam is concerned about issues of homelessness and mental illness, and for people who find themselves on the margins of society.

Author's Note

Dear Reader,

I hope you enjoyed reading *For This Little Time* as much as I enjoyed writing it. Support from readers like yourself is crucial for any author to succeed, particularly in this E-book era.

If you enjoyed this book, please consider writing a review at amazon.com and if you are inclined, follow me on Facebook at https://www.facebook.com/PamelaDeRaddoAuthor/

The reviews are important and your support is greatly appreciated.

Thank you,

Pam DeRaddo